THE

TWELVE

by

James K Burk

Wolfsinger Publications Security, Colorado

For Tara Elaine-Renee (Olive), Whitney Dawn,
Erika Alana-Morgana,
and the next generation;
Orion Salvador and Olivia Isabelle

ANTON

Anton groaned as he dropped into his chair. The sides of his tent had been raised to admit the cooling breeze and he helped himself to a cup of water flavored with lemon. Despite his momentary contentment, he still had doubts and misgivings. Although he could appreciate the pleasure of accomplishment, the battle three days ago had left a foul taste in his mouth. Battle? It had been more a slaughter. The Valtierrans they'd maneuvered into a hopeless position had been inept at everything but dying. Their leader, a man in a mask or helmet of some sort had been gulled into fighting on ground of Anton's choosing, where he had been able to bring only part of his army into the action. At least the man had died well. A pity he could not have led well.

Anton's own army was a mob with only a trace of the discipline they needed. He'd been in more danger from his own men for putting a stop to the butchery than he'd ever been from the Valtierrans. And as soon as they'd won what they were pleased to call a battle, they'd begun to pillage and plunder the local farmers. He'd had to kill one man himself and order two more hanged and half a score flogged before they'd learned their commander gave his orders seriously and expected them to be obeyed.

Tatros, the prince who'd bought Anton and his services, had only been interested in using part of the skills Anton had brought from the south.

Anton could almost forgive the prince's indecision. Almost. He hadn't allowed Anton time to make this mob into an army but had dithered so long before deciding to attack the harvest had been gathered and most of it sent away to Valtierra before it could be seized. Now Anton had to contend with hungry soldiers whose supplies had to be hauled from Shicassa, and the locals would probably be robbed into starvation.

At least he'd put the men to work, putting up a wall between most of the mouth of the valley and Valtierra. They'd still have enough energy to carouse at night, but it kept them out of trouble during the day.

He'd just become comfortable when Khaimon, his First Captain, entered the tent. "There's an envoy from Valtierra to see you. He's carrying a small chest. He said it's for you."

"Let him come in. And stay. I am not sure how well I can speak their language." Khaimon left the tent, then returned ushering a middle-aged man with a dark wooden chest bound with black iron.

The stranger tilted the case and opened it, exposing a mask. The mask portrayed a stern face, the head a helmet with a red horsehair crest ending in a long black tail. "The Council asks you to accept this." The man spoke a dialect of the same language Khaimon spoke, but with a lilting accent.

Anton looked at Khaimon, an eyebrow raised.

"He's—they're asking you to join their Council of Twelve." His expression was bemused.

Anton thought a moment before he said, "I am deeply honored. I hope you will not be offended if I consider my answer carefully. I will see you again in the morning and will have an answer for you then." Turning to Khaimon, he said, "Have a tent set up next to mine for our guest."

The man closed the chest and followed Khaimon outside. Anton drained his cup, appreciating the tart flavor that slaked thirst better than water alone.

He poured another cup of the water and sipped at it, then put it aside to reach for flint and steel as the sides of his tent were hauled down and pegged. Striking a spark into tinder, he held a candle to the flame until it flared, then he waited.

Khaimon returned. "I thought you might need the privacy more than the breeze. I've given orders for the guards to be stationed twenty paces away and to allow no one to approach any closer than that."

Anton gestured at the other chair. "So, what is the significance of the mask?"

Khaimon helped himself to a cup of water. "Valtierra is governed by a Council of Twelve. Every two years the city holds a festival and, at the end of the celebration, they choose the Council. They select a Wise Old Man, a Crone, a Fool, a Harlot, a Rash Youth, and so on. I gather that the ones chosen spend the next two years in near-seclusion, and they can only appear in public wearing their masks." He drained his cup in a single drink. "You could do worse than accept the offer."

"Do these people know I am the one who led this army against the city?"

"I'm sure they do. It's a measure of their respect that they're inviting you to be the Warrior."

Khaimon leaned forward and lowered his voice. "And it's a measure of my respect and affection that I'm advising you to accept the offer. Or, at least, to get away."

Anton frowned. "Why should I do that? I have won the battle I was sent to win, and I have not been paid yet, except for that," he gestured at the elaborate suit of armor, stained dark blue with silver-inlaid patterns. "Your prince believes strongly in incentives. I was shown the heads of the commanders who had failed."

Khaimon lowered his voice even more. "I haven't seen the heads of the successful commanders, but I assure you they're just as dead. Tatros fears one thing more than failure, and that is a successful leader who might turn the army against him or become too popular with the people."

Anton felt as though the ground had just swallowed him. Everything on which he'd based plans and hopes had been suddenly snatched away, and the feeling that remained was anger. "Why do you serve such a scavenger hound?"

"I have family. Tatros knows I'd rather die than be the cause of their deaths. Fear is a greater incentive than profit."

"So…?"

"So don't go on any long walks with the petty-captains, and don't return to Shicassa with the army. One more word of warning—if you take the offer, be aware Tatros has spies in Valtierra, perhaps even on the Council. I'd make sure you always have a weapon to hand."

After a gesture for silence, Anton considered his options. With no time to plan, he had to improvise. He didn't doubt a thing Khaimon had told him, and his years as a soldier and leader had at least prepared him to react quickly. One question occurred to him. "Why are you warning me?"

Khaimon stared into his eyes. "Because of that respect and affection I mentioned. You're a good commander and, more importantly, a good man. You care about the men under you and you even care about the enemy. And I want to keep my self-delusion that I'm also a good man." He refilled his cup and drank half of it. "And think of it this way—I'm a prisoner, but I can help the condemned man escape."

After another moment's thought, Anton nodded. "Tell the envoy from Valtierra I will meet him where we signed the truce. Tell him to leave immediately. Order the petty-captains to prepare their men to return to Shicassa tomorrow. And have my horse saddled and ready."

After finishing his water, Khaimon nodded. "Good luck. And don't forget the weapons." He rose and strode out of the tent.

It wouldn't do to leave before full darkness. Anton glanced at his weapons and chose his war hammer, which was devastating against an armored opponent, more so than a sword. Setting the weapon beside his chair, he looked over the map spread on his table.

Valtierra lay a day's ride to the southwest, Shicassa a day and a half's ride due north.

The warning was a gift and a curse. It had probably saved his life, but it left him starting at shadows. Out of habit, he'd kept a day's trail rations and a skin of water by his kit. While they might not be as palatable as the meal soon to be delivered to his tent, they were probably safer.

He damned the famine that struck the south and his former leader who had sold him to the northern prince, causing him to leave the honest warfare in the south for what had seemed a golden opportunity. The northern city-states held themselves more cultured, but it seemed their sophistication bred only more devious treachery and a taste for unnecessary violence.

"Your dinner, commander," said a voice from outside the tent.

Anton reached the chair in a single step and slipped the haft of the war hammer up his sleeve, holding the head so it was mostly masked by his hand. "Enter."

Two men, helmeted and in half-armor, stepped into the tent, one of them bearing a steaming bowl of stew. The man set the bowl on the table and stood waiting. While Anton couldn't recall the names he recognized the men as a petty-captain and his lieutenant.

"I seem to have lost my appetite. Eat it for me." He watched them eye each other and prepared to move.

"You'd better regain your appetite soon," the petty-captain said. "We have orders to escort you to Shicassa, and it's a long ride." As the man spoke, his hand crept toward his dagger.

Anton stepped forward, letting the hammer drop until he clutched the haft and swung the hammer up and into the man's face. Before the man could fall, Anton swung an overhand blow at the lieutenant, burying the spike end of the hammer in the man's helmet and skull.

He left the hammer in the skull and quickly drew on and buckled in place the rich armor. Take what payment one could was a tenet of the mercenaries' creed.

Hands long-practiced made quick work of donning the armor. He stopped to tie to his belt a pleasantly-heavy pouch of coins and finally removed the hammer from the dead lieutenant. The heart had been stopped long enough blood welled out of the wound instead of gushing. He cleaned the head of his hammer as best he could on a blanket, then snatched up the pouch of rations and the waterskin.

As he stepped outside the tent, he noticed the guards who had stood outside had apparently been dismissed.

Most of the men were gathered around a great fire, eating, drinking, and laughing. With their night vision gone, they'd have trouble seeing him if he walked among them, but he stayed in the shadows until he reached the horses.

His horse had been harnessed and saddled and left tethered at the near end of the pasture. A tug freed the reins and he was in the saddle in an instant.

The animal was reluctant to move at night but he urged it into a walk around the camp, and by the time the moon was full-risen he was on his way to the place of the treaty.

THE WISE OLD MAN

The old man finished his prayers as always, asking for guidance from the Sustainer, then donned his mask. As always, he experienced the odd feeling, a mixture of reverence and claustrophobia.

Opening the door of his apartment, he snatched up the gnarled staff and walked as quickly as his age would permit to the Council Chamber.

The Crone and the Fool had arrived before him. The knotted features of the Crone's mask faced him for a moment, then turned again to stare down at the table before her. The Fool's mask had remained fixed ahead, the odd shape of the eye-openings giving its wearer a perpetually cross-eyed appearance, and the usual grin was absent from the mouth below the mask.

As the Wise Old Man took his chair, the Harlot hurried in, followed by the Merchant and the Farmer. The Mother arrived, her hair still damp from a bath, and the others followed. As usual, the Artisan was the last to take his place at the curved tables forming an arc.

The Crone slowly peered around the table. "As you know, it falls to us to choose a new Warrior."

They all paused to remember the man. Receiving news of the Warrior's death had been a shock to the Wise Old Man and, he supposed, to the others as well. It was always a blow to learn of the death of a member of the Council, and a reminder of one's own mortality.

"This being the Month of the Crone, I've sent a message to the commander of the army who beat us, offering him the mask… "

"Are you completely senile?" the Old Man snapped. "Without consulting us, you offered the position to an outsider?"

The Mother slapped the table with her hand. "He's not a son of Valtierra."

"Loyalty," the Merchant observed, "is not a commodity easily bought, and the price comes high."

The Farmer's harsh voice added, "He took from us our most fertile valley."

The Crone waited for the objections to run out before she replied. "You are all correct, but we need a Warrior. The one chosen at the Festival was our greatest Warrior. Since we have no one better, then our best choice is the man who beat him. If the gods favor him and the city still stands by the next Festival, he will have become a son of the city."

"I won't be a part of this desecration of the city's traditions," the Wise Old Man said.

"Is that the wisdom speaking, or just the age?" the Fool asked, and emitted the giggle that so annoyed the Old Man.

"You may vote against him," the Crone said, "but one of the responsibilities of the Twelve is to consider the decisions we make."

"It sounds as though the decision has already been made," the Wise Old Man grumbled.

"No," the Crone replied. "I've asked that he present himself to us, so we can ask questions of him and he of us. It seemed the fairest course."

While they waited for the outlander, the Wise Old Man looked at each of the others in turn. Their masks revealed nothing, of course, and he might as well have been studying paintings, but he tried to read their postures. Another useless exercise, as no one leaned forward eagerly or leaned back, then he realized he was leaning back and tried to move to a more erect position without drawing attention to himself.

When the man entered, he walked with an arrogant strut. His face was brutal, with broad features.

"Welcome," the Crone said. "I've invited you to this Council, but these others also have a vote in the decision, as do you." Her mane of white hair stirred as her mask turned to each of the others. "Who wishes to ask the first question?"

After a moment's silence, the Wise Old Man spoke. "How do we know you'll have the interests of Valtierra at heart, when you're only a hired blade?"

"I did not know that would be an issue." The man had a barbaric accent. "I understood you wanted a Warrior. That is my profession. I choose whether or not to ply my trade and to whom I rent my talents. Once the agreement is made, I honor it faithfully."

The Mother leaned forward. "But you are not a son of the city. How do we know we can rely upon you?"

The Wise Old Man was surprised to see a wry smile appear on the dour face. "Are adopted children less loyal than those born to a family?"

The Merchant ran his finger around the rim of his chased silver goblet. "Why are you available, rather than still serving your former employer?"

"Some agreements are a matter of faith. I did not break faith. The prince wanted me dead and tried to order it. I considered that a breach of our agreement."

The Wise Old Man tangled his fingers in his beard. He'd heard nothing of this treachery. "Does that mean you are ready to lead Valtierra's warriors against Shicassa?"

"Only if the Council determines it is for the good of Valtierra. My personal feelings have less to do with the decision than does the threat posed by Shicassa."

The Wise Old Man leaned back into his chair again. Whether the answer was honest or not, he had to admit the man had spoken well.

"What should we pay you, and why?"

The man turned his head toward the speaker. "I'm not yet familiar enough with the masks to know which is which, but from the rich robes, I would guess you are the Merchant. Your profession has paid you well. Mine is more chancy. My last employer offered me a thousand marks of silver a year. I am willing to serve for a thousand marks of copper."

The Wise Old Man, despite his misgivings and his dislike, found himself giving grudging respect to the man before them.

"I propose that we—and this man—delay our decisions for a fortnight. We scarcely know him and he, on his part, knows us and Valtierra not at all. For that time, he will attend all the meetings of the Council but he may not vote until and if he is accepted. Until then, he need not wear the mask, except in Council."

The Fool gave his obnoxious giggle again. "Now I think I hear some of that wisdom speaking." He turned his face toward the Merchant. "I'd buy a horse with more care than we've shown so far—and still more if it came from your stables."

The Crone tapped the base of her staff three times on the floor. "All in favor of this proposal, raise your right hand."

The Wise Old Man hesitated a moment, then raised his hand, noting that almost all the others did the same.

"All opposed, raise your left hand."

The Priest raised his left hand. "I cannot welcome an unbeliever onto the Council."

The Crone turned to the Fool. "I noticed you didn't vote."

Through a broad grin, the Fool replied, "I'd have thought neither side would want a fool voting with them, but the Priest makes a compelling argument that, as a Fool, I should've voted with him."

"If no one else has a matter to bring before the Council…" The Crone paused for several moments of silence, then finished, "…I declare this meeting ended."

The Wise Old Man was surprised to see the outlander approach the Priest and speak with him in undertones. After a brief conversation, the man walked toward him. The Rash Youth stopped him and they exchanged a few words, then the outlander loomed over him.

"If I might, I would like to visit with you after the evening meal."

Taken aback by the request, he paused before replying. "I'll meet you in the garden in the courtyard."

The big man smiled with half his mouth. "That seems a popular place for meetings."

He seemed unaware the garden was chosen because it was more public and, therefore, a safer place to meet a man one did not completely trust.

The Wise Old Man ignored the proffered hand, using his stick and the table to haul himself erect, then, with a nod, returned to his apartment.

THE PRIEST

The Priest had known at first glance the man who might be the next Warrior was a man of violence. It might be contained, but it always lurked below the surface. His face, with its broad cheekbones and predatory nose, short and curved like the beak of a bird of prey, betrayed that pent-up violence as much as his aggressive stride.

When the man had approached him he'd been surprised and somewhat intimidated, but he knew the Trinity protected him. Still, he'd chosen a place for the meeting where others could see them.

Then the man had turned away and spoken, in turn, with each member of the Council.

Turning his back on the crowd, the Priest made his way to the garden. The heat of the Council chamber had been oppressive, but here in the garden he found shade and a breeze. Even the faint rustling of the leaves seemed to carry away some of the heat and he let himself be soothed by the colors and scents of the late summer blooms.

His sandaled feet followed the gravel path to his favorite bench under a skeleton tree. He reached out and touched the bone-pale trunk. Higher among the branches remained clumps of the old dead outer bark that reminded him of rotting flesh clinging to the white of the inner bark.

The heathen was only another burden to the Faith, probably the least of its load. The Faith was losing its hold on the people and he wondered if he weren't seeing the twilight of the Faith in Valtierra.

When had it changed? When he'd been a boy, the temples had been filled to overflowing on the Sabbath. Now they were hardly filled on Fest Eve. Once, the altars had been covered with flowers and fine cloth. The altars that remained had only a linen covering, if they weren't bare wood, and flowers were seldom placed on them.

Something had gone from the city or, perhaps, from the Faith. Few people gave to the temples, not a tithe, not a jot. And fewer seemed to observe any of the requirements of the Faith. Drunkenness was no longer seen as shameful. Now, the only marriages were simply alliances among the Houses. Almsgiving, when it was practiced at all, was only another display of wealth.

He shook his head. Such dark gray thoughts were out of place in a garden.

Looking up at the sounds of booted feet on gravel, he watched the outlander approach.

"May I sit beside you?"

Wordlessly, the Priest moved to make more than enough room for the other man.

The man sat, moving his sword so he could sit comfortably. "You were half-right at the Council. I'm not really an unbeliever, just as I'm not a believer. I am ignorant of your faith, but willing to listen."

"Are you thinking of converting?"

"I do not know. As a priest, you think of conversion. As a warrior, I am not sure what I will learn."

Curious despite himself, the Priest asked, "What gods do you worship?"

"Where I am from, in the south and west, we worship no gods. They have their affairs and we have ours. Hetah is simply the father. He was the one who made the world and the race of men, but he built many worlds and seldom gives attention to any of them. Ojile is the Prince of Battles. He expects us to fight bravely and well. But if he favors anyone, it is the strong and the skilled. He cannot be implored. He is the Prince of Battles, not the lord of the beggars."

"You have harsh gods."

"We live in a harsh land and, I suppose, we are a harsh people. What gods do you worship, and why are they worth worshiping?"

The Priest paused to order his thoughts. "We worship the Trinity; the Creator, sometimes called the Builder or the Maker, the Destroyer, and the Sustainer. The names are the functions. All things are born, all last for a time, all die. Death is a part of the great cycle. To worship a god is not to praise Him, it's to acknowledge His or Her supremacy. We cannot shape the gods, we can only accept and try to live the cycle as they've established it."

The outlander leaned forward. "I can understand your gods. I might even believe in them. But I could never submit to them."

The Priest's breath caught in his throat at the blasphemy, then he considered the statement before couching his reply. "You'll submit, willingly or unwillingly. You were born, your life is sustained, and you will die. Or do you think you can be the one thing, besides the gods themselves, who will live forever?"

"Not forever," the man replied, "but I intend to postpone the inevitable for as long as possible."

The Priest released a held breath. "We're not so different, after all. Almost everyone fights for that last breath, but we know it will come. We'll talk more about this later."

"I would be pleased. But what do your gods ask of you? And what do they expect of you?"

"They expect us to live speaking the truth, to respect the persons and goods of others, to be faithful to our vows and our spouses, and to teach our children well."

The outlander turned the mask in his hands, apparently studying the detail. "That seems very simple and sensible. And what are the rewards and the punishments?"

Even with the shade and the breeze, the Priest wanted to remove his own mask and wipe the sweat from his face. "The only punishment the Faith may give is for a priest to refuse the last rites and to refuse to invoke the gods at the grave. And they may shame those guilty of drunkenness or licentiousness."

The Warrior stood. "I find I rather like your Faith. I appreciate candor. Too many faiths promise another existence as bribe or threat. We will talk again."

The Warrior's long strides quickly carried him out of sight among the trees. With a glance around to be sure he was truly alone, the Priest untied the laces below his jaw, took off his mask, and wiped his face with the sleeve of his robe. With the other sleeve he wiped out the inside of the mask, then again lowered it over his head and tied it.

He found himself rethinking his opposition to the Warrior. Knowing the man was an outsider from beyond the southern mountains, he'd expected an idol-worshipping killer who practiced every vice known in Valtierra and perhaps a few unknown on this side of the mountains. Instead, he'd met a man with respect for virtues and traditions. He'd have felt better had many who gave lip-service to the Faith tried to live as well as this heathen seemed to.

THE CRONE

From decades of practice, her fingers went about the knitting, letting her mind wander. She wondered if, so long ago, when she'd been the Mother, how she might have felt about being the Crone. She was certain that young woman would never have dared make such a decision or would have had the iron to stand by it.

The discomfort in her fingers was only one of the penalties of age, but she'd still won the trade. As one approached the inevitable, one saw more clearly, both backward and forward. The future was very nearly as clear as the past, and she'd grown the iron to help the future unfold.

Choosing the leader of the Shicassan army had been a gamble, but the reports she's heard of him had been encouraging. He'd ordered the slaughter stopped after the Valtierrans had fled the field. He could easily have destroyed most of their army and seized more land, but he'd stopped after achieving his goal. That bespoke a man with a respect for life and one who exercised restraint. Such qualities would not have endeared him to Tatros.

He'd survived the tyrant's displeasure, so he was obviously resourceful, and Valtierra needed a resourceful man to lead its army. The Warrior who had died had been a fine fighter but timid in his role as leader and unwilling to assert his command.

Her reveries were interrupted by the sound of knuckles rapping lightly on her doorpost. She decided to avoid another penalty of age; the difficulty of rising and walking. After donning her mask, she said, "Enter."

The Warrior swung the door open and stepped inside. As at the Council, he strode confidently, his strong features composed.

Waving toward the stool, the Crone finished her line of knitting, then set it aside.

"Thank you for seeing me." His clipped accent with the rolling r's, while pronounced, didn't make him difficult to understand.

"You presented yourself well in the Council. And I noticed you spoke with each of us after. How did your conversation with the Priest go?"

A smile flickered across the broad face. "I think we understand each other better and will have more time to know each other. That is what I must do with all of you."

"Why?"

"Because I must understand your parts in government so I can understand my own part. Some of the Council I can understand, and I can see how alliances might form. The Wise Old Man and the Priest are obviously traditionalists. I suppose each has a role. At a guess, the Rash Youth is there to confront tradition and represent the passions of the young and the sense of outraged justice."

"You're very clever." The Crone leaned forward and stared into his dark eyes. "Is that because you're a warrior or in spite of it?"

He shrugged. "I had never thought about it." She watched as he toyed with the ties of the mask. He was either working up his nerve to say something unpleasant or trying to find the proper way to express it.

He looked up into her eyes. "How much authority will I have over the army?"

"What do you mean? If you're talking about going to war, that's a decision that has to be made by the Council. What, precisely, are you talking about?"

He dropped his gaze. "Your soldiers fight like little boys playing at war. They need training. And your army needs more archers and slingers. I need to know if I can demote, reassign, or punish soldiers who cannot or will not do their work."

"In those circumstances, your control is almost total, although death warrants must be reviewed by the Council." Obviously, the Crone thought, he is considering the position. This reinforced her opinion that he was the man to be the Warrior. Valtierra didn't need a man who didn't think about responsibility. He was apparently a man who chose his words carefully, then stood behind them.

"I doubt there will be many death warrants, although men learn from shame and the occasional flogging."

The man stopped fidgeting with the mask's ties. "Do you always lead the Council?"

"No, there are twelve of us, and twelve months in a year. Each member leads the Council in his or her turn."

"I would be interested in attending the Council during the Fool's turn."

The Crone laughed. "It can be entertaining, but don't sell the Fool short. He's remarkably clever and quick-witted. There are times when he echoes back our statements in such a way that we realize we hadn't looked at our ideas from both sides."

He shifted on his stool. The Crone knew it was an uncomfortable seat and lower than her couch, which is why her guests were usually offered it. It kept conversations short and it reminded them that, at least in this place, she was the one in charge.

Apparently giving up any hope of comfort, the Warrior asked, "Are the decisions of the Council unanimous, or by simple majority?"

The Crone cackled again, but this time it turned to a cough and she reached for her cup. The watered lemon and honey drink soothed the throat, gave her the moisture to swallow. "When have you heard of twelve strong people agreeing on every issue? And it's too easy to get a majority to agree to an ill-advised decision. In the Council, a decision requires nine votes.

"And don't think that since the consideration of your nomination won ten votes, you have ten votes to become the Warrior. They voted to take the time to think on the matter, not to accept you as the Warrior."

The Warrior stood. "I am aware of that. I will meet each of them in turn and we shall see." He tucked the mask under his arm. "What do you see as the greatest problems facing the city?"

"So far as you're concerned, it'll be the rivalry between Valtierra and Shicassa. That valley you helped seize from us was a great resource. It was fertile enough to make the difference between enough and starvation in a bad year, and enough and food to sell to others in good years. We've always been rivals but Tatros is nibbling at all his borders, especially the border with Valtierra."

The Warrior snorted. "If war with another city-state were the only problem facing the Council, I would see your Priest for conversion. It will be the first place I have ever seen so blessed. Let me guess. If I were to ask the Priest or the Wise Old Man, I would learn that the young have no respect for their elders or the old ways, and that their fashions are shameless. Other members of the Council would have other issues they felt were not being addressed, or were being addressed badly."

The Crone laughed again, took another sip to avoid coughing, and said, "As I said, you're very clever. I think you're going to be a surprise to some on the Council. I'll let you discover the rest from the others."

As the Warrior turned and left, the Crone took off her mask and drank the rest of the liquid in the cup, then took up her knitting again. She'd been right about his cleverness, and it disturbed her a little. He was obviously clever enough to be dangerous, and she could only hope he was honest enough to be trustworthy.

THE RASH YOUTH

The Rash Youth found himself rather liking the Warrior. He was a large man, not massive but with an air of solidity, and he bore himself with pride. His accent, which clipped most words a bit short, seemed businesslike and proper to a Warrior.

He took a mouthful of the finely chopped salad then wiped his fingers on a piece of flatbread, which he used to gather a mouthful of hummus. He ate lightly, taking only a little of the spiced meat and sipping at a cup of watered wine. He'd be getting some exercise soon, and he wanted to keep his edge keen.

The Warrior entered the dining hall, glanced once around the room, and approached the table at which the Youth sat. The man sat, cross-legged, across the table.

"You might want to get something to eat," the Youth said. "The kitchen is through that door." He nodded toward the door.

The Warrior rose, strode into the kitchen, and returned with a platter containing the same tabouli, hummus, baba ganoush, and flatbread the Youth enjoyed, along with a portion of moussaka and a cup.

"How do you like the wine?" the Youth asked.

"I have not developed a taste for it," the Warrior replied. He raised the cup in his hand. "The lemon is new to me, but I like it. The wine I have tasted is either too sweet or too bitter for my taste."

The Youth laughed, showing his even, white teeth. "I'll be happy to sample until I can find something to your tastes. How do you like the food?"

"Actually, very much." Still a little awkwardly, he used the flatbread to scoop up a bit of hummus then did the same with the moussaka. "You people have a taste for slightly sour foods, but this pale yellow paste still lacks something."

The Youth opened a small pot on the table, drew out a pinch of red-brown powder, and sifted it onto the hummus. "See if this helps. I'll warn you, it should be used sparingly."

The Warrior sampled the spiced hummus and smiled broadly. "Excellent! Just what it needed."

"What sort of food did you eat, where you were from?"

"Almost anything we could kill. I never liked wolf, but bear is very good, and I am partial to panther. Most of the time, of course, it was beef or mutton."

The Youth wondered what panther might taste like. "Only meat?"

"No, there were several kinds of roots, herbs, and berries, along with some fruits that grow well in cold weather. Nearer the coast, there were settlements of farmers, but most of the land had a short growing season, so we were herdsmen and hunters."

"What did you drink?"

The Warrior replied, "Ale," and gave his attention to his meal until he'd finished his platter and drained his cup. "An alemaster was a man of standing. A good alemaster was given more respect than your princes, and it was deserved."

Having long since finished his light meal, the Youth leaned forward, resting his elbows and forearms on the tabletop. "Did you come here over the mountains?"

"No, nobody crosses those mountains. The mountains themselves are not so dangerous or treacherous as the wild men who live in them." Finished eating, the Warrior seemed to be looking for something. After a moment he stood and strode to the kitchen, then back to the table. "I could never abide anything sticky or oily on my hands."

"You were talking about the wild men of the mountains."

The Warrior nodded emphatically. "Each new generation has its doubters, and now and then someone, usually a trader with the scent of profit deadening his smell for treachery, will accept an offer to guide them safely across the mountains. I have yet to meet the man who has made the trip.

"No, I came by ship. It is riskier than it might seem, for the mountains march right into the sea, and ships still have their bellies ripped out by the hidden peaks. At first, they are islands, lessening in size and height as you reach the deeper water, but it is at least two days' sailing to reach a completely safe passage—if you consider monstrous waves safe."

The Warrior chuckled. "I will never be a sailor, and I will never return to the south. I puked for two days, and for the rest of the voyage I was too stricken to do more than lie in my bunk and hope to die. I wanted to vomit but could raise nothing but bile and water."

"You sound afraid to return," the Youth observed.

"I have been in battles in which I was afraid for my life. That sea voyage was the only time I ever wished for death."

"You might've gotten your wish from Tatros. Why have you been so quick to forgive? This forgiveness doesn't seem a warrior's trait."

The Warrior's mouth settled into a grim line. "I have forgiven nothing. I will never agree to a truce with Tatros, should he offer one. But I doubt anyone outside a few people could find a way to kill him. In the meantime, I take some satisfaction in knowing he must sleep with a dagger under his pillow, and he fears death. If I do not kill him, someone else will."

The Youth uncrossed his legs and sprang lightly to his feet. "If you've finished your meal, let's take a walk to my room."

The Warrior uncoiled and rose, not as lightly but still effortlessly. "I have to meet the Wise Old Man after the meal."

"His meal hasn't been taken to his room yet, and he dawdles over his food. You've time for a little exercise."

As they walked together, the Warrior spoke. "You have learned about me. I have not yet learned about Valtierra."

"Perhaps," the Youth said, "the best way to learn is to have a guide. I could show you the city." He smiled. "In some ways, it's best seen at night." He stopped before a door and drew it open.

The Youth enjoyed his quarters. His pallet, on a wooden frame, with a large cedar chest at its foot, stood against a wall. At the other end stood a wicker framework laden with cloaks and tunics, and with a top shaped to hold his mask. Against the opposite pale tan wall rested a chair and a small table with inkpot, quills, and an oil lamp. This left the rest of the room open and the ceiling, too high for him to touch even if he sprang, conveyed a sense of spaciousness.

He walked to the chest where he caught up two wands. "Choose one," he said.

With a quizzical look, the Warrior took one.

"We'll pretend these are light swords." The Youth had practiced with a handful of soldiers and had learned that, in the use of the light sword, he was their superior. Used to fighting armored opponents with shields, most of them stood and hewed like woodcutters, and his agility and quickness were enough to let him beat their best.

"If you do not mind," the Warrior said, and unbuckled the belt with his dagger and the light sword and laid it across the bed. He raised the mask and lowered it over his head, tying it in place. "I do not want an advantage and, since you are masked, I will limit my vision as well."

Picking up the wand again, the Warrior whipped the air with it to make an intimidating hiss then took a stance sidewise to the Youth.

Relying on quickness, the Youth lunged, trying to touch the Warrior's side with the tip, coming in to the right of the Warrior's stick. A deft movement to the Warrior's right, the rod held palm-up, deflected his wand and the man beat the Youth's stick aside then whipped his own wand around for a slash at the Youth's head.

Desperately, the Youth swept his wand up to parry but the slash had been a feint and as he missed the parry, the Warrior's wand touched him lightly in the ribs. The man was cat-quick, the Youth realized, perhaps as fast as he was.

"Again?"

The Youth feinted a thrust, this time to the left of the Warrior's rod, found it deflected by the Warrior moving his hand only a little to his left, again gripped palm-up.

The Youth sprang back to clear his 'blade' and the man followed, thrusting.

Trying to copy the other man's defense, the Youth attempted to beat aside the stick but another flick of the wrist brought the wand down against the top of his mask.

"Enough," the Youth said, lowered his wand then tossed it onto the top of the chest. "When we have more time, you'll have to teach me some of your magic."

The Warrior placed his stick beside the other and drew on his belt again. "No magic, just practice. In the south we long ago learned different swordwork is needed for an unarmored man than an armored one. The technique, especially with light swords, is very different from a man using a shield, and still different from the ways to fight a man using no shield but wielding a heavier blade." He untied the mask and ducked out of it.

"You're not doing my reputation for rashness any good," The Youth said. "Let me regain part of it by showing you Valtierra. We'll see if we can find a wine to your taste, and one of the Harlot's sisters."

"I thank you for the offer," the Warrior replied, "but I still have to meet the other members of the Council. And I am afraid my own thoughts and impressions will give me more than enough company for the next night or two. If the offer still stands three days from now, I will take you up on it."

"I'm sure I'll see you before then to remind you," the Youth said. "And you can repay me by teaching me proper fighting skills."

"Looking to become the next Warrior, eh?" the Warrior asked. "You have the quickness for it, and the wit." He turned to leave, paused by the door as though reminded of something then went out.

The Youth glanced once around the room, slipped a purse full of coins onto his belt, and left the room. As he paced the corridor he decided he needed to talk to the Merchant. It shouldn't be too difficult to order a barrel of ale. He wondered what the stuff would taste like.

THE WISE OLD MAN

The Old Man had lost interest in many of the pleasures of life, including food. Eating had become just another duty, and his jaws and teeth made it an uncomfortable one. He finished his light meal and a cup that contained more water than wine then donned his mask again. The woman who'd brought his food would return later to take the cup and tray back to the kitchen. Catching up his stick, he hauled himself as erect as his aged body could get, and hobbled out of his rooms, down the corridor to the garden.

Torches guttered and flared in the faint breeze and the Old Man, using the stick, carefully made his way to the bench beside the small pool. When he reached it his breath was shorter and his heartbeat faster than they would have been after running half a league when he'd been a younger man, a condition that annoyed him more than the stiffness of his joints. Still, the pool provided rest and solace, and was worth the effort it cost to reach it.

He'd just composed his thoughts when the outlander towered over him. Looking up, he said, "Please sit," gesturing at the other end of the bench.

"Thank you," the man said, and seated himself. "Obviously, we have no way of knowing whether or not I will be accepted to the Council, but if I am, I need to know as much as possible about Valtierra and my duties. So, I am asking each of the Council to give me some of their time and the benefit of their knowledge."

The Old Man snorted. "You can save your time with the Fool."

"Perhaps, but courtesy requires I give him at least a hearing."

The Old Man felt he'd somehow been gently rebuked, but he considered the question. "To be honest, I'm afraid of a real war with Shicassa, a war for which we are very poorly prepared. It would mean the death of Valtierra. So it's only natural I should fear a Warrior who might rush us into disaster. Particularly a Warrior who is an outlander."

"If war comes," the Warrior said, "it will not be because I bring it. And I think preparing for war may be the best way to prevent it." He gestured broadly with his left hand and arm, the sweep apparently indicating all the land around them. "Yours is a wealthy city, and they always attract the hungry and the greedy.

"Further, while I am an outlander, I have no reason to wish you or your city ill. I fought you because my talents were for sale, not because I wanted your city to fall."

After a long pause, the Warrior added, "I think a number of the city's problems can be resolved by restoring a sense of duty and pride. I can only do that with the army and, perhaps, the militia."

The Old Man tried to conceal his surprise. The man had named the monsters that lurked in his sleepless nights. "When I was a child, I remember my grandfather speaking of the city with pride. The only thing he cared for more than the city was his own family. Now, many of the people take the city for granted, and give nothing to it."

"How do you think you can change that?"

The Old Man slowly shook his head. "I don't know. If we pass laws we can't enforce, we weaken ourselves. If we enforce them, we run the risk of becoming a tyranny like Shicassa."

"Who commands the militia when they are not under arms?"

"No one. They're only called upon to aid the army or the constables." The Old Man flexed his hands, trying to work some of the stiffness out of his joints. "I'd forgotten you might not understand how we've tried to balance power. The army may not enter the city of Valtierra. They have a permanent camp two leagues from the city. Order is maintained in the city by the constables, who have their own leader who answers to the Council."

The Warrior stood. "I shall have to visit the city, probably within the next two or three days. I have only heard about it, but to know the place I must walk its streets, see its markets, talk to its people. Until I'm more familiar with Valtierra, I will not be able to add anything to the Council." He nodded. "With your permission, I will take my leave."

The Old Man nodded in reply and watched the man's long strides carry him away.

The surface of the pool before him rippled at the breeze. In a couple of months, that breeze would be much colder, and his joints would ache more fiercely but, for now, it was a pleasant respite from the late summer heat.

Sandaled feet scuffed the ground softly and he looked up to see the Priest standing across the pool from him, his gray robe making him almost invisible in the evening's gloom. "May I join you?" the Priest asked.

He gestured at the bench.

As the Priest seated himself, he asked, "What's your assessment of that man?"

The Old Man chuckled. "Much less certain than it was when he first entered the Council chamber. What do you think of him?"

The Priest stretched his legs out before him. "I was predisposed to dislike him."

The Old Man was quick to catch the word. "Was…?"

The Priest nodded and from the pocket of his robe drew a prayer-stone. "Obviously, he's an outlander who doesn't know our customs or worship our gods, and he could be a dangerous man." He raised his face upward to the stars beginning to appear. "I was a bit reminded of the Destroyer. Do we make offerings to him because he can throw lightnings, or because he refrains from doing so? I think that one," he nodded in the direction the Warrior had taken, "is a little like the Destroyer, but even more like the Sustainer."

"How so?"

The Priest shrugged. "It's hard to say, but I have a sense he respects tradition and virtue. I also believe he would rather build than destroy." He shrugged. "Just a feeling."

"Your feeling may be correct. I'm beginning to have those same feelings. I just wonder how much we can trust feelings." He thought a moment. "From what I've seen, his wits are as keen as his sword but swords have two edges and we don't want to cut ourselves."

"Cleverness is facile but shallow," the Priest replied. "I see real depth in him."

Using his stick and accepting the help of the Priest, the Old Man worked his way up until he stood. "Walk with me as far as my rooms?" As they entered the building, the Old Man asked, "And what about the fact he doesn't worship our gods?"

"I'm beginning to think," the Priest replied, "that I'd prefer an honest heathen to someone who ignored the gods except to use Them for an occasional display of piety."

They finally reached the Old Man's door. The Old Man said, "I'm also beginning to think I might vote for him." He opened his door. "Pray for me, if you would."

"I do, every day, and all the city as well."

The Old Man hobbled to his bed and untied and removed his mask. The heavy leather seemed an appropriate symbol of the weight of their authority.

After noticing the cup and tray were gone, he undressed and laid on the pallet. For the first time since he'd first put on the mask, he felt hope, and his mind, instead of perceiving everything in shades of dread, spun with possibilities.

THE HARLOT

She lounged on soft, brilliantly colored cushions until she heard the rap at her doorpost. "Come in," she said.

As the Warrior entered, she stifled an impish smile. In contrast to his confident stride and stance at the Council, he seemed wary and almost deferential. She waved her hand at another nest of cushions and watched him try, unsuccessfully, to find a comfortable way to sit.

"Thank you for seeing me." His accent added a touch of the exotic to his deep voice.

Most of his face was in shadow, the room's only light coming from two candles. She decided the trade was a good balance—his strong features looked attractive either way.

She smiled. "It seemed a proper time to meet you. Harlots always look best at night."

One corner of his lips curled up. "I have no idea what you look like."

"So," she said, "I can keep the mystery alive for a year and a half." She leaned closer. "Have you come to beg me for my vote?"

He shook his head. "You will give it to me or not, as you choose…"

She laughed. "Well, you've passed the first test. Groveling isn't something a Warrior should do well."

"Actually, I was curious about how you see your part in the Council."

"I'm one of those who must be convinced. The Rash Youth represents the spirit of rebellion, while others uphold tradition—the Priest and the Wise Old Man. Some others—the Crone and the Fool particularly—seem to have their own interests. Most of the rest of us are there to provide the balance."

He stretched and the muscles of his arms rippled. "I get the impression the Council is a place of shifting alliances, like clouds on a breezy day—coming together, merging, separating again."

"In some ways," she said. "There are reasons for alliances because of common interests. For instance; you, the Merchant, and I are, in one way, natural allies. We all sell something, although your wares and mine are more intimate. It's ourselves we're selling."

"You are very sharp," he said. "I admit to being a bit surprised to learn you are such a realist."

She laughed, hard enough the bells tied to the leather ribbons the mask used to represent hair tinkled. "Every harlot is first and foremost a realist."

"What do you want from the city?" The question was direct and unexpected.

She had to consider the question, never having asked it of herself. "I want the people of the city and around it to respect what my sisters and I do. Part of it is to weave illusions. That's probably why you were surprised to find I am a realist."

She lowered her voice, as though imparting a trade secret. "The ones who cast the illusions must never believe in them, else the illusion will fail."

She considered his question again. "I think I'd like the city to respect tradition but not be bound by it."

The Warrior smiled. "You give the impression you're not bound by many conventions."

"Actually," she replied, "my role is very much bound by tradition. Although, I must admit, I sometimes pay little attention to which ear a man wore his ring in."

She noticed the raised eyebrow and knew he was unfamiliar with the customs of Valtierra. "You won't be able to be so subtle if you decide you're going to wear the mask. In Valtierra, it's the custom for a boy or girl, when they become a man or a woman, to wear a ring in their left ear. If they marry, or if they become a priest or priestess, they remove the ring and wear it in their right ear.

"A harlot should never sleep with someone with a ring in their right ear. The only ones who wear no rings are those who've lost a spouse and have chosen not to partner again."

"Thank you," the Warrior said. "There is still much for me to learn about Valtierra. I should ask if there is anything you want to know about me."

She caught her smile just an instant too late. "I think I already know quite a bit about you—it's a harlot's gift, you know, and I'm sure I'll learn more at the appropriate time."

For a man his size, the Warrior got to his feet gracefully. "Then," he said, "I will bid you a good night."

As he closed the door lightly behind him, the Harlot rolled onto her belly and lay, her hands propping her chin. She'd expected the directness, but the Warrior had displayed surprising depth. She'd already decided he'd be a good addition to the Council and the conversation had confirmed it.

THE WARRIOR

Alone in his room, Anton turned the mask in his hands. It was a work of art, as were all the masks. Like the others, it ended at the tip of the nose, the bottom running wide of the mouth, so it didn't interfere with breathing or eating. At the edge of the cheekbone it plunged down to about the line of the jaw, where it ended in cords used to secure it. The back of the mask reached to the base of the skull. Ears molded into the mask funneled sound to the wearer.

The masks were formed of cunningly shaped leather and, with the exception of that of the Priest and his own, all had some representation of hair. Two or three had the suggestion of hair molded on and painted, like that of the Youth with its golden brown ringlets. The Wise Old Man's mask and that of the Crone bore wild white manes, while the Harlot's was topped with thin, curled ribbons with bells bound in them. Her 'face' was comely but almost garishly made up, pale with bright pink cheeks, blue around the eyes, and artfully arched eyebrows.

He'd liked all those to whom he'd spoken and he appreciated the fact they were men and women who were doing their best to become the masks they wore. All were striving to become something greater. That was worthy of respect.

He hadn't told them of the possibility that there was a traitor among them. It would have accomplished nothing. His own position was too precarious for them to believe him, and it would warn the spy, make him—or her—more wary.

If there were indeed a spy, the danger to Valtierra was greater than all but one of the Council knew.

The difficulties he faced were not unfamiliar—he'd fought one campaign in which the leader had been too dense or too reckless to use scouts in strange territory—but groping in darkness for a mortal enemy was as dangerous as it was stupid. Now he was forced to fight the same sort of battle. The first thing he needed to do was to learn what forces he faced and what resources he had available. Just as important was the terrain of the battlefield, which was the culture of Valtierra. He was hobbled, somewhat, by his unfamiliarity with the language. He barely understood the way they shortened and bound words together, and he still thought in his native Ragdan. He wondered if he'd ever be able to think in this northern language.

He'd begun his exploration of Valtierran culture by learning about the others on the Council. He still had to meet with more than half of them, but he also needed to see the army he'd lead. They hadn't impressed him in battle, and he had yet to learn whether it was a sword of soft lead or of steel only needing to be tempered. After he met with the Fool in the morning, he'd ride to the army camp. And, he had yet to visit the city. He'd only seen the city's walls and nearest gate when he'd been escorted to the residence.

The residence itself was impressive, with its tiled floors and plastered walls. It had been been built of tan stone, with doors and shutters for the many windows made of dark wood bound with ornate patterns in black iron that still showed the marks of the hammers. Tapestries and paintings decorated the walls and a few small statues rested on dark wooden pedestals. The largest sculpture stood just outside the dining hall; the Trinity carved of some hard, black stone. The Warrior found the figures fascinating. The Artisan might've been the model for the Maker while the Sustainer was represented as a woman with ample breasts, and the Destroyer leaned on a long, curved sword. For such a fearsome figure, his features were almost pretty. When he looked at the figures more closely, he realized that despite her obvious attributes, the Sustainer stood in a decidedly masculine pose and the nose and chin were certainly not effeminate. All the figures, he realized, were sexually ambiguous.

The building appeared larger than it was because it was an open square, with the garden at its center. Along the front ran a corridor from the kitchen and dining hall to the Council chamber, intersecting at the ends with other corridors leading to apartments for the Council members and, he presumed, rooms for the women who cooked and cleaned and the stableman, unless the man slept with his charges. A few outbuildings, including four latrines, a couple of buildings he didn't recognize, and what appeared to be a forge, stood behind the residence proper, along with a small grove of trees.

Yes, he'd need to see the city he was expected to defend. He'd take the Youth up on his offer in a day or two.

Turning the mask in his hands again he realized that, while the decision was not solely his to make, he'd decided to become the Warrior. The office represented a challenge and, to a warrior, a challenge was something to be met.

Meeting challenges hadn't come easily to him. In his first battle, he'd failed miserably. At the beginning of the battle he'd stood beside a half-brother, part of the shield wall beyond the wagons. When the enemy had rushed toward him it was as though he'd been turned to stone.

He could still close his eyes and see it; large men in leather armor and studded mail, their teeth showing in either grins or snarls, charging forward to kill him.

Life hadn't been pleasant but it was still new and he had dreams and hopes and wants, and all of them, he knew, would die with him; a short life ending in pain. He'd taken to his heels. His half-brother had died fighing, and other men of the household had dashed toward the gap in the line. Some of them had died fighting as well but, at day's end, the other house had become less than a memory.

His father and other half-brothers had led the hunt that found him cowering in a wagon. The memory of it and of his cowardice was still enough to make his cheeks burn with shame. He'd been beaten senseless and treated as something lower than a dog until the next battle. In that battle and the two after it his task had been to hold the house banner, unarmed and with a half-brother to 'protect' him. He suspected the half-brother was there to cut him down if he fled, but he'd learned that even a painful death was preferable to shame. He'd gotten a few scars—an arrow through his right leg and another through his right shoulder, as well as a gash across his chest from a badly-parried sword cut, but he'd stood his ground.

His punishment was actually a boon. He'd never deserted one of his own men since that first battle, and being forced to stand in the middle of the fray with nothing to do but watch had let him observe and evolve tactics to give advantages to his house. His father had been willing to accept the advice—as long as Anton took the most dangerous parts in the feints and ambushes he planned. His standing in the family improved, but only barely. He'd never been allowed to forget that he'd run from danger and abandoned a half-brother when he was fourteen.

He supposed that was why his father had sold him for a week's provisions and a couple of goats.

His position had changed only a little with the trade. While he'd had nominal command of the Shicassan army, Tatros had never let him forget he was a disposable hireling and he wondered whether the gift of armor and some money hadn't been merely an ostententatious display more for Tatros' benefit than to curry Anton's gratitude.

Now he was free. He was winning respect and acceptance by both the army and the Council, and he knew he'd never falter. He was no longer reminded of his flaws or inferior station, and he fully intended to earn what he'd been given.

THE FOOL

The Fool woke, yawning, and washed his face and hands from the ewer and basin. The water, night-chilled, helped shock him more fully awake and he dried himself with the blanket. From the chest he drew a bright red tunic and brighter blue trousers. A soft pair of ankle boots and a studded belt finished his wardrobe for the day. He was just reaching for his mask when he heard someone rapping at his doorpost.

After ducking into his mask and tying it in place, he opened the door and waved the Warrior into the room. Two chairs stood by the window and he said, "Choose one."

The Warrior took the chair in the shade of the wall and the Fool sat in the other, basking in the morning sunlight. "Always meet and talk with a fool the first thing in the morning," the Fool said. "That way, nothing worse will happen to you all day."

The Warrior chuckled. "I had been wondering why the Twelve would include a Fool…?"

"It's not an easy task, being the Fool." He throttled the smile that threatened to turn his lips up. "Some days, I wake up just aching to feel passionately about some cause, or to think deeply about a problem, but that's work for someone else. I must always see the humor in things. And that isn't always easy."

The Warrior did smile. "I suspect you feel as strongly and think as deeply as anyone on the Council. What only you can provide is a sense of proportion, which can sometimes come only from humor, and tension is often best dispelled by a good laugh."

"Careful," the Fool said. "Now you're treading into the realm of the Wise Old Man. And if you think about it too long, you might be chosen the next Fool."

The smile remained. "I could never carry out the task as well as you."

The Fool pretended a transparent outrage. "Now that's a fine thing to say! We're all Fools, it's just that some of us acknowledge the fact."

"Being a stranger, I find myself looking for advice."

The Fool shook his head slowly. "Who is the bigger fool, the Fool or the man who asks advice of him?"

The Warrior had a rich, distinctive laugh. "As you say, some of us just acknowledge the fact." He paused. "I am going to visit the army camp."

"Then pray to the Sustainer for a head cold. Otherwise, you can smell the place a league away. And I wouldn't eat or drink much while I was there. The food is awful and the wine indifferent at best."

"Something all armies seem to have in common."

"That I couldn't say." The Fool tried to smooth back the unruly red mop of hair crowning his mask. "You're much more well-traveled than I. One thing I might suggest is a visit to a tailor's. You look as though you've found the last Warrior's chest of clothes, but they don't fit you well. He was almost as tall as you are, but heavier."

"I was thinking of going to the city tomorrow night. Do tailors keep late hours?"

"That's probably their busiest time. The young people prefer the evening hours and they provide most of the business. Staying in fashion is as expensive as it is pointless."

The Warrior's grin returned. "I thought being pointless was a desirable quality for a Fool."

"There's too much competition," the Fool replied. "They're amateurs. Fools are best appreciated alone. When everyone around them is a fool, they become tiresome."

The Warrior chuckled again. "Have you any suggestions about what I should buy?"

"What did I just tell you about seeking the advice of a Fool? Choose what's comfortable for you. You may even start a new fashion."

The Warrior stood. "I thank you for your time and for the pleasant conversation."

The Fool got to his feet. "Have you broken your fast yet?"

"Not yet."

"Then let's go get something to eat. If you don't eat at the camp, you'll be hungry, and if you eat at the camp you'll probably be dining on slop." He led the way to the dining hall.

The Fool took water and, seeing the Warrior add lemon to his cup, did the same. Loading his platter with cheese, grapes, melon, and olives, he added a small bit of baklava.

As they sat at the table, the Fool observed that only other people in the room were the Mother, nursing her infant, the Crone, and the Farmer, each eating alone.

He and the Warrior shared a companionable silence as they ate, the Fool deciding he liked the taste of lemon in the water.

Finally the Warrior unfolded his legs and got to his feet. "Thank you, again," he said, and carried his platter back to the kitchen.

After the Warrior had gone, the Fool carried his own platter back to the kitchen and refilled his cup with more water and lemon. After a moment's thought, he decided it would never do to take it back to the table and sip. It would be too plain to everyone he was thinking. Sometimes, it was hard being the fool. He drained the cup and skipped back to his apartment.

Alone, he could take off the mask and be just as thoughtful as he wished. He suspected the Warrior would be brimming with proposals for the Council, and waiting a fortnight wasn't in the man's nature. He'd want to move swiftly. The trick was not only to hurry the vote on the man's membership but to make it look as though it had been the Council's idea.

The next meeting of the Council was over a week away. In that time he'd be sure the Warrior was ready. Absently, he picked up the small sandbags he kept in a bowl, juggling them until he had eleven of them in the air.

THE WARRIOR

The Fool was right, the clothing of the dead Warrior fit badly, although it helped the man had a taste for sleeveless shirts. In this warmer northern climate, less was better.

Stopping in his rooms, he exchanged the light sword at his belt for his war hammer. Going into a strange camp of armed and armored men, the hammer, with its greater authority, was a comfort. He was tempted to put on his armor but in the late summer heat it would be stifling.

In the stables he saddled his pale gray stallion, noting the animal had been well cared for. He led the horse out, mounted, and gave him his head.

Apparently bored with inactivity, the charger set a good pace and the Warrior, after letting him gallop off some of the energy, held him to a canter that still made quick work of the two leagues or so to the camp.

Observing the fields through which he rode, he saw signs of a good harvest. Plots of some gourds and melons remained but the grain crops and most of the vegetables, cultivated in small plots, had been gathered.

If this land was richer than that of the south, its peoples were far more expressive. The southerners were taciturn and used to bearing hardship with stoicism. These northern people spoke more and seemed to laugh easier. Among the Council members, the Crone seemed the most like the people he'd known. He hadn't missed her scrutiny and he suspected she possessed a shrewdness that would match that of any southern matriach.

The Rash Youth was at the other extreme; voluble and volatile. The Fool pretended to be more like the Youth but his cleverness was a sharp tool and he plied it well. He might not fight with weapons but in a battle of wills or intrigue he'd be a dangerous enemy.

The Fool had been correct when he warned him about the odor; he smelled the place before he ever saw it.

The encampment's gray stone wall was nearly as high as that of the city, at least the height of six tall men standing on each others' shoulders, and sprawled across the lower slopes of two hills and the valley between them. Horses grazed and goats browsed in a fenced pasture to his left, and two score of them were heavy chargers like his own mount, while twice that number of lighter horses and draft horses also cropped the dying grass. To the right of the fortress a herd of cattle grazed.

A horn winded a single drawn-out note and a few more guards appeared at the top of the wall. The gate ahead of him stood open and he slowed his mount to a walk.

The walls might be of stone, but most of the buildings inside were of wood, and most of them were hovels.

If anyone were in command of this camp, it seemed a carefully kept secret. Even the guards wore only light tunics and trousers, and only they seemed to be carrying weapons. Chickens scratched in the dirt, goats browsed the weeds. And he saw women the Harlot would probably be embarrassed to meet. Overlaying it all was an almost palpable air of despondency, the mark of the garrison soldier.

A man hurried to meet him, still buckling his breast and back plates together.

"Are you in command here?" The Warrior's tone was a warning.

"No sir. He sent me to meet you."

Fixing the unhappy man with a glare, he said, "I want every captain, petty-captain, and lieutenant assembled by that wall," he gestured at a section of wall where stairs rose to the walkway, "and I want the rest of the camp as far away as possible. Now, where is the commander of this sty?"

The soldier pointed to one of the few stone buildings, then took to his heels.

The Warrior handed the reins of his horse to the next soldier he saw and strode to the building the man had pointed out, which, while it was of stone, was ill cared for. Not deigning to knock, he thrust the door open and stepped inside. If anything, the smell was even worse inside the building, and he accidentally kicked a bottle spinning.

"Who…?"

"Your commander." The Warrior stared into the shadows until he saw a pudgy middle-aged man still drawing up his trousers. A woman, barely awake, lay on the pallet behind the man.

For a long moment the Warrior battled his rage and when he spoke, he controlled his voice enough to keep it soft but still steel-edged. "You will be needing new quarters. I am having this pigsty cleaned."

Despite the sullen scowl on his face, the man had enough sense to remain silent.

"Do you know how to build a proper latrine?" The man nodded, his scowl deepening.

"It does not show. Well. You can have fifty men to help you. You seem to be in the Sustainer's favor. I am amazed plague has not wiped out this camp. When you have finished dressing, you can join the assembly."

His anger remained, even after he'd walked outside and seen men rushing about, most moving to the opposite side of the camp. While the leaders gathered, he strode to the stairs and climbed halfway to the catwalk near the top of the walls. From this higher vantage he could see the movement of people more clearly. When the number of stragglers had shrunk to only a handful, he glared at the faces staring up at him.

"This camp is a pesthole. That will change and it will change quickly. Tomorrow morning, we begin a three-day march. I expect all the soldiers to be carrying everything of value they own, along with their armor, weapons, and supplies enough for three days. Any men unable to march will be expected to build enclosures for the animals, clean any stone structures, and demolish the wooden ones.

"Every man is to be given a ration of one cup of wine a day. If a man wants more, he may buy it. I expect warriors to drink. I do not expect to see them drunk. If I find a man drunk, we will see if a flogging of ten stripes improves his ability to drink without becoming a sot. If I find a drunken man on sentry duty, or other duty, it will be fifteen stripes.

"Some of you may be here to serve the city. The city is being poorly served. Some of you may be here for the money. You are not earning it. If you are here because you are too lazy to farm, too inept to be craftsmen, and too ashamed to beg, you will either earn pride or lose it altogether. I was told you were soldiers. You should at least try to look like soldiers. In this camp, beginning today, you will all wear your armor and carry or wear your weapons, unless you are doing hard, menial labor.

"Now," he roared, "return to your men and prepare them for tomorrow's march."

Muttering broke out below him and he heard one voice ask, "Where are we marching?"

"This is not the Council," the Warrior bellowed, "and your opinions were not solicited. If you are unable to lead your men, take your valuables and get out. If you think you might be warriors or want to become warriors, see to your men." He paused to note where his horse was tied to a post and marched down the stair and to his animal, mounted, and rode back to the residence.

THE ARTISAN

He saw the Warrior riding past on a well-lathered horse, then returned his attention to the forge and the glowing metal in it. Drawing out the steel bar, he set it on the anvil and hammered it, rough-shaping a blade.

He supposed the man had visited the camp. He had his own visits to make. After the evening meal he'd walk to the city and visit his family. It'd be good to hold his wife and son again. They'd accepted his absence with a measure of grace but were always pleased to have him visit. Eighteen months seemed even longer, but the Council was a duty to be borne.

At least he had no worries about the shop. While his wife knew nothing about smithing, she was the daughter of a master tanner and was very familiar with the business of running a shop, and his senior jorneyman could well be a master in most cities. He'd promised, however, to remain at the smithy until the Artisan could hang his mask on the wall and return to trade.

Even as part of his mind wandered, his hands and eyes had continued their patient shaping of the metal.

After a time he became aware of the Warrior standing patiently by the door. After finishing the shaping while the steel was still hot, he set it on a brick shelf built onto the forge, then trudged to the door. He nodded to the Warrior. "Let's talk outside."

The breeze was a relief from the heat of the forge. He wished he could remove his mask and wipe the sweat from his face, but he'd had six months to become accustomed to the discomfort. "What can I do for you?"

"I need someone who can teach men to build in stone. I do not want them to work, I want them to teach others how to work."

"That's sometimes harder than the work." The Artisan stretched and flexed his arms.

"Could we ask the Council to pay the man?"

"Of course. The Council pays the army and the constables. What do you want built?" The Warrior obviously had something in mind.

"I want to re-build the camp. It is a slum."

The enormity of the task appealed to the craftsman. "You'll need a planner; someone who can look at what you want and what you have available." He led the way to a barrel of water, drew a ladle and drank, then handed the gourd dipper to the Warrior.

The Warrior grinned. "A drink to seal the agreement." He ladled up more water and drank deeply. "Are tailors and cobblers among the artisans?"

"Anyone who works with his hands and mind is an artisan. We have different guilds, but we're all craftsmen."

"Who should I see in the city for new clothing? I did not really have time to pack a trunk when I left my last employer."

"I'm sure the Rash Youth can lead you to the best places."

"Do the tailors and cobblers keep their shops open so late?"

The Artisan grinned, but with a touch of vinegar in the expression. "The ones who want to prosper do. Young wastrels account for most of the clothing and boots bought in Valtierra."

The Warrior gestured toward the forge. "I am sorry I interrupted you. What were you working on?"

Shrugging, the Artisan replied, "Just something to amuse myself. When I can't work with my hands, make the metal do what I want it to, I feel—useless. And since I have no apprentices or journeymen here, I do all the work from start to finish; the shaping, grinding, filing and polishing. In my own shop, I only draw the plans, supervise the work, and add the touches that make my wares exceptional. In many ways it's a pleasure to do all the work."

"What do you make?"

"Anything with a blade. Tailors are still using shears I made when I was an apprentice. That's another source of satisfaction—knowing you've made something that lets another man do his work better, something that will be useful for decades."

After a moment's thought, the Artisan asked, "Where are you getting the stone to build with?"

"We can begin by tearing down the wall. There is no need to fortify a camp; it is the city that needs protection. If I were attacking, I would send a small force to lay siege to the camp and use most of my men to take the city, which would only be defended by militia. Besides, hiding behind a wall reminds the soldiers they are garrison warriors. I want as few garrison soldiers in my army as possible."

"Makes sense," the Artisan agreed. "I'll talk to some planners and masons tonight. How soon will you need them?"

"I needed them today. I will need them even more tomorrow."

The Artisan chuckled. "At least you can't be accused of inaction. Do you know how you want the camp laid out?"

"Have you something to draw on and draw with?"

The Artisan led the Warrior back into his workshop, handed him a stylus and a wax-covered board.

The Warrior laid out a series of rectangles and squares. "The two largest squares will be the dining hall and the brothel. The rectangles are barracks. The smaller squares, connected, will be living quarters for warriors who are married and for the captains, petty-captains, and lieutenants. There are already a few stone buildings. If they can be scoured and used, we will modify the plans to include them. Otherwise, we will use their stones for proper buildings."

"I'll take that with me tonight." The Artisan looked over the plans. "I'll also have the planner modify them for wells and latrines."

"I am in your debt."

"I'll remember that." The Artisan paused. "You haven't mentioned my vote in the Council."

"That is your decision to make. I doubt very much I could beg or cajole your vote and we both know I have nothing to bribe you with, even if you could be bribed."

The Artisan returned to his forge and picked up the steel he'd been working. "I'll talk with you again very soon."

With a nod, the Warrior strode toward the residence.

Thrusting the steel back into the fire, the Artisan worked the bellows with his left hand. He'd been favorably impressed before, and the conversation had reinforced his opinion. The man, outlander or not, was obviously capable, and the Artisan respected his direct manner. Had the man not been a Warrior, he'd almost surely have been a craftsman.

Withdrawing the glowing poker, he shifted hands and wielded the hammer again, beating sparks out of the heat-reddened metal.

THE MATRON

The crimson was still too bright, so she mixed in white and a trace of blue, then brushed it onto the board. The sunset she was painting affected her as sunsets always had and for the thousandth time she tried to sort out the feelings. A trace of melancholy, a daub of satisfaction, a brush-stroke of reflection, all as complex as the composition and the colors that made it up.

A rap at her door caused her to start, then she put on her mask before pacing to the door and opening it. The Warrior, wearing his mask, stood waiting. "Come in," she said, then returned to her painting to clean her brushes.

The Warrior stood gazing at her work and nodded once.

"Sit down." She gestured at one of the two chairs with the brush she was cleaning. After making sure the bristles were clean, she set the brush in a jar with half a dozen other brushes, all bristle-end up, and sat in the other chair.

"You seem to have decided to accept the part of the Warrior—if we choose to accept you."

"Until then," he said, in his deep voice with the bitten-off accent, "I have work to do, and I will need the help of you and others on the Council."

"What do you need of me?"

"The soldiers in the camp have nothing but slop to eat. It is very hard to give men pride when they are fed like swine. I was wondering if you might help me find women who can teach some of the soldiers to prepare a proper meal."

"No women but the lowest of the harlots, or women desperate to marry ever go into the camp."

"I will vouch for the safety of any woman who goes into the camp."

She studied the man through narrowed eyes. "I hope you understand that if anything happens to any woman in that camp, my vote in the Council will be the least thing you need to fear."

"I expected as much." He gave her a half-smile. "You remind me of matriarchs in my own land. They are fiercer than the men, and much more calculating."

"If you're prepared to protect the women, I'll speak with them."

"But not for a day or two, at least," he said. "I need to know which men I can rely upon, and most of the men will be gone from the camp for the next three days."

She raised her eyebrows, then realized he couldn't see the expression. "And what will they be doing for those three days?"

"They will be marching. They have been too long in camp, grown too soft. I need to find out their mettle. While we can hope they will never have to show it in battle, I have to know before the battle whether they have the determination they will need."

Her natural suspicion goaded her to ask, "And where will they be marching to?"

"That is something I need to ask you and the other members of the Council. I am a stranger here. I know most of the crops have been harvested but I want to do no damage. Also, I would like, as much as possible, to have water nearby. I have ordered them to carry all they need for three days. I can promise you that most will not bring enough water, and I want to test them, not cause them to die of thirst. They can do without food, and those who neglect to bring a blanket will lose sleep, but they will need water."

She found herself grinning. This man didn't believe in half-measures. "Talk to the Farmer. He's most familiar with the country outside the city."

"Thank you."

"What do you think of the other members of the Council you've met?"

The Warrior leaned back in his chair and stared above her head, his eyes looking at something only he could see. "I have only met a few, but all of them have impressed me. I can see why they are on the Council."

"Even the Fool?"

"Especially the Fool. I think he helps you all remember what you are supposed to be. He helps you strive to be greater than you are."

She poured water into a cup, offered it to him then poured another cup of water for herself. "And you respect them all?"

"Yes. I do not always agree with them, but I do not need to agree with someone to respect him or her."

"I wouldn't have expected that point of view of a Warrior."

The Warrior stared into her eyes. "You seem to think there is only one sort of warrior. A man who fights while angry or in hatred may be a dangerous enemy but he will never be a true warrior. Respect for your opponent is a warrior's trait. I have never seen an army of warriors. An army needs to be a benign tyranny. The trick is to find the balance. The spirits of the men can be destroyed by either too much tyranny or a leader who is too benign.

"A city or a state cannot afford a tyranny. Where I was born, if you were not born to a family of standing, you could never be more than a highly honored servant or a bandit. In Shicassa, everyone is a slave but the tyrant. From what I have seen of Valtierra, birth means less than ability or determination. You have the freedom to grow, so the city can also grow."

The Matron smiled. "You have an endearing naivete. We have families of wealth and standing here, too."

"Of course, but it is possible to become one of them if one is capable. That is the important difference."

Intrigued, the Matron leaned forward. "You said a city can't afford a tyranny. What did you mean by that?"

Gesturing at the window, as though to indicate the city, or perhaps the world, the Warrior replied, "Too many talents are wasted in a tyranny. In a place where talent means less than breeding, everything must bend to the leaders. There is no…," he paused to search for the word, "…innovation. Nothing new is permitted unless it serves the ends of those in power. The city cannot grow and neither can its people. If a thing cannot grow, it dies."

"I hadn't looked at it that way," the Matron admitted.

"But what of the other city-states?" the Warrior asked. "Valtierra and Shicassa are not the only city-states in the region."

The Matron thought a moment. "Benett, the port city to our east is ruled by merchants and ships' captains. They have no real government. Lancar, to the south, is a matriarchy. Shicassa is to our north, of course, and to the north and west is Sheilba, while to the west stands Ravanna. Sheilba is a princedom like Shicassa, while Ravanna is ruled by a council of guilds. Further north lies Amarr, where the people elect a council like ours, but much larger; something like sixty men."

"Interesting," the Warrior said. "Where I am from, you could wear out a horse every day for a week and still be in holdings ruled by families."

"From what I've heard, your land is a cold place. Perhaps you grew that way because you had to. Here, the land is richer and our only enemies are our neighbors, and we aren't given to trust enough to form alliances, so all the city-states balance each other, and we can have as varied a menu of governments as of foods."

The Matron stood. "It's been pleasant talking with you. You will probably need to speak with the Farmer. He should be in the garden."

The Warrior was apparently intelligent enough to take the suggestion. He got to his feet, bowed, and strode from the room.

Returning to the painting, the Matron chose a smaller brush and began to pick out the ripples of light on the river and the highlights on the cottage.

She'd need to use her contacts with the matriarchy in Lancar to reassure them Valtierra had no designs on them. Benett would take no action unless it was actually attacked. She suspected the Artisan had contacts with the guilds in Ravanna, and would likely reassure them as well.

She'd voted to delay the vote on the Warrior for a fortnight because it postponed a problem. While she'd personally opposed the appointment of the Warrior, she hadn't wanted to annoy the Crone. Now, it seemed, such a choice was unnecessary. While she still harbored reservations about appointing an outlander, this one seemed to be earnest and capable. He seemed to take his duties seriously.

THE FARMER

Collecting dead leaves was his major distraction in the fall. Spring and summer were his busy times, when he had to prepare the ground, plant, keep the plants fed, watered, and give them at least a chance against the weeds. Now, some of them were preparing to die or, at least, to sleep, and he only needed look after their beds.

Except for a few herbs, none of the plants in the garden were truly useful. In the plot outside the residence he grew vegetables and tended fruit and olive trees, but it was their time to rest, too.

At first, he was too engrossed in the work and his own thoughts to hear footsteps on the gravel and noticed nothing until the booted feet stood before him.

He looked up at the mask of the Warrior and tried to hide the scowl that was his first response then realized the other man probably couldn't detect it under his mask.

"May I speak with you?" the Warrior asked in his deep voice with the strange accent.

The Farmer gestured toward the nearest bench, tossing the weeds and leaves he'd gathered on the gravel, and sat down on the bench, wiping dirt and bits of leaves from his hands.

"The Matron tells me you know the land around the camp and for several leagues beyond it."

"And…?"

"I am leading the men on a march tomorrow. I would like to stay only a short distance from water and I do not want to trample any fields. I would also prefer to stay a good distance from towns and homes. Could you help me prepare a route?"

"How long are you going to march them?"

"I would like them to march at least eight leagues a day, for three days. Nine would be better, but I do not know what they are capable of. That is one of the reasons for the march."

At least the man had respect for the farmers. The Farmer motioned for the Warrior to follow him and found a bit of ground that could be cleared. Finding a stick was easy enough.

Poking a hole in the dirt, he said, "This is the camp." A twisting line. "This is the creek near the fort." He drew a line connecting the two. "That's two leagues." Another line approximately followed the course of the creek. "Two more leagues up, you cross the creek. There's no bridge but a ford." Another curving line. "Three leagues to this second creek then you follow it for four leagues. You can set up camp beside the creek anywhere along the line of march. Be careful with fires. The stubble will likely be dry."

"There will be no fires. The men must learn to pitch a cold camp."

For the first time, the Farmer felt a grin fight to crack his face. "That won't make you a popular man."

The Warrior shrugged. "They did not give command of the army to the Matron or the Mother. We will have to see if they have given it to the Fool."

The Farmer chortled. "After four leagues you should find the springs. Several streams spread from there. If you take the next one, you can follow it," he scratched a jagged loop, "till it brings you to within a league and a half of the creek you'd left. You can decide for yourself how you want to go from there."

"Thank you." The Warrior studied the lines, probably memorizing them.

"One thing's in your favor. Tomorrow will be cooler, although the coming storm will leave mud." The Farmer scratched the beard on the right side of his jaw. "Is this going to help get back the valley you took?"

"That is a matter for the Council to decide. >From what I know of Tatros, getting that valley back will mean war with Shicassa. That is a decision I am not prepared to make. It is your land and your blood. It must be your choice which you value more."

The Farmer raked his short beard with his fingers, smoothing it. "For a Warrior, you don't sound excited about the prospect of war."

"I am not. Any man over thirty years old who looks forward to a war is insane. The glory is fleeting and most of the memories foul. Sometimes one has to fight a war but enjoying war is a young man's delusion."

"But you still call yourself a warrior."

"And you still call yourself a farmer. I do not have to enjoy my work to be good at it. Do you enjoy all the things that make up being a farmer?"

"Only sometimes."

The Warrior shrugged. "There you are." After a long silence spent staring at some middle distance, he said, "I think that is why I like those of you on the Council. You are doing work you do not always enjoy, and most of you are doing it for others, not yourselves."

After another moment's silence he stood, stretched, and strode back to the residence.

The Farmer, absently stroking his beard, watched him go. He wasn't sure yet he'd forgiven the man for taking Sweetwater Valley, but he felt a grudging liking for him.

He returned to his work but he kept thinking of a real war with Shicassa and the ruin it would bring to the land and the lives it would cost. Nothing, it seemed, was ever as simple as it appeared.

THE RASH YOUTH

When he entered the dining hall the Youth noticed the Warrior at a table, attacking his moussaka with a horn spoon. The Youth found a platter in the kitchen and filled it, then carried it to the same table and sat down across from the Warrior.

"I was hoping to see you," the Warrior said. "Do you remember your invitation?"

The Youth grinned broadly. "I do. And my promises, too. I still haven't found a wine worthy of your palate, although I've worked tirelessly sampling for you."

"I must be back early. I will have a busy day tomorrow. But I was told you would know the best tailors and bootmakers." The Warrior dipped some flatbread into the spiced hummus and took a bite.

The Youth swallowed his first mouthful of moussaka and sipped a sweet wine. "I'll make you a trade. After we get you measured for new clothes, you spend half an hour at a tavern."

"Very well, half an hour."

"Excellent!" The Youth hurried through his meal and finished at the same time as the Warrior. He let the Warrior wait outside his rooms while he added a pleasantly weighted purse to his belt and together they walked to the city, a quarter of a league from the residence.

"Someone decided," the Youth said, trying not to pant, "that the Council would be freer of the momentary passions of the crowd if we were not actually in the city."

"A wise man," the Warrior said, wrinkling his nose.

To the Youth, the city's smell was heady and exciting. He'd grown up breathing that air. To the Warrior it seemed an odor, while to him it was an aroma.

As usual, the cobbled streets were filled with people walking as though on missions of great importance or stumbling with great inebriation. Others stood talking or arguing, and a few yokels visiting town gawked at the sights. The Youth thrust a thumb in the direction of one of them. "Try not to look as though you had ridden into town in the same farmer's cart as our friend there."

The Youth noticed a faint smile lurking under the Warrior's stern mask. "I will try to look more worldly-wise."

Vendors hawked sweetmeats and fruit and bread, and even some of the tradesmen stood outside their shops, cajoling passersby to examine their wares or try their services.

The Warrior was obviously uncomfortable with the presence of so many people and with the assumed familiarity of the more aggressive hawkers. His hand seldom left the grip or guard of his light sword and he walked widely around the people thronging the streets.

"Why so nervous?" asked the Youth.

"Too many people. I still have not become accustomed to having so many people around me. And almost all of them are staring at me."

"They're staring at the masks."

"I would have thought they would have become used to members of the Council walking among them," the Warrior growled. "You, at least."

"They never truly become used to us," the Youth replied. "We're novelties that are always new. And they aren't used to the Warrior being among them. Even the other Warrior seldom visited the city, and you are unknown to them. They've heard stories and are trying to decide what to believe."

"They can believe I prefer to be left alone," the Warrior grumbled. "Do they expect my mouth to be dripping blood from the last baby I ate?"

The Youth couldn't resist a grin and said, "No, they probably think you have better table manners than that."

The Warrior's eyes narrowed, then he laughed.

People around them stared silently, so it was as though a wave of silence followed them through the noisy throng, but as they'd walked deeper into the city the crowd noises had become louder.

"What did you want to shop for?" The Youth had to raise his voice almost to a shout to be heard above the noises of the crowd.

"Boots, leather trousers and jerkin, and a tunic or two."

The Youth motioned for the Warrior to follow and pressed into the crowd, leading him down two curves in the street before turning down another narrow, winding street. Within two hundred paces he stopped and gestured, then followed the Warrior into the shop.

The air of the shop was redolent with the scent of leather, and the Youth introduced the Warrior to the master, a tall, thin man with a drooping moustache and hair just turning gray. "My friend needs boots, the best to be had."

The man studied the Warrior a moment then asked, "Hard or soft, and how high do you want them?"

"Hard boots," the Warrior replied, "and to here." He indicated his upper calf.

The man had him remove his boots and stand on a piece of heavy leather and drew around his feet with a nugget of chalk. With scraps of leather he measured around the Warrior's calves and the distance from the upper calf to the heel. "What color?"

"Dye them a dark oxblood red," the Youth said, before the Warrior could reply. "And can you make him trousers and jerkins as well, or must we see a tailor?"

The bootmaker snorted. "A tailor is a master with cloth, but with leather they haven't the feel for the work." Taking out more scraps, he measured the Warrior from shoulder to ankle.

With a trace of amusement, the Youth watched the Warrior's discomfiture with some of the measurements taken.

"Do you want those with the finished side out or the rough side out?"

Again the Youth interjected. "One of each."

"What color do you want them?"

"The finished ones chestnut brown and the unfinished ones a light tan." The Youth was thoroughly enjoying himself.

"Did you want laces or a codpiece on the trousers?"

This time the Warrior spoke first, snapping, "Laces."

"But codpieces are the fashion," the Youth informed him. "The bigger the codpiece, the more man you are."

"From looking at some I saw in the street, their owners are part horse," the Warrior said, "but I suspect most of them are padded. There were a couple whose owners probably use them as a place to carry a spare tunic."

The Youth looked at the bootmaker and shrugged.

"I should have all these in three days," the bootmaker said. "It'll come to about five marks of silver."

"Five marks of silver! We're just buying the leather, not the whole cow," exclaimed the Youth. "And that's enough for two cows and a calf." The Youth motioned at the shop. "I can see why your shop is so well-appointed. A mark of silver and ten copper would be an outrageous price, but we're willing to go two."

"Two marks?" The bootmaker stood, arms akimbo. "For a butcher who'd just toss you the hides and tell you make them yourself, a mark and ten would be more than enough, but you're paying for craftsmanship. But, because you're a good customer, I'll make it four and ten."

"But," the Youth protested, "the materials are going to cost you no more than a mark or so. Three."

"Cheap materials, perhaps," the shopkeeper retorted, "but we use only the best. And I have to pay and feed my apprentices as well as my family. The apprentices alone will eat more than the four."

As the Youth drew a breath to reply, the Warrior growled, "I have an army to lead. You two are going to haggle to four marks. I will pay it." He dug into his pouch and drew out two large Shicassan coins. "This should cover."

The bootmaker shook his head. "Shicassan coins? Where will I change them?"

"Silver and gold are whores," the Warrior said. "They have no allegiances."

The shopkeeper's doleful expression was transparently false as he looked at the Youth. "Your friend doesn't appreciate art. Done."

As the Warrior strode out of the place, the Youth had to hurry his steps to keep up with him. "You need to learn our customs. You might've offended that man by not haggling."

"I am sure the extra silver in the coins will pay for enough ointment to tend his bruised feelings. Let us visit that tavern you spoke of."

"We still have the tunics to purchase, and you'll need a cloak; the weather's turning."

"Only if we can do it quickly."

The Youth nodded and directed him to another shop where the Warrior was again measured. He chose a simple pale blue fabric but the Youth remarked he'd be taken for a farm laborer and added an order for another tunic, a red soft, shiny fabric. The cloak was already made, a dark gray-green woolen piece with a hood and the Warrior took it with him, leaving another mark of silver.

From the tailor's to the tavern was a brisk walk to a cross-street, then another. The sounds of laughter and a babble of voices led them to the door and the Youth recognized two friends and half a dozen acquaintances sitting at a table. He led the Warrior to that corner of the tavern.

He also recognized the barmaid and patted her soft rump as he ordered a cup of wine someone had recommended.

An acquaintance was holding court, leaning back in his chair and gesturing expansively as he told a bawdy story.

When the barmaid brought the wine, the Youth looked at the color. As nearly as he could discern, by the light of the tallow candles, it was pink. A sip was enough to verify the flavor was so mild it was almost fragile, and only suggested sweetness.

"I think this will do for you," he told the Warrior, and gestured for the barmaid to bring another cup and a cup of a more flavorful red wine for himself.

The Warrior studied the tavern as though it was an enemy's citadel and the Youth motioned toward a pair of chairs, which he drew to the table.

Still watchful, the Warrior moved his chair around the table so his back was to the corner. With a shrug, the Youth followed him, asking a friend to make room.

When the barmaid brought their cups, the Warrior thanked her and reached for his pouch but the Youth waved away the offer and paid for the wine.

The storyteller, perhaps a year or two older than the Youth, finally finished his tale to a chorus of laughter, then looked at the Youth and the Warrior, who'd just taken an experimental sip of the wine.

"It would seem wit is lost on some."

"Perhaps half of it," the Warrior said in a mild voice.

One of the other young men at the table guffawed and the face of the storyteller, already flushed with drink, turned a deeper red. The young man's voice acquired a bit of a rasp as he said, "Humor's a quality rare in the butcher's trade."

The Warrior's voice remained soft. "Better the butcher's trade than no trade at all." He pointed at the young man's hands. "Your soft hands say you are a stranger to work."

"These soft hands can still hold a sword," the young man said loudly.

"That would be a greater mistake than not having a trade." The Warrior still hadn't raised his voice. "Getting yourself killed to protect false pride is not only a waste, it is a burden on others."

The Youth watched with fascinated horror as the gathering he'd intended to be a pleasant diversion had turned tense and ugly. He took a deep drink of his red wine and said, "I've had enough to drink for the evening and you have to be up early. Shall we go?"

The Warrior took another sip of his wine and nodded. "I would appreciate it. I am not sure I could find my way back to the residence alone. Your city seems to follow the path of a drunkard, and I am too sober to find my way through it."

As they stood to leave, the storyteller lurched to his feet. "You've insulted me. Apologize or draw steel."

"You don't want to do this," the Youth said.

"I wasn't talking to you," the storyteller snarled.

"There is always enough time for someone to die," the Warrior said. "After you have sobered up, you can decide whether it is worth your trouble."

"I'm ready now."

"No, you are not." The Warrior still hadn't raised his voice and he turned, his hand moving toward his sword, then, snake-quick, he struck the other man's face with the back of his hand and, with his left hand, whipped out the other man's sword, which he tossed to the floor.

The storyteller stumbled backward, collided with a chair, and fell awkwardly.

Stepping over the downed man, the Warrior told the others, "Take your friend home. And keep his sword for him until he is sober."

The Youth followed the Warrior into the street. "I hadn't meant for anything like this to happen. I was hoping we could drink some wine, laugh a bit, and perhaps visit a harlot."

"I understand that." The Warrior turned at the corner. "I had forgotten that youth is not only a time for passions but a time when trivial things are seen as important."

"You seem to know your way around," the Youth remarked, having to walk quickly to keep up with the Warrior.

"But I thought it better to get you out of the tavern. If I had left and you had remained, you might have had to kill him."

Surprising himself, the Youth laughed. The relief from the tension in the tavern and the unexpected remark from the Warrior had lifted his spirit, and suddenly he realized how much he loved the city. Even the smells and the babble of voices all around seemed precious to him. He laughed again.

As they reached the city's gate, he remembered to ask, "How was the wine?"

"Not bad. If I have to drink wine, it is the best I have had."

The Youth resolved to return to the inn tomorrow and buy a bottle of it.

THE WARRIOR

The rumble of thunder woke him sometime during the night but dawn was still hours away and the blanket was warm. He remembered the evening before and realized the Youth was, in some ways, more mature than he'd been at that age.

He woke again just before sunrise and groped for his flint, steel, and tinder. Locating the candle by touch, he struck a spark and lit the candle from the tinder. The one small light caused the items near it to cast huge shadows. He thought there might be a lesson there but left it for later reflection.

After dressing and masking himself, he crept to the kitchen, not wanting to disturb the sleep of the others. Embers still glowed in the bottom of the oven and he welcomed the warmth. After fixing a breakfast, he found some of the dried meat mixed with berries and covered with tallow. That should last through the day's march, along with some of the flatbread.

Carrying the food back to his rooms, he prepared a rucksack. He undressed then donned the padded arming clothing, then the armor.

While the plate armor was heavier than the armor he'd worn when he was younger, its weight was much better distributed and it was cunningly designed to allow more freedom of movement than armor that offered less protection.

After tying on his mask he shouldered the rucksack and a waterskin, which he filled at the well in the garden. The sky was turning to rose and gold as he saddled his horse and added a nosebag and oats to the rucksack. The early morning was cool and he hoped the Farmer was right, that he'd picked a cool day for the march. The saddle creaked as he mounted and he turned his horse's head toward the camp.

Yesterday's riding had apparently taken the edge off his charger's enthusiasm for speed and it settled into an easy canter that still ate leagues.

He again smelled the camp before he saw it but the place had changed. The guards on the walls wore armor and carried shields and weapons, and he could see movement in the camp that appeared more organized than random.

A horn sounded, a long, single note that was doleful but still drew the captains and petty-captains rushing to the gate. After passing through the gate he looked around at the men assembled around him and at the other men behind them falling into varying degrees of order, most of them still fumbling with their rucksacks or settling their helmets.

"Are your men ready?"

One of the captains had apparently assumed the role of spokesman. "All of them fit to march."

"Very good." The Warrior swung out of the saddle. "Have them form a file four men abreast and each of you lead your company, starting with the ones nearest the gate."

He heard a little furtive muttering but ignored it, instead turning and striding out the gate, leading his horse. He'd marched half a league before he turned to look behind him. The line of men following him was irregular, with few files even. After he'd ascertained their stamina, he still had to turn them into soldiers. Some of them might even become warriors, but they'd have to become soldiers first.

He'd also noticed three of the captains riding. He climbed into the saddle and rode back along the line until he'd reached the nearest of them. "Dismount and lead your horse," he ordered.

The man glared at him but swung out of the saddle. When he looked for the other two, he saw them already dismounting so he rode back to the front of the line, dismounted, and again led the march.

Within an hour he was grateful for the day's coolness. He was already sweating under his armor and had drunk half the water in his waterskin. In another hour he stopped at the creek, which was clear enough to let him count the pebbles on the bottom. He refilled the skin and, from his rucksack, took a flask of vinegar, adding a little to the water to prevent flux.

The men behind him were doing the same and some of them had sat down beside the stream. He hoped they were careful so the water downstream would still be clean for the men at the rear of the line. As soon as he'd taken a drink he slung the waterskin and rucksack over his shoulder and resumed the march.

Perhaps three and a half hours from the beginning of the march he crossed the ford, the water barely lapping over his ankles, and he marched them for another hour before he called a halt. While the men rested, he ate some of the dried meat and drank water then rode back along the line. Some of the companies were only a herd, but he'd noticed three of them, along the line, who'd managed to march in step. They were also the groups whose armor and weapons showed care. He stopped by each of the groups' captains and praised them and their men, and he carefully remembered those captains' names.

The ride from the front of the line to the rear and back again took half an hour and, reaching the front, he dismounted and began to march again.

In the south country he'd often marched ten leagues a day, sometimes more, and he'd been expected to fight a battle at the end of the march, carrying heavier loads.

As he neared what he judged to be eight leagues, he again mounted and rode back along the line. All the men seemed tired, some near exhaustion, and he observed a long line of stragglers, men who hadn't been able to keep up with the pace he'd set. He also noticed the army had left a trail of possessions and even rucksacks.

If he wanted to turn them into soldiers and not corpses, he'd best call a halt. Returning to the head of the line, he ordered a halt and had the message relayed back for all the captains and petty captains to join him. Most of the men simply dropped where they'd stopped. Glancing at the man with the signal horn, he guessed the man hadn't enough breath to wind the signal.

The late afternoon was pleasantly cool but he knew that, before long, the night chill would make the sweat in his arming clothing uncomfortably cold, but discomfort was one of the lighter burdens of command.

When the captains had assembled he studied them before he spoke. Most were in pitiable condition, at the edge of collapse.

"Order the men to set no fires. They will either eat their rations cold or do without. And they will use their blankets for warmth." Looking at the men before him, he saw several who looked as though they'd have argued, had they the breath. "If we were in the field, nearing battle, we would not want to warn the enemy of either our position or our numbers. Fire would do both."

Some of the faces were still stubbornly set. "Are you prepared to lose a battle because your men are unable do in peacetime what they will desperately need to do in war?" he demanded. "Tonight I want sentries posted. Each man should watch for one hour, and that includes you captains as well. The men sleeping may take off their armor but should be prepared to don it quickly, and they should keep their weapons to hand. I will take the first watch."

He named the captains of the three companies whose men had remained the best organized. Two of them he ordered to move to the vanguard of the column, and the third he moved to the rearguard. To them he said, "It will be your task to drive the stragglers."

"Finally," he added, "on tomorrow's march I want scouts forward, to the rear, and on both side of the line of march. I want them at least a bowshot away from the column. In better circumstances, I would have cavalry for that purpose, but the men already know how to ride. They still have to learn how to march.

"See to your men, then to your horses."

As the captains trudged back to their companies the man he'd chosen to lead the rearguard approached him. He was a stocky man with pale blue eyes. "You haven't done my men or me a favor." The man's tone made it an observation, not an accusation.

"Ruthlessness is a valuable trait in a soldier and a necessary one for a warrior," the Warrior replied. "If the men cannot learn, they will die a useless death in battle."

"The good side," the captain said, "is that the men are too tired to mutiny." He strode away into the mob of men.

The Warrior returned to his horse and led him to water, careful not to let him drink too much. Returning to his rucksack, he withdrew the nosebag with its ration of oats and, while the animal ate, the Warrior rubbed it down with one of this blankets. Only after he'd hobbled his mount did he eat his own rations.

He compared this new army he led to the one he had quit. Prince Tatros' forces were about as numerous, and better soldiers, but not by much. When he'd started to train the men, Tatros had told him to fight with what he had. Apparently, successful commanders were not Tatros' only fear.

He would have to build this army into something better than a mob. When he finished with them, they'd be at least as good as Tatros' best troops.

Khaimon had been a good leader and the Warrior hoped he wouldn't have to fight the man and his company. He wondered if Khaimon had been given control of the army or whether Tatros already had another mercenary ready to assume command. Given the prince's suspicious nature, he'd probably prefer to have another foreigner under his thumb.

After finding a place to lay his blanket, he flattened the area with his war hammer, laid out his blankets, and walked down the column. Sentries were taking vantage positions. Seeing one of them sitting and nodding, he said, "I suggest you pace to stay awake. If I catch a sentry asleep, we will see if two lashes will help them stay awake."

The young man sprang to his feet and began to pace.

He repeated the warning to the captains he saw and told them to pass the information down the column.

Most of the men had already shed their armor and, while some gnawed rations, most of them were already snoring. After seeing to the men within a quarter hour's march from the front of the column, he paced back. By the time he'd returned to his bedding, the colors in the west had been lost in the darkness and the quarter moon had risen.

He made his way out of most of his armor, although he kept the breast and back plates on. As he was sure would be the case, his sweaty arming garments chilled almost immediately, but he'd felt colder before and he stood the hour's watch.

At the end of the watch, he laid down on his blanket and drew the other blanket over himself. Finding a comfortable position in which to sleep was almost impossible. His armor allowed a little comfort only when he laid on his back, but the mask, with its crest, required him to keep his head turned to one side or the other. He was still fidgeting when sleep overwhelmed him.

* * *

The dawn light against his eyelids woke him and he observed four men stood sentry around him. He rose, strode a dozen paces further from the creek and relieved himself then returned and asked one of the soldiers who their captain was.

He recognized the name, Hondros, as one of the men he'd chosen to lead the vanguard. "Captain Hondros said he'd been told to post sentries but you hadn't said where, and he thought we'd be most useful here," the soldier told him.

"Tell him I am grateful." He put his armor on then found the man with the horn, woke him, and told him to signal the men to wake and assemble.

When the men began to fall into ranks he motioned for Hondros to join him. "Thank you. I slept soundly last night and safely because of you and your men."

Hondros, a tall, slender man with hair and eyes that were almost black, nodded.

While digging into his rucksack for a bit of dried meat, the Warrior said, "I am going to leave the march to you to lead a couple of hours after noon. We should reach the springs in a little over an hour and we will follow the first stream to the east of this one. It should bring you back to where it will only be a short march to downstream of this creek. Take the ford and lead them back the way we have come. That should make the third day's march shorter and you can have them pick up and carry back the gear they have shed."

The two of them strolled to the creek and filled their waterskins, again adding vinegar.

"Most of the men won't be sorry to see you go," Hondros said. "You've marched most of them into the ground, and in heavier armor than any of them wear."

"Except for the shields." The Warrior had noticed most of the men carried shields about half the height of a man, curved, with a flat base and a curved top, while some companies had smaller, lighter oval shields. "Those," he said, pointing to the men with the oval shields, "are the cavalry, I suppose."

Hondros nodded, settled his rucksack and waterskin, then slipped into the sling that secured his shield, and slung his helmet by the chinstrap to the sling holding his shield.

After taking the hobbles off his horse, the Warrior and the commander of the vanguard set a brisk pace. The Warrior could hear the tramp of the men, marching in step behind him. "You and a few others have done very well."

"My men understand the importance of their duty. Valtierra has too many enemies to afford the luxury of a show army."

"What sort of leader was the Warrior before me?"

"A good man but intimidated by some of the captains. Most of them were chosen by the Warrior before him. That one had once been a great fighter but had taken to his cups and he promoted his drinking companions."

"Most of them will be building latrines and commanding work details or teamsters. I would be grateful if you could give me a list of capable petty-captains and lieutenants."

Once or twice the Warrior looked back. To him, it looked as though some of the men had caught a second wind.

When he ordered a halt at noon, he passed the word down the column for the captains and petty-captains to meet him in the vanguard. After the men assembled, he announced he was appointing Hondros as his second in command. A few frowns and furtive looks told him he'd chosen well, that some of the less capable were beginning to worry about keeping their captaincies.

An hour after resuming the march he climbed into his saddle and left the column at a canter. Despite having walked for over half a day, his horse was eager to move. As he rode back to the residence, he considered the challenges he faced. Tents would have to be provided. If his orders were being followed at the camp, the hovels were being torn down and the men would need shelter until more substantial housing was built.

Hondros had seemed capable of protecting the women he hoped the matron would send, but he'd go to the camp with them. With such a large number of men, some crimes and derelictions would be inevitable, and he'd need to enforce discipline with a heavy hand, at least until they learned. He hoped examples would be few, but they'd need to be harsh.

He'd need to talk with the Wise Old Man to arrange for some men to be able to visit the city. It let them see what they might have to fight for, and the time visiting the city could be used as a reward.

The sun had nearly gone down by the time he reached the residence. Leading his mount to the stable, he found the stableman pouring oats into troughs for the horses. "Don't let him drink too much water, but give him an extra half-ration of oats. And would you rub him down and put a blanket on him?"

The man nodded and took the reins.

In the kitchen he took light portions of everything, seated himself at an empty table, and ate slowly, too tired to really attack the food. After the light dinner, he forced himself to stride to his quarters. Removing his mask was a great relief, and he stripped off his armor and the padded tunic and trousers. The pallet had never seemed softer and he slipped into a deep, dreamless sleep.

THE MOTHER

Her baby still slept as she ate the morning meal. She glanced down at the perfect little face, smiled as it pursed its lips, then sighed. She could never have imagined how much she could love until she'd become a mother.

The Warrior strode into the dining hall and, after a glance around the room, approached her table.

He kept his voice low as he asked, "May I join you?"

A bit surprised that he would show consideration for the sleeping baby, she paused then nodded.

He looked at the infant she held and, because of the stern visage of his mask, she couldn't read his expression, but he kept his voice low. "I am trying to meet each member of the Council to learn. Part of our responsibilities are to create laws for Valtierra, but most of us have other responsibilities as well."

Again she shook her head, careful not to let the motion disturb her son. "Being the Mother and being a mother is all I have time for."

"Are you from the city or the outlying country?"

"I was born in the country, moved to the city." Her curiosity overrode her caution. "I take it you were from the country?"

He shrugged. "I am not sure whether you would call it the country or a village on wheels. As hunters and herdsmen, my people followed the cattle and the game."

His accent made some of his words harder to understand, and he spoke a little more slowly and more haltingly than most people she'd spoken with. "Why did you leave?"

"Because Tatros bought me from my lord. It had been a bad year. We lost cattle and sheep to wolves and bandits. I was not sorry to go because I would never have been more than a servant. I would always be my lord's sword and, if I had children, they would never have been more than servants either."

The Warrior seemed to have sharp eyes and sharper perception, seeming to read her expression through her mask, because he added, "Yes, I had a mother, too."

Embarrassed he had found her so transparent, she asked, "What sort of woman was she?"

"Probably a good woman, but a servant who was badly used. I was my lord's bastard, but he had plenty of those, as well as three sons by his wife. Sometimes a snatch of melody will remind me of the songs she used to croon to me."

He seemed open but not vulnerable. He had apparently accepted his life without rancor. The Mother finished eating her melon and drank the remaining milk in her cup. "What do you want?"

"I would like a little land of my own. Perhaps a few cattle or sheep. Or goats. I would like to have a wife and children and know they could be whatever they wanted to become, to have the chance to work for themselves."

She hid her surprise better this time. "I'll wish you well, then."

"How do I call a meeting of the Council?" he asked.

"You don't." She smiled to relieve the unintended severity of the words. "It's the month of the Crone. You ask her to call the Council and, if she believes there's a need, she'll call for the Council to gather."

"Thank you." He stood and nodded then strode into the kitchen.

Her baby began to fuss, so the mother lifted him to her shoulder, hummed softly to him, and patted his back as she worked her way to her feet and walked to her rooms.

THE CRONE

Answering the light tap at her doorpost, the Crone found the Warrior, masked, waiting for her. She waved him into the room and sat on her couch, waiting.

"I would like to ask you to call a meeting of the Council."

"Why?"

"Because I want to be sure I am not exceeding my authority."

"What have you done?"

"I have appointed a new man my second in command. The previous commander of the camp has been reduced to overseeing menial labor. I intend to make other changes as well. I will also have to ask the help of the Matron and the Wise Old Man and probably others on the Council."

The Crone chuckled. "It sounds as though you haven't let things rust, but I don't see any difficulty. I assume you chose new commanders on their merits, since you haven't had time enough to gain any drinking companions. As for assistance from the others—I suspect you'll be able to convince them."

He nodded acceptance of her decision.

Before he could turn to leave, she gestured toward the stool. "Don't be in such a hurry to leave. We have only had one conversation. What do you think of the other members of the Council you've met?"

"I like them and I respect them. I think everyone here is well chosen. That includes the stableman. He seems a little slow, but he knows horses, and he cares about them."

"What do you want?"

He smiled. "You are the second person to ask me that today, and those may be the first times anyone has asked me that. It is a little like a deluge after a drought." He paused before he spoke again. "In the near future, I want to build an army Valtierra can take pride in, an army with its own sense of pride. The city needs defenders. Later, a little land of my own. I am no farmer but I could raise cattle or goats."

"That seems little to ask."

He shrugged. "It is more than I had before."

"Perhaps we should bring in more foreigners," the Crone said, smiling.

"I would not wish that sea voyage on anyone."

She chuckled again. "Was it that bad? I've always been curious—I've never seen the sea."

"You have not missed much. It is just a lot of water."

She leaned forward. "But you've seen foreign lands, visited cities where they speak strange languages and practiced different customs, eaten strange foods."

Again he shrugged. "Cities and buildings do not impress me. You must remember I grew up in a place where gatherings of more than five hundred were rare. Strange languages are interesting. Some are even melodic. But, in the end, it is all to let one man or woman talk to another. And if foods are your interest, you need never leave Valtierra-it has the best food I have eaten. In both the port cities I've seen, the people eat mostly fish."

The Crone was surprised. "Fish are a delicacy here."

"Perhaps because of their rarity, but I'd rather eat my horse, hooves and all, than ever eat another fish."

"You've apparently seen the army. Has your opinion of them improved?"

"It may. If the best men cause the others to improve, we may have a chance to build an army worthy of the name. At least we have some companies of good men who have not been dragged down to the level of most of the soldiers. All of them need to work harder, but it will take time to build stamina and determination. The worst of them will be given menial work to do. They can decide for themselves if they want to take the trouble to become soldiers. If they do not take the choice to improve, they will either spend their days as laborers or quit the army."

"How will you decide whether they're considered deserters?"

"If they admit to their commanders that they are not fit to be soldiers they will simply be mustered out. If they leave without informing their commanders, they are deserters and will be dealt with harshly."

The Crone had noticed his fidgeting. "You look as though you have things to do and little time in which to do them. Thank you for the conversation."

"No, I thank you." He stood and strode out the door.

She found her knitting and began the next row, smiling to herself. She'd chosen well. She wondered, idly, if she'd be remembered as the one who'd chosen the Warrior. She loved Valtierra, but it had rusted and needed a man who'd scour it clean.

THE MERCHANT

Hearing a rapping at his door, the merchant set down the parchment he'd been reading, turning it face-down on the table, and said, "Enter."

The Warrior stepped into the room and the Merchant got to his feet. "Welcome. What can I do for you?"

Always sensitive to posture and expression, the Merchant smiled. "Please forgive my professional insincerity. It's a habit of my class."

The Warrior grinned, and the Merchant realized the man could be dangerous in more ways than with a blade in his hand.

"I have met with each of the others," the Warrior said, "but I had not had a chance to talk with you since the Council meeting."

"You seem to have decided to accept the office of the Warrior." The Merchant held up a bottle but the Warrior shook his head.

The Warrior leaned forward. "I understand the aims of the others and am beginning to appreciate my own duties, but I do not know your duties or what you want for the city."

The Merchant leaned back in his chair, steepling his fingers. "My duties are to improve trade, which was never easy and became more difficult when we lost Sweetwater Valley. Besides foodstuffs, we have only luxuries to trade. Now we have less food to trade. Even in foodstuffs, we had nothing exceptional—our wines and olive oils weren't noticeably different from those of our neighbors, and now we have less of those and other crops. This means our craftsmen, who are the best, now have to carry more of the weight of trade. The problem is that they produce luxuries which, in hard times, are more difficult to sell." He leaned forward and handed the Warrior his chased silver cup. "You'd have to travel very far to find anything near the craftsmanship. And the bottle is almost as exquisite."

Turning the cup in his hands, the Warrior grinned again. "Does the cup make the wine taste any better?"

Concealing his irritation, the Merchant accepted the cup back and placed it beside the blown glass bottle. "No, but the profits from selling it are sweet. Such profits are how the Youth can afford to order a keg of ale from the south."

Noting the Warrior's surprise, the Merchant realized the man must have known nothing of the order. "I'm sorry. I seem to have spoiled a surprise. I'd be grateful if you'd forget I mentioned it."

The Warrior nodded and the Merchant leaned back again, appraising. "A fortnight can be a very long wait. I believe that, with a few others on the

Council, we can convince the Crone to call a gathering in the next two or three days."

"Thank you. But what do you want?"

"Nothing I don't already have. I eat well, live in a fine house, and I can appreciate art like the cup and bottle, even afford to own a little of it. My words carry as much weight on the Council as anyone else's. And we share an interest in battles. You contend with other warriors and other leaders. For me, driving a bargain is less bloody but the challenge is the same—to win a battle of wits against someone else who fights by the same rules."

The Warrior leaned back in his own seat. "Yes, the Harlot mentioned that you, she, and I were in similar lines of work."

"I suppose, but neither you nor I need worry about getting the pox from our work."

The Warrior opened his mouth but closed it again without saying anything and the Merchant would've almost given the cup to hear those unspoken thoughts. Instead, the man paused a moment before asking, "What do you want for Valtierra?"

The Merchant considered his answer for a moment before he replied, "Greatness. I'd like it to be more than just one of a score and a half of city-states. I'd like to see it lead the north."

"Wealth and leadership bring their own risks," the Warrior warned. "Make the plum too large and sweet, and it will be picked."

"That's why we must have alliances, so attacking Valtierra will bring other cities to our aid."

The Warrior snorted. "That is a dangerous game. Any alliance would also commit us to defend other cities and, if we fail to honor the alliance, we will anger them more than if we had left them alone in the first place, as well as showing that our alliances are worthless. And if we were attacked, what is to keep our allies from either deserting us or even joining our attacker for a share of the spoils?"

With the back of his hand, the Merchant irritably swatted away the ideas as though they were annoying flies. "We're a Council of Twelve. Surely we can study those who we'd be best allied with. And we needn't make only one alliance. While a single alliance might not keep us safe, many could."

The Warrior continued to lean back, his mouth set. Obviously, he hadn't been convinced. The Merchant smiled and said, "I'll talk with the others and we'll see if we can't call the Council sooner than a fortnight."

"Thank you." The Warrior stood. "I presume I can ask your assistance if I need it?"

"Of course." The Merchant watched the man stride out of the room. He appeared to be an honest barbarian but he also had an unsettling shrewdness about him. The Merchant could understand why Tatros would try to kill such a man.

THE WARRIOR

The Merchant had been the first member of the Council he hadn't liked, and he wasn't sure about respect. That didn't make him a traitor or a spy. The Warrior clenched his fists. Did he expect the spy to be transparent? Whoever it was, he or she was a spy, and concealment was their sword and shield. As for the Merchant, he might simply be deluded, a man building a castle in the air.

When the Merchant had remarked that, unlike the Harlot, he wasn't likely to catch the pox, it had taken restraint not to suggest greed was only another pox.

He found the Matron in her rooms, nearly finished with the painting. It was of a cottage by a river at sunset, and it was executed well enough the painted board could have been a window. "Is that something on your land?"

"My father's. He and my older brother still farm there."

"Very good work." He turned from the painting to the painter. "The men will return to the camp today, most of them limping and few of them caring about food as long as there is enough of it. If you could ask several women to be ready to go to the camp tomorrow, I will arrange for wagons for them and the supplies they will need."

"I'll take care of the wagons," she said. "Just remember what I said about the promise of their safety."

"It is impossible to forget," he replied, with a smile, then left to search for the Artisan. When he asked the Youth, he was told the man had already left for the army camp.

When he saw to his charger, he found the beast as eager to run as ever. Apparently, the extra oats and a good night's rest were all it had needed. He kept it waiting until he was armored, then gave the animal its head.

He found the ride almost as exhilarating as his mount until he topped the rise and again smelled the camp. That would take time to dispel. It would never completely disappear, but work could make and keep it bearable. In the south they believed that smells carried fevers, and he needed an army in good health.

Men were breaking up the top of the wall and the shanties were gone, with only bare earth and heaps of wood to show where they'd stood. He'd only had a quick look when the horn was winded and he observed the men on the walls were armed and armored. Much better. He rode down the slope, across the small valley, and up to and through the gate. The Artisan and two other men waved to him. As he dismounted, he observed the goats were penned.

The Artisan gestured broadly at the torn earth and the piles of wood. "We've already laid out the lines of buildings and mortar is being prepared. Any man without a fever was ordered to tear down the huts, which wasn't difficult." He pointed. "The latrines are off that way."

"I am impressed," the Warrior said. "You have accomplished much with half a day's work."

The Artisan grinned. "Don't be too impressed. We started yesterday. Tents should be up in another hour or so. With more manpower, we can start the first buildings by noon tomorrow."

"I will be bringing women to the camp tomorrow to cook and to teach some of the men to cook. They will need a place to work."

The Artisan nodded toward the stacks of wood. "There's plenty of wood for fires and the weather looks to be fair. We still have the kettles and pans for making food. We can throw together ovens tomorrow morning."

"From what I have heard," the Warrior replied, "the pans and kettles have not been used for making food for some time." He studied the lines of rocks laid out for buildings and noticed they were uniformly straight and with wide, straight streets between them.

The Artisan noticed his study of the future camp. "Stemos felt the army camp should be orderly and allow men in formation to march in straight lines. And he's laid out two or three large buildings with no purpose in mind. He said one never knows when one might need another building."

One of the men, an older man with heavy brows and a grizzled beard, looked up at the mention of his name.

"Thank you, Stemos," the Warrior said, "and I have already found a use for one of them. One should be a temple."

"From what I've heard of this army," the Artisan said, "you could probably make it the size of the smallest quarters and it still wouldn't be half full."

"Things change."

"We had them bury the excrement. The offal from the latrines can be covered with lime and buried or burned. But better to have it carted to the fields and buried. The Farmer says it makes the land more fertile."

"I am in your debt."

The Artisan grinned. "Warriors aren't the only ones who enjoy a challenge. Stemos would like to build a city. This will do."

The Warrior paced around the camp. The ground was churned and men dug or carried stones. The only wooden buildings still standing were the latrines. Stemos, who, with the Artisan, had followed him, pointed. "It makes them easier to move. When a pit is full, it can be limed and covered, bailed out, or, after the walls are moved, burned."

The wells had been covered and two of them had windlasses. "The others will be the same," Stemos said. "The granaries were already made of stone. Besides the walls and two or three buildings, they were the oldest and best-built parts of the camp."

By the time they'd circled the camp the men began to raise the tents. To the Warrior, it looked like a meadow of huge, drab flowers blooming. And he watched builders from the city oversee men digging trenches, then lining them with stone, applying mortar, and adding more stones.

The sun had fallen almost to the horizon before he heard the horn winded again and the army appeared, Hondros and his troops in the lead. Hondros halted the column and the Warrior strode out to meet him.

Hondros nodded to the walls, which had lost most of their top rows of stones, and the torn earth and piles of wood. "It looks as though there's been a war, and we lost."

"No," the Warrior said, "but the camp will look better within a fortnight or so." The Warrior looked past Hondros to see the expressions of surprise on the faces of the soldiers still fresh enough to have expressions.

"Between you and me," Hondros said, "it looks better already."

"Pass the order for the captains to lead their men to tents, then return here."

While Hondros relayed the orders, the Warrior studied the men who trudged and stumbled past him. Some of them seemed dazed, while others clung to the ragged hem of exhaustion. He doubted more than a score of them could've fought a battle, and most of the captains and petty-captains were in no better shape. At a quick count, he saw each company contained about fifty men.

When the men had settled into the tents and the commanders returned, he stepped atop a pile of stones. "Let your men rest tomorrow. By noon, I hope to have a proper meal prepared for them fit for men. The day after tomorrow, they will begin to help rebuild. The day after that, they will begin training. In ten days, I hope to give each man a day's rest. We will rotate the men so we will always have nine men out of ten training. And we will have more day-long marches.

"You will be responsible for your companies. If you have three men or fewer who cannot meet their duties, talk with me. There will be at least one company who will cook or dig latrines. That company will be made up of men unfit for more warlike duties. The men who performed best on the march will be the first to receive new quarters. Any company that excels, whether in marching, training, or building will be next to move out of the tents. All the men will be treated fairly and with respect, but performance will be rewarded."

He made his way down the pile of rocks and by the time he strode to Hondros, the rest of the captains had turned away to return to the tents.

"Wearing your armor is a very good idea," Hondros observed, "and I'd stay away from the walls while they're being torn down."

The Warrior couldn't tell, from tone or expression, whether the man was joking or not.

"Return to your men and rest. But have a dozen men ready to protect the women I will be bringing to the camp tomorrow. I have vouched for their safety, so, if they are even offended, someone will be wearing stripes under his tunic."

Hondros nodded and marched away to his company's tent.

The Artisan, Stemos, and the other workmen from the city gathered by the gate. Most of them climbed into a wagon; the rest had ridden their own horses.

Riding back to the residence, the Warrior and the Artisan shared a companionable silence until they reached the stable.

As the Warrior unsaddled his horse, he asked, "How soon can the men do the building without your help or that of the others?"

"Perhaps a month. I'd want them to put up two or three buildings, with someone able to make sure they're doing it properly."

They turned their horses over to the care of the stableman, strolled into the residence and parted in the corridor to their apartments.

After removing his armor and mask, the Warrior washed himself, put the mask back on, and walked to the dining hall. The Priest and the Wise Old Man shared a table, conversing in low tones. He filled a platter and returned to their table. "May I join you?"

The Priest nodded to indicate the open spaces at the table.

"Thank you." The Warrior concentrated on the food on his platter until he'd taken the edge off his hunger, then gazed at the Priest. "Do you think you could find a priest willing to serve in a temple in the camp?"

The Priest concealed his astonishment well. "There's no temple in the camp."

"There will be." The Warrior swept up the last of the moussaka with a piece of flatbread and followed it with a sip of water. "I think it would be a good thing, both for the Faith and for the camp."

"To what end?" The Priest was obviously curious.

"The men have little respect for themselves." The Warrior slowly turned his cup with his fingertips. "Men who respect themselves find it easier to respect others. I believe a priest might bring out that quality. >From what you have told me about the Faith, I think the values would be important to the men."

After several moments of reflection, the Priest nodded. "I'll ask some of the priests I know."

To the Wise Old Man the Warrior said, "I would like to see about a different interpretation of the law. I agree the army should never enter the city except to defend it, but I would like soldiers, unarmored and armed only like the citizens, to be able to visit the city."

Watching the Old Man stroking his beard, obviously considering the request, the Warrior pressed on. "There are about eight hundred men in the camp who have not visited the city since they joined the army. I think it would be good for them to see what they might have to die for."

"The city doesn't need any more brawlers." The Old Man's tone was a warning.

"I intend to send only men whose captains trust them, and they will be reminded that if they create trouble, after the constables are done with them, they still have to face the penalties we will impose."

"How soon do you want to do this? And how many men will you be sending us?"

"I would like to start within a month, and we would only allow a score—two score at most—to visit the city at one time."

The Old Man continued stroking his beard. "I'd want to speak with the constables and magistrates, but I'll speak in favor of it."

After finishing his meal, the Warrior asked, "What sorts of laws and punishments do you have in the city?"

The Old Man spread his hands. "There are so many. Small thefts are punished by servitude or flogging. Large thefts can mean the loss of a hand. Brawling is punished by a night or two in the city prison and payment of damages or servitude. Those who can't learn or refuse to learn are branded and banished."

"Perhaps a different punishment might help. I would suggest some of the minor infractions might be punished by cleaning some part of the city. You might add drunkenness to the list, too."

The Old Man smiled. "It might help curb their high spirits if they had to clean offal and vomit. That idea has real merit."

The Priest had long since finished his meal and sat staring at the Warrior. "You've been away from the residence quite a lot."

The Warrior finished his last piece of flatbread. "I have been seeing to the army. They have been neglected, and the last Warrior had not had time enough to change that."

"And how have the changes been welcomed?" The Warrior thought he detected a hidden smile.

"Change, even change to the good, is seldom welcomed. It will be some time before I wear anything but armor in the camp, but that will eventually be another change." He shrugged. "Ask the Artisan how one shapes steel. It must be beaten, heated, and quenched."

The Old Man chuckled. "And I'll wager the steel doesn't like it either."

THE MATRON

She woke early, washed, and dressed in her plainest clothing, finishing with the mask. She wondered if her nervousness was simply another sign of reluctance, but she couldn't ask her friends to do something she wouldn't or couldn't do herself.

Breakfast was quickly eaten; some fruit and flatbread, and she hurried out to the stables. Four wagons and their teams awaited her. The first and second wagons were for the women, and the Warrior sat beside the driver of the first wagon.

All but two of the women she'd asked were already in the wagons, and she saw those hurrying to join them. She climbed up to the seat beside the second driver and tried to make herself as comfortable as possible on the hard wooden seat.

The wagon lurched forward and she swayed on the seat. As they jolted ahead, she tried to admire the countryside but the fields looked dead and brown, almost lifeless. Something seemed missing and it took her a moment to realize it wasn't something outside the wagon but something inside it. The usual chatter when she and her friends gathered was missing. They were just as nervous, just as reluctant as she, but they'd come, and she felt prouder of them and closer to them than she ever had before.

In a little over an hour they smelled the place, then topped a hillock and the camp lay before them. The smell wasn't much worse than that of the city, and she was able to ignore it. A long note on a horn announced their arrival. She hadn't expected the camp to sprawl as it did. She'd never seen the place and had somehow imagined it as more compact; tightly packed buildings with a wall, atop a hill.

The first wagon passed through the gate, drew aside, halted, and the Warrior sprang down from the seat. She'd almost expected him to collapse in his armor, but he moved as though he'd never worn anything lighter.

A troop of soldiers marched toward him. After a few words from the Warrior, the group fanned out among the wagons and marched beside them as they moved again, finally stopping beside a tent, before which yawned a fire pit.

The Matron carefully climbed down and joined the other women as they looked at what they had to work with. Someone had thrown together makeshift ovens, and they had pots and pans. It was crude, but she'd done with less. With scarcely a word from her, her friends had organized themselves and formed teams to share the labor. Some of the men guarding them helped them unload the supplies until the women were able to set to work preparing the noon meal.

The Warrior approached her, his grin clearly visible below his mask. "If I could get the men in this army to work as smoothly together as your friends, my work would be almost done."

Despite herself, the Matron felt a glow and, after a curt nod, hurried off to join the others.

While the women were too busy for conversation, they were also too busy to be nervous. The men who were helping them were respectful almost to the point of shyness, and finally the work was done, with meals prepared and placed on trays. Men carried away the trays at which ten men could eat, and she noticed all the men were at least clean to the elbows.

She watched two of the nearer groups of men eat and found it almost painful to see. They were men the Mother would've called sons of the city, and they ate as though they hadn't tasted food for years. She found herself sympathizing with them. Most seemed to be good men fallen into bad habits. She was surprised to see about a fifth of their number were hardly more than boys, unable to even grow beards. When she remembered her distaste and fear, she felt the burn of shame. It'd been easy enough to think of them as something less than human, never having met them, but now they were just men, like her father and brothers.

After making sure they'd left enough food for the evening meal, she approached the Warrior. "We've done all we can do here for today."

The Warrior ordered the teams and wagons readied and, as soon as the women had climbed into the wagons, they set out for the residence,

The women spoke more than they had on the ride to the camp, but still less than they usually did. They were tired, and most of them, when they spoke at all, spoke of the men. When they reached the residence, she thanked each of the women, pleased to see that the Warrior did the same.

Walking to the dining hall with the Warrior, she said, "There's rather more to you than I'd expected."

"That is true of almost everyone," he observed. After a short silence, he asked, "Have you talked much with the Fool?"

She shook her head. "Conversations with him often make me feel dizzy."

"They have the same effect on me, but I notice when I stop spinning I am looking at things from a new vantage. There is more to everyone on the Council than one can see with one glance—or even two or three looks."

As they entered the hall, the Youth approached them. "The Crone has called for a meeting of the Council tomorrow morning."

The Matron turned to the Warrior. "We'll both have to be there, of course, but I think the women will be happy to go to the camp tomorrow, even without us." To the Youth, she asked, "Did she say why she's calling for the meeting?"

The Youth gave an odd gesture with the palms of his hands up. "The Crone never tells anyone what she's thinking, except in Council, and I'm not even sure about then."

"Excuse me," the Warrior said, "but I need to speak with the Harlot. Would you care to join us?"

The Matron's attempt to hide her distaste was half-hearted. "I'd rather dine alone. I have some thinking to do."

The Warrior nodded to her and the Youth and strode to the kitchen.

Glancing around the room, she saw the usual groupings; the Merchant and the Artisan, the Wise Old Man and the Priest, and the Mother, the Crone, the Fool, the Harlot, and the Farmer eating alone. As would she. The day had been one of discovery, and most of what she'd discovered was within herself. She'd always thought herself broad-minded, unable to see her own blind spot. She wondered what else she'd taken for granted or thought she'd known when she only supposed.

THE HARLOT

She'd noticed the Warrior entering with the Matron and wondered what they might have in common. When she'd glanced up again the Warrior had carried a tray from the kitchen and was approaching her table.

"May I join you?"

"Absolutely. I want to see how you're going to sit in that armor."

Ignoring the clatter, he actually managed some grace. As he settled himself, he asked, "Have you visited your sisters in the camp?"

"They're not part of the Sisterhood."

"Perhaps they should be. We have almost leveled the camp, and one of the first buildings put up will be the brothel. I would like for the women in it to know how to take care of themselves—to stay healthy and not become pregnant. I would guess most of what they think they know are old wives' tales."

"Why a brothel?" the Harlot asked. "I understood they were living among the soldiers."

The Warrior had just used his horn spoon to deliver a large bite of moussaka to his mouth and he had to chew, swallow, and sip at his cup before he replied. "Several reasons. It gives them some control over their situation. A woman in a hovel of eight or ten men is likely to be passed around like a bottle of cheap wine. In a brothel, she can choose her partners. And if a man has a woman constantly around him, anger can boil into rage and then the woman is abused. If he has to earn her companionship, even if only for an hour, it becomes valuable to him."

She let him eat his meal while she pondered. When he'd finished his food, she said, "You're a very strange warrior. Why do you care?"

He grinned. "It is impossible to shrug your shoulders when you are in plate mail. Why should I not care? I must be concerned for my men. They are the people I have to fight beside. And everyone else in Valtierra is someone I have to fight for. If you care enough to kill and perhaps die for someone, you care enough to help when you can."

"All right," she admitted. "You've shamed me. I'll visit the camp within the next few days."

THE FOOL

He'd noticed the Warrior enter with the Matron and dine with the Harlot, then leave the hall alone. The Warrior was a bit of a puzzle. He moved easily in all the circles of the Council but he remained as alone as the Fool. He seldom needed the armor he wore because his armor was confidence.

Most of the others were far easier to read. The Farmer's craft and the Artisan's cunning were all in their hands. They were straightforward men. Both overcame their natural antipathy to the Merchant for their self-interests. The Merchant's hands were only skilled with coins but he was as slick as ice and at least as cold. His geniality was a thin veneer.

The Wise Old Man would've been wiser had he seen more, and seen past the customs of the city but, to be fair, he and the Priest at least tried to perceive broadly. The Mother was, in many ways as bound by tradition as the Priest and the Old Man, as limited in view, although some of her problem was simple shyness.

Shyness was a quality notably lacking in the Rash Youth, and the Fool liked him more than the rest of the Council, despite the Youth's weakness for frivolity. His passion for what was new and popular sometimes overwhelmed his common sense, but he also had a strong sense of fairness.

Of all of them, the Harlot, with the possible exception of the Merchant, was the most cynical. He had, however, noticed most cynics were idealists who'd bloodied their noses against reality at least one time too often. The Matron was more complex than most, a mixture of velvet and iron but with several blind spots. The Crone was very perceptive and, while she seemed to have no specific plans, she obviously thought she saw the direction in which she wanted to move the city.

He remembered to take a sip of his wine.

All of them represented their own class or group, which was the principle behind the Council, but he suspected the Warrior was shaking them awake, making them look beyond their comfortable views.

He finished the rest of the wine in a single swallow and carried the tray and the cup back to the kitchen before strolling to his rooms.

When he was alone he took off his mask and stared at it with distaste. The wild horsehair mop dyed a color never seen in nature and the distorted eyes that made him appear cross-eyed and the comically long nose were all part of his own armor, but tiresome.

His best armor was his sense of humor, a quality he'd developed as a child.

He'd always seen the world differently, been moved by things others couldn't perceive. Being different meant paying a high price, and so, as recompense, he'd embraced humor, partly as a balm. In many ways it was the most natural armor for him because his knack of seeing relationships others missed was fodder for wit. It also protected him from most conflict because people didn't generally want to attack someone who made them laugh.

The weakness of his armor was that he craved respect, and the qualities that protected his vulnerable parts also meant he was tolerated, but almost never respected.

Nothing was perfect.

He lit a candle against the growing darkness and considered putting on a cloak against the evening's chill. He also considered walking to the city. The noise and bustle might take the edge off his loneliness. Sometimes, false intimacy was better than none at all. He decided this wasn't one of those times. The advantage of armor was you couldn't be touched. The curse of armor was you couldn't be touched.

He was sure everyone else had his or her way to spend the time. The Mother had her infant, the Matron her friends and her painting. The Youth was probably already in the city, the Merchant again counting his profits, the Artisan at his forge, the Farmer was probably already abed—the man rose at an unseemly early hour.

He realized there were two he couldn't account for; the Warrior and the Harlot—unless they were together.

Any sort of company was worth a brief stroll. He slid the glass sleeve around the candle and seated it in the candleholder, picked the holder up by its ring, and left his room. He strolled the corridor, turned right at the cross corridor, and knocked at the second doorpost to the left. Hearing the soft ringing of bells, he knew the Harlot was putting on her mask, meaning she was alone.

"Enter." She had a soft voice to go with her other soft charms. When he entered the room he found her still tying the laces of her mask. She gestured toward a table on which another candle rested.

The Fool blew out his candle, then set the holder beside the other candle. "I wasn't sure you'd be here."

The smile under the mask seemed sadder than any other expression could have. "As long as I'm the Harlot, I can't simply be a harlot." The eyes behind the mask narrowed, calculating. "I'd guess you're another member of the Council who wears the mask reluctantly." She gestured at the other mass of cushions.

"You're exceedingly sharp." The Fool sat down and crossed his legs like a tailor.

"Not especially," she replied. "I just know men very well. It's not the same thing, but it's a necessity of my profession."

He chuckled. "You seem to have a poor opinion of men."

"For the most part, it's warranted. I see men under the worst circumstances. They're all need. Some seem to believe their coins buy them everything. Some of those are the same ones who try to take their money back after their needs have been met. Others are only trying to get what they want with a few words dipped in butter and honey. Now and then, I'm pleasantly surprised but those encounters are rare enough to be memorable."

"What about the Warrior?"

"He's one of the rare ones; he and the Youth. Both of them seem to realize I'm more than a vagina."

"The Youth?"

"Yes. He has the same needs as other men. Perhaps more than most. But he treats me with the respect he treats others. Most men treat me with contempt because they have contempt for themselves and their needs, and most women treat me with disdain because they hold me responsible for the weaknesses of their men."

The Fool wanted to say something clever but some bleakness defied humor. "I'm sorry."

"What brings you to my rooms?"

Her honesty seemed to require the same of him. "I was feeling lonely and felt the need to talk to someone."

Again that sad smile. "At least it's a different form of intercourse than most men seek."

"I hope you know I respect you as much as I do anyone on the Council."

The smile became more genuine as it reached her eyes. "I'd already noticed you are courteous or discourteous with a fine impartiality. I think part of your problem is that you sometimes forget we're people, not just objects to be manipulated."

He'd obviously not hidden his surprise well enough, as she'd continued, "I saw you in the garden, once or twice, juggling, and I noticed you were juggling eleven of the small bags."

"A juggler always juggles an odd number of objects," he interjected. "It's somehow easier to handle than an even number."

"Then why not thirteen, or nine? It took me a little thought to realize there were eleven of the bags and eleven members of the Council besides yourself." She'd apparently read his expression again. "No need to worry, your secret is safe with me. Again, you treat me no differently than you do anyone else, and your manipulation, as far as I've seen has been for what you feel is the good of the city."

After a pause, she added, "It must be very lonely."

She'd reached through his armor and touched him.

He shrugged. "It's always been lonely, but at least this way, I can do some good." He paused, looking into himself. "Sometimes I don't know, myself, what is manipulation and what is honest."

They shared a silence then he grinned. "We're both supposed to be light-hearted and a little silly, and we're as somber as the Priest. As I mentioned to the Warrior, sometimes being the Fool is hard work, and I'd guess it's the same for being the Harlot."

She produced an impish grin. "And sometimes it's harder when it isn't hard."

He chuckled again. After another silence, he said, "I'm sorry this is the first time we've really talked. I find I like you."

She stood, poured two cups of wine, handed him one, and sank back onto her cushions. "I like you, too. I'm still a little wary of you but, since you're a man, it's nothing personal."

A sip of the wine informed him it was a white wine with a trace of sweetness. "To change the subject, why do you think the Crone is calling a meeting of the Council?"

"I'd hazard a guess that it's to vote on accepting the Warrior. What do you think?"

"The same. I've noticed the Merchant speaking with several members of the Council, then most of them speaking with the Crone."

She sipped then set her cup on the floor. "Why do you suppose the Merchant is calling for an early vote?"

"The answer to that question, my pretty, is something I can only guess at. I think he's worried our large friend is becoming too popular. If the vote runs against him, the Merchant can get him off the Council. If the vote goes the other way, he'll vote with the majority and gain what he hopes is gratitude from the Warrior and credit from the others for advancing the Warrior's position."

Her laughter was a sweet sound. The Fool had become a connoisseur of laughter and hers was almost music. "That's very astute."

He snorted. "The Merchant believes he can move things from behind a sheet, like those who perform shadow-plays in the street. He's not an especially talented beginner. I'd wager the Crone sees through him as easily as through a crystal goblet." He sipped at the wine again. "The answer I'd pay more to own is why he seems to fear the Warrior."

"How will you vote?" she asked.

"That will depend upon the others. If he's in danger of being voted out, I'll vote for him. If he receives ten votes, my vote will do him more good if it's cast against him." He finished his wine, stood, placed the cups on the table, lit his candle from hers, and replaced the glass. "I thank you very much for the companionship. If I may, I'll visit again."

"I'll be here for the next eighteen months."

He nodded to her and made his way back to his own rooms. After taking off the ugly mask, he undressed, blew out the candle, and crawled into the chilly bed. By burrowing deeply into the blankets and covering his head, he warmed himself until he fell asleep.

* * *

The morning was chilly and the bed warm, and he took nearly half an hour to work up his resolve. The morning light was so pale it seemed to be ill, and the floor cold against his bare feet. He began to shiver before he'd prepared the fireplace, and his hands shook so badly he'd barked his knuckles before he'd gotten a spark into the kindling.

Still shivering, he retreated to the bed and warmed himself enough to let him get out again to set the basin by the fire and pour water from the pitcher, then climbed back under his blankets. When he finally rose again and dipped his hands into the water it was only tepid, but he washed himself quickly, shaved, dried himself with an old blanket, and dressed. Feeling stronger, he strolled to the pleasantly warm kitchen. Most of the other members of the Council were already in the dining hall, the Warrior dressed in new clothing, including a leather jerkin and trousers.

As was usually the case before a meeting of the Council, each member dined alone, the meeting on everyone's mind, no one wanting to be seen trying to influence the others. To the Fool, they all seemed to be trying to be their masks.

When the Crone rose, she stopped by the Warrior and murmured a few words in his ear, then led the way to the Hall of the Twelve, followed by everyone but the Warrior. Each member took his or her seat, and the Crone announced, "I've been told the Wise Old Man wishes to change a proposal he made earlier."

"I do," he said. "I had thought it would take a fortnight to know the man the Crone had nominated to be the Warrior. I should like to change my proposal and have the Council vote on his membership immediately."

The Fool noticed the Old Man glance at the Merchant, as though for support or confirmation,

The Crone tapped her staff three times on the floor and said, "I call on a vote on the amended proposal. All in favor raise your right hands."

Everyone on the Council but the Fool and the Crone raised their right hand and the Fool felt a twinge of doubt. If the Merchant had managed to find just three other votes, he could block the Warrior's nomination. Was the man really gambling, or was he playing with loaded dice?

"All opposed, raise their left hands."

He sat motionless, as did the Crone.

"Since the measure has passed, all those who wish to admit the man to the Council as the Warrior, raise your right hands."

One of the advantages of a mask, even an ugly one, was that it shadowed the wearer's eyes and so he could watch the Merchant. As he'd suspected, the man raised his hand when he saw the others had voted in favor.

The Harlot turned her head slightly, tipping her face back far enough he could see her wink. She'd evidently been watching the Merchant, too, and she let the Fool know she was sharing their private joke.

"All opposed, raise their left hands."

The Fool drawled, "I like the man and I think he'll bear his responsibilities well, so only a fool would vote against him." He sighed dramatically. "I suppose it's my duty," he said, and raised his left hand. As he'd intended, his remark brought chuckles from most of the members and he could almost feel the tension flow out of the room.

The Crone rang a bell sitting before her and, a moment later, the Warrior strode through the door, his face a mask under the Warrior's mask. He halted just outside the arc of the tables.

"Warrior," the Crone said, "take your seat on the Council."

After the Warrior had paced to the empty chair and sat down, the Crone asked, "Are there any other matters to bring to the Council?"

"I have a question," the Warrior said. "I understand the residence is the home of the Council, but my obligations will require me to spend much of my time at the army camp. Will this be a problem for the Council?"

The Fool fought back a grin as he watched the other Council members looking at each other, none having anticipated such a question. Finally, he drawled, "The army needs a leader, and it's better to let you go to them rather than having them pitch camp around the residence. I propose that, as long as you attend the Council meetings, you be allowed to carry out your tasks where you must."

Almost to his surprise, the Fool was the only one who voted against the proposal.

"If there is nothing more to be proposed or discussed…" the Crone waited half a dozen heartbeats before she announced, "I call this meeting ended," and tapped the floor three times.

THE HARLOT

If she wanted her words to mean anything, she knew, she would have to honor them. She paused outside the Matron's door, working up her courage and building her defenses doubly tall and thick, then knocked at the door.

Within moments the Matron opened the door and even the mask couldn't hide her astonishment. "May I come in?" the Harlot asked.

The Matron gestured into the room and toward a chair, As the Harlot entered, she observed one wall almost filled with paintings, two more incomplete works leaning against another wall and one, almost finished, on a framework. She'd heard the Matron was a painter but hadn't realized she was so talented. While scenery or pictures of fruit or flowers were not to her taste, the execution was excellent. As she lowered herself into the chair, she said, "Your work is very fine. I'd never seen it before."

The Matron sat in the chair across from her and, with her characteristic asperity, said, "I doubt you came to see my work or discuss it. What do you want?"

The directness of the attack caused the Harlot to take a moment to quell her annoyance and couch her reply carefully. "We haven't always agreed." The understatement was the honey in the medicine—they'd almost never agreed, but now wasn't the time to raise a torch to their differences. "However, in this case, we're both working at the behest of the Warrior. You and your friends have been visiting the camp. The Warrior has asked me to speak with the women in the camp. Could I ride with you tomorrow?"

The Harlot was forced to hide another impish smile. The Matron wasn't good at hiding surprise, and two of them in a few minutes seemed to exceed the woman's limit.

With thumb and forefinger stroking her chin, the Matron remained silent for an uncomfortably long time before she said, "We leave very early in the morning. You will have to be ready to travel before sunup."

"I'll meet you at the stable then, and thank you." The Harlot stood, walked to the door, and closed it behind her. In the corridor, she heaved a sigh of relief. If she were the sort to keep track of such things, the Warrior would be heavily in her debt. He only had to fight other men, not beard the lioness in her den.

* * *

She woke at the knocking on her door. "Thank you," she shouted to the Farmer through the door. He was usually the first to rise and the Harlot had asked him to wake her as early as possible. Donning a robe and her mask, she visited one of the bathhouses behind the residence and bathed. Feeling somewhat refreshed, she returned to her room, examined again the contents of the bag she'd packed for this occasion, then dressed in the clothing she'd wear for the day. After a light breakfast with two cups of sweetened tea and a brisk walk to the stable, she found herself among a group of women waiting for the stableman to finish harnessing the teams.

The other women seemed as wary of her as sheep of a strange dog, and the only conversations were muted as one woman would murmur to another. Finally, one of the women approached her. "Are you riding to the camp with us?"

"I am." She studied the woman, who she guessed to be at the bottom of the social ladder and she'd probably been chosen to speak to the Harlot because the rest had feared contagion. "What's your name?"

After a moment, stammering, the woman managed to say, "Kondrake."

"Well, Kondrake, I thank you for your interest. The Warrior has requested me to help the camp women. You may tell your friends they can behave as though I'm not really here."

Kondrake turned to walk back to the flock of matrons and wives, but not before the Harlot detected a hint of a smile.

After the wagons had been brought out and the women had climbed into them, the Harlot remained to herself at the front corner behind the driver of the first wagon. As the ride progressed, a little conversation started but, since the Harlot already knew how to prepare food and wasn't interested in learning the intricacies of knitting or embroidery, she let herself drowse.

After being jostled for a time she hadn't marked, she smelled the camp. She'd been warned about the odor but it didn't seem much worse than the city. In less than a quarter of an hour they passed through a gate and the wagon drew to a halt.

With the rest of the women, she stood and, like them, hobbled to the end of the wagon. Sitting too long on a hard wooden floor in a cramped wagon bed left the legs weak and the body stiff.

Seeing the Warrior among the men waiting for them, she approached him with an impish grin. "You owe me a huge debt. I was willing to forgive having to rise before the sun, I was even going to forget the ride in the wagon, but the insipid conversations on the way were too much."

He smiled. "I already owed you more than I could pay with my Warrior's wages. Perhaps a good meal will help balance the account. Are you ready to meet the women?"

She nodded and together they walked to one of the drab, stained tents, the Warrior carrying her bag for her. She was amused to see men stop their work or their drilling to stare after them, but none spoke. It was as though a look at the pair had turned them into statues.

The sides of the tent had been drawn up and half a hundred women stood together, silently waiting. Most of them, had they tried to ply their trade in the city, would've starved. Almost all the faces staring at her were as plain and as hard as a clenched fist, and some of them were as hostile. Care and hard lives had etched deep lines, most of them around the eyes, into all the faces but the youngest.

They were what she would probably have been had she been less lucky or had a plainer face. The Warrior had been right – they were sisters.

"The Warrior has asked me to speak with you." She spoke softly, partly so the men around would be less likely to hear, partly to force them to listen closely. "I hardly know where to begin. I've brought some herbs and the ways to use them to avoid pregnancy. There are no herbs to avoid the pox, but some to help relieve it." She reached into her bag and withdrew a pale, translucent tube. "There are less dangers of pox or pregnancy if you require your men to use these. It's a bit of sheep's intestine, tied off at the end. I suppose you know to mix a bit of vinegar with your water to avoid the flux."

A few of the women nodded, while most stood in motionless silence, as if they were stones.

"I cannot change the past," the Harlot said. "And I certainly can't change your pasts. The greatest changes are those the Warrior has already made. You can now control who you see. He's assured me your choices will be respected. And, while the past is gone, you now have some choices you can make for the future. If any of you choose to leave the camp…"

"And where would we go?" snapped a woman with more wrinkles than most and with gray in her mouse-brown hair.

"Ask the Warrior to speak with me. There are harlots in the city who have enterprises, and they employ former harlots. If you can learn to sew, to cook, or to clean, they'll have work for you.

"I understand some of you have been badly used and even abused, but to dwell on a hurt is to make the pain last longer. You all have value. If you didn't, the Warrior wouldn't have the men building you a brothel."

A few of the faces remained stubbornly set, but more of them seemed thoughtful as they weighed their possibilities.

"For now," the Harlot said, "we must deal with the practical matters you face each day." She removed the herbs from her bag, showing the women what they looked like, where to find them, how to prepare and use them, and in what quantities. She also showed them unguents and explained how to make them. Most were medicinal but some were to smooth the skin. She showed them how to apply kohl to the skin around their eyes and vermillion to their lips.

The older woman who'd spoken before gestured at the ointments and cosmetics. "A waste of time. They just want to bed us, huff and hump us and relieve their needs."

"Since you can now decide who you will take to your pallets, you can put a higher value on your company," the Harlot replied. "And if you are more attractive, the men will value their time with you more."

A soldier stopped just outside the tent. "The meal is ready," he shouted.

The Harlot sent ten of the women for platters and ate with her new sisters. To her, the food was about the same as the food in the residence but she noticed most of the women savored their meal and realized why the Warrior had enlisted the Matron and her friends. To the camp women, the meal was apparently a feast.

By the time they'd finished eating, the Warrior himself stood outside the tent. "The Matron and her friends are preparing to return to the residence."

The Harlot nodded, then turned to the women. "Remember what I've told you. If you need anything else, you can tell the Warrior you need to speak to me. I'll visit you once or twice a fortnight. And also remember you can help yourselves and each other."

Walking back to the wagons with the Warrior, she said, "I told them you'd honor their decisions, including which men they chose not to bed, and allowing them to leave the camp."

"Of course…"

"I also said you'd support their choices. That means discipline for men who don't believe a woman should be able to reject them."

"Leaving their blood on a lash is likely to make the men understand matters they hadn't known before. It will only take one or two of them before the rest can learn without paying the price themselves." As they neared the wagons he added, "I am still in your debt."

"I think we can call the account balanced."

The ride back was more pleasant than the one out had been. Kondrake and two of the other women spoke to the Harlot, their curiosity apparently winning over their need for the approval of the other matrons.

The wagons stopped first at the city and the Harlot was able to ride beside the driver to the residence, grateful for even the tiny relief afforded by the springs under the seat.

She'd assumed her place on the Council had simply been a nod to tradition but now she realized she had much work to do and found the prospect unexpected but pleasant.

THE CRONE

She'd risen early and eaten slowly and, after finishing the fruit, cheese, and bread, returned to the kitchen to refill her cup of tea. As she sat nursing the tea, she watched the other members of the Council arrive.

The Farmer had already finished his breakfast before she'd arrived. He was like the land he worked—solid and earthy. He commonly rose before the sun and was usually in bed shortly after sunset.

The Artisan was another solid man. She suspected he left the running of the shop to someone else, perhaps his wife. Like the Farmer, he seemed content only when he was working. While not as unimaginative as the Farmer, his gift was only for his work.

Hobbling into the hall, using his staff almost as a crutch, the Wise Old Man was another one who sought comfort in routine. She could almost feel the stiffness in his joints, which matched the stiffness of his mind. Not a bad man, he sometimes failed because he was unable to wear someone else's skin, look out through their eyes. He was honest; he'd almost certainly never taken an unfair advantage, but he'd never felt the sting of an unfair disadvantage. She'd known him before he'd put on the mask, and the old man's family had never been wealthy, but they'd never been poor, either. He'd been a rash enough youth, in his day, although he'd never worn that mask, but he'd settled into his work as a stonemason and had become a dependable man. His wife had died three years ago and he'd grieved and removed the ring from his ear, but they'd had children and grandchildren, and the old man had devoted himself to them. He could be counted on to favor the young while harboring a distaste for their frivolity.

As the Warrior strode into the room she smiled to herself. His energy seemed contagious and most of the Council members had become infected as well since he'd visited with them. The Wise Old Man had become more active in dealing with the constables and magistrates and had seen the new ordinances were enforced. She'd noticed he'd enlisted the Matron and the Harlot in his campaign to improve the lot of the people at the camp. She'd listened carefully to the stories about him before she'd chosen him and, from all she'd heard, she'd been sure he and Tatros had been oil and water. She was just glad he'd escaped in time to serve Valtierra.

Watching the Mother enter the hall, she tried to guess at what made her so quiet. It wasn't mere shyness, That was a puzzle she'd need to study more later.

The Matron still sat at a distance from the Harlot at meals but at least acknowledged the other woman and was polite if not friendly. That was more of the Warrior's magic. She watched the woman disappear into the kitchen.

When the Priest entered he walked to an empty table and sat. He was probably fasting. That seemed a sort of ritual with him on the days the Council met. So strange that someone who could wrap his mind around a Trinity one couldn't see could be one of those with little imagination. She supposed his concern was so bound in prayer and meditation he sometimes forgot what one prayed for or pondered on. Still, he was another good man, and less judgmental than she'd thought, although he carefully avoided the Harlot. She wondered if that might be less his distaste for her or her profession than fear of his reaction to her.

The Merchant, who padded into the room on soft slippers, was probably no more pompous or dishonest than most of his class but, just as the Priest had his Trinity, the Merchant had his moneybags. His attempts to manipulate the Council were probably as transparent to the Fool as they were to her.

As though her thought had been a summons, the Fool appeared in the doorway, glanced around the room, then walked to the kitchen for his meal. Deceptively deep, he was easily a match for anyone on the Council and his machinations made him a match for almost all the others. Sometimes she almost felt guilty for liking him.

The Harlot walked into the room as though it was her court. To the Crone, it had been like watching a rose bloom. Since the Harlot had visited the camp she'd begun to emerge from a sort of exile inside herself. She'd found a cause and was ready to devote herself to it. In its turn, the cause gave her a vivacity she'd lacked.

Her favorite, the Rash Youth, was the last to arrive. He was as rash and brash as his archetype but with a sort of innocent joy. Her affection for him was tinged with a trace of sadness. He was about the age her grandson would've been had he and her daughter and son-in-law not died seven years ago of the bloody cough.

That plague had been a dark time for the city and most members of the Council had lost some members of their families. She wondered whether it had been harder for her to watch her family die or to have to go on without them. That's when she'd begun to lavish her love on the city. If one stopped loving, one died. So, an useless old woman had accepted life for herself and nurtured it for the city.

Had her grandson lived, she could wish he'd have been very like the Rash Youth, with his wild enthusiasms and facile mind. And she saw evidence he was becoming a good man, dependable but with ideals and the imagination to make them real.

She'd noticed others on the Council had also been charmed by the Youth. The Harlot treated him as a friend rather than as someone to seduce or be seduced by, while the Matron displayed an unwonted patience for the young man. In fact, the Rash Youth seemed to be liked by all the Council. And she'd observed he and the Warrior had apparently become fast friends, something that benefitted them both. The Youth's joyous good nature seemed to lighten the Warrior's dour character, while the Warrior's resolve and respect for the abilities of others were seeds being planted in the Youth's fertile mind.

She waited until he'd finished his meal before she touched her lips to the last of her almost-forgotten tea, which had cooled from tepid to cold. The taste of cold tea repelled her so she set the cup down and, using her staff, hauled herself to her feet and walked slowly to the Council chamber.

After taking her seat at the chair in the center of the table she allowed the others to take their places before she rapped the staff on the floor. "Does anyone have a matter to bring before the Council?"

The Fool laughed. "In three days' time? Things have begun to change, but they're not moving that quickly, I hope."

"Then this will be a very short meeting. My only remaining duty is to hand over the staff to the Rash Youth."

From his place at the left end of the arc the Youth stood and walked to the chair at the center and gravely accepted the staff. The Crone stood and returned to her accustomed chair to the left of the Wise Old Man.

"Since there are no matters for the Council to discuss, I call the meeting ended," the Rash Youth said, as he tapped the floor three times.

Part of the satisfaction the Crone felt was for the Rash Youth, who only needed seasoning, but most of it was for having used her time as head of the Council well.

THE RASH YOUTH

Alone in his apartments he idly toyed with his sword. He'd anticipated becoming head of the Council but hadn't looked forward to it. While hardly strenuous, the behavior required of the head of the Council conflicted with his temperament and the role of the Rash Youth. Visiting taverns and consorting with prostitutes were expected of the Rash Youth, while considered unseemly for the Council's leader.

He wondered how some of the others managed. The Harlot seemed to have accepted being cloistered throughout her term on the Council. She'd had her own disadvantage—her profession and role were disdained by many people in the city and even by some on the Council. She had, however, served her time as head of the Council with dignity.

Some members seemed able to assume the leadership easily. The Wise Old Man, for instance, commonly saw only magistrates and the Chief of Constables and leaders of delegations from artisans and farmers. He seemed to have only one or two friends who weren't titled in some way, but he'd probably outlived most of his old companions.

The Crone had been exceptionally able and he'd been impressed with her choice for the new Warrior. She'd kept a firm hand on the reins and he hoped his time leading the Council would be even a third as successful as hers had been.

Idly, he wondered how the Fool would fulfill his obligations in a few months. He found himself liking the Fool although one could easily find oneself impaled on the man's barbed wit. The Fool's irreverence was, however, a welcome antidote to the pomposity of some on the Council and some of the people with whom they'd had to deal. He'd noticed the Merchant's superficial joviality often evaporated after a comment or two from the Fool.

None of which solved his problem. He slid the blade into its scabbard and walked to the dining hall. As he entered the room the Warrior emerged from the kitchen with a well-laden platter. In the kitchen, the Youth quickly filled his own platter and returned to the hall, stopping at the Warrior's table. "May I join you?"

"Yes, please do."

Sitting cross-legged from the Warrior, he started on his own meal. The tabouli and falafel were excellent. "I suppose you'll be riding out to the camp after the meal?"

Caught with a mouthful of moussaka. The Warrior nodded.

"I wish I could go with you, but I have to visit the Crone to find out what duties have been planned for me." He chuckled. "Better a quick death by sword than a slow one from boredom."

The Warrior answered the chuckle with one of his own. "Somehow, I've never found my meetings with the Crone boring."

After swallowing a bite of tabouli the Youth replied, "That will be the least boring part."

The Warrior sipped at his water. "Are you bound to the residence when you become head of the Council?"

"Not really," the Youth said, "but the less I am the Rash Youth, the more the others will approve—not that I'm desperate for the approval of others, but it's my duty to at least look responsible."

"I will wish you well, then. Is there anything I can send you?"

"I don't know how you'd deliver a gift of patience. I suspect that, for the next month, that'll be the thing I need most."

The Warrior's eyes crinkled with a half-hidden smile then became serious. "Just be careful. Remember, there are those who wish the city ill and, for the next month, you represent the city."

The Youth realized he was being warned. "Do you know or suspect some danger?"

"If I did," the Warrior said, "I would have already told you anything I could put a finger on, but Tatros is a devious man and a vengeful, avaricious one. He has designs on Valtierra and no compunctions against doing anything that would hurt the city. Continue to wear your sword."

For the first time, the Youth realized war was not merely armies facing each other in the field and he had the choice of being a warrior or a victim. "Thank you for the advice."

The Warrior stood and strode out of the hall, and the Youth gazed at the other Council members. Until he had some idea what he faced in the way of duties and problems, there was no reason to seek their advice or assistance.

THE MERCHANT

As he fell into the line of members following the Youth to the Council chamber, he hoped for a quick meeting. Merchants from Benett would be waiting to haggle with him. They'd undoubtedly want more grain cheaper but meeting the possible needs of Valtierra left him with little surplus. It hadn't helped that the Matron had warned him if the quality of the foodstuffs sold to the army didn't improve, she'd denounce him before the Council. The men in the army hadn't been able to tell good from bad, but the Matron and her flock of old hens had noted it immediately.

As he took his temporary seat at the end of the table opposite the Wise Old Man, he tried to guess what business they had to discuss. They were halfway through the Rash Youth's term as head of the Council and he'd heard nothing to suggest the meeting would consist of much more than six taps of the staff.

As soon as the Youth asked what matters needed be addressed, both the Harlot and the Warrior spoke. After a moment, the Warrior nodded to the Harlot to continue.

"Thank you," she said to the Warrior, then looked for a moment at each member of the Council. "I propose we pay the women in the camp the same as the men. Their services are just as important to the city."

Caught off-guard, the Merchant cleared his throat until he could stall for enough time to phrase his objection. "Why should we pay them? Don't they receive payment from the soldiers? It's an unnecessary expense to the city. And what would they do with the money? They receive their meals from the city, and I understand the men in the army are building a bordello, so they have a roof over their heads."

The Harlot seemed to bristle like an angry cat. "How much can a soldier, who is paid five coppers a month, pay? The women have never received payment, and they deserve better. Theirs is a hard life. If anyone on the Council believes otherwise, I urge them to try it."

The Youth seemed to be biting back a comment, but the Fool said, "At least one other member of the Council has, but he's a high-priced whore."

The Merchant clenched his fists, wishing he could use them to batter that insolent grin off the Fool's face. The fact that others could see his rage only added kindling to the fire.

"I agree with the Harlot," the Warrior said. "These women help keep the men an army rather than simply an armed mob. Not only are their lives difficult, they are also often short. If they are not killed by the pox, they grow old quickly, and no one seems to have any use for an aged harlot. To be sure, the city gives much to some, but from others it only seems to take. I believe the Council should...," he stumbled over a word and took a moment to remember it, "...redress this wrong."

The Merchant ached to answer this insult to his class, but too heated a reply would only antagonize the others, most of whom stared at the table, still examining the idea.

Without giving away her opinion by expression or tone, the Crone asked, "Are you stating this as a proposal?"

"I am," the Harlot replied.

Tapping the Council staff on the floor, the Youth announced, "There is a proposal before the Council. All in favor raise your right hands."

The Crone's hand shot up immediately, as did those of the Warrior, the Harlot, and the Rash Youth. After a moment, they were joined by the hands of the Mother, the Farmer, the Wise Old Man, and, with obvious reluctance, the Matron.

With a laugh, the Fool raised his hand. "Even I can count to nine."

"Those opposed," the Youth said, "raise your left hands."

"This will mean more taxes," the Artisan grumbled, as he raised his left hand.

"You'll recover them the next time you overcharge a customer with more money than sense," the Fool drawled.

"I would prefer not to vote," the Priest said. "I'd rather have had the time to meditate and pray on the question, but I won't simply oppose it, either."

Part of a merchant's skills were knowing when one had been bested in a trade and the ability to hide one's chagrin. The Merchant sat motionless.

"The proposal is accepted," the Youth announced, as he tapped the floor.

"I also have a proposal," the Warrior said.

The Merchant groaned to himself. So much for a quick meeting. The merchants from Benett would be more primed to haggle.

"As some of you know," the Warrior glanced around the table. "I have brought discipline to an army that sorely needs it. There will probably not be many more lashings than before, and those will be for just cause, but I also need to be able to offer more. I would like to be able, each month, to offer awards to the companies who do best. It would only be double their usual pay. In time of war, of course, it could be two or three companies who distinguish themselves, and we might even treble their usual pay."

"And where do you propose we find the money to pay them these awards?" the Merchant demanded.

The Warrior stared into the other man's eyes. "I will give a quarter of my own wages. Perhaps others might also contribute. We are speaking of taxes, but my men will be paying theirs in blood."

The Wise Old Man tapped his staff against the floor. "I don't think that will be necessary. Some in the city gain more than others from the city. It seems only fair that, in their prosperity, they provide for the safety and health of the city. I propose a tax of one copper mark for each mark of silver paid for items. If someone wants a luxury, I doubt a tax of one-twentieth of the price will dissuade them from buying."

The Merchant found his voice at last. "You are proposing to drive prices up. This will cause some craftsmen and merchants to leave the city, and the tax will make our items more expensive. We'd be losing business to other cities."

The Artisan shook his head. "You exaggerate the problem. Every city levies taxes, and we enjoy lower taxes than the neighboring cities. Most of the added costs to our items are not from taxes but from the merchants' profits and from other cities' tariffs. Rewarding good men is an expense I understand. I agree with the proposal."

"Does anyone else have an opinion to state? No?" The Youth glanced at the masks around the table. "Then I call for a vote. Those in favor of the proposal…"

Only the Merchant and the Fool failed to raise their right hands and the Fool giggled. "Being a Fool isn't as lonely as I thought it might be."

Glaring at the Fool, the Merchant tried not to hear the chuckles the Fool's remark had wrung from some of the Council. He'd remember the insults and payment would cost the Fool dearly.

"Are there any more matters to bring to the Council? Then I call this meeting ended." The Youth tapped three times and the Merchant hauled himself to his feet and hurried from the chamber. He supposed some of the Council members would think he was fleeing, his tail between his legs. Well and fine. He'd be able to recover his lost prestige, and it was always better to be underestimated.

Breathing deeply, he cleared his mind of everything but what he could gain for the city in haggling with the other merchants. He was confident of his ability and the struggle would be on familiar ground where he'd won before.

THE WARRIOR

When the Warrior arrived at the camp it had acquired a different air, even if the odor remained. Hondros met him at the gate, armed and armored, and led him to the quarters of the former commander. From the smell of lye soap and the condition of the place, it seemed even the walls had been scrubbed. A pallet that looked new had been placed in a corner and a frame had been constructed for his armor.

"Hardly palatial," Hondros commented, "but it should keep the rain out. What are your orders?"

The Warrior set his possessions near the pallet. "First, we will look this place over."

In contrast to the almost surly inactivity he'd noted on his first visit, the camp bustled. In a large square, two companies in full armor practiced, facing each other using trimmed greenwood saplings for swords and spears.

After watching them for a few minutes, the Warrior waved for Hondros to stop the practice, something the man did with a bellow that would've impressed an outraged bull.

"You are not fighting like an army," the Warrior shouted. "A battle is not the place for each man to show his prowess. You must each be capable of fighting well, but you will need that most in heavy woods or steep hills. Did any of you see either in your three days of marching? I did not. Most of your battles will be fought on level or nearly level ground.

"You must learn to fight together or you will learn to die together." He drew men into a line, placing them apart by the width of a shield. Next he taught them to use their swords for thrusting, so that as they advanced at his command they looked like nothing so much as a moving wall with constantly grinding teeth.

"You may wonder," he shouted, "why you do not use spears. You five, with the spears, line up abreast and face me."

Thrusting his war hammer into his belt, the Warrior drew his sword and took a shield from one of the men watching, then walked toward the five, who held their line, the sapling spears pointed at his chest. As he approached the line of sticks his sword lashed out, trimming the saplings by the length of a forearm then, using his shield and the sword to beat aside the 'spears', he charged ahead, driving between two of the men, shoving one aside with his shield and striking with the flat of his blade.

"If an enemy can break through your wall, your spears are useless. If a man can cut off the head of the spear or get between you and the spearhead, the spear is useless. If you must carry a spear, you must learn its uses better, and always be sure the head is not too tightly secured."

He borrowed a spear and managed to loosen its head, then hurled it at a shield braced by another shield. The point drove half the length of a finger into the heavy, leather-covered wood. "Now," he said to the man he motioned to draw it out. "Throw it back at me." As the man wrenched the spear free, the head was left buried in the shield and the Warrior easily deflected the shaft with a blow of his sword.

The Warrior gave the soldiers time to understand what they'd seen and learn from it. "There will be times when a man or a small group must fight alone, but first you must learn to fight together."

Looking beyond the men training with weapons, he observed almost all the workers in sight had stopped in their labors and were watching the training. "You men," he shouted to them, "will also learn to fight. Everyone will work, but those who learn well will be those who spend more time training and less time toiling."

He nodded to the captain and petty-captains training the soldiers and, with Hondros, followed one of the wide streets toward the top of the nearer hill.

"It's a beginning," Hondros observed.

"Well said. It is only a beginning. They also have to learn to fight in formations at least three lines deep. And we have not even begun to retrain the cavalry or the archers and slingers, and we need more of the archers. Archers cannot win a battle by themselves, but we can use them to force the enemy to move to ground of our choosing."

As he watched other men piling stones and slapping on mortar, he continued. "A soldier's craft is as demanding as any, and the men must be trained until they fight and adapt to changes by habit. At the same time, we need them to learn other crafts as well. Only the very best fighters will be only soldiers. We also need builders, armorers, cooks, and herdsmen, all of whom can also fight. And teamsters, because most soldiers will not be able to carry enough supplies for more than a three days' march. And the cavalry must learn to tend their horses in the field. A sick horse means one set of eyes less to find the enemy or a better march route."

Hondros drew a deep breath. "I'm not sure how many of the men are ready to be craftsmen."

"That is why we must teach them to take pride in their work. Until they begin to realize they are better at their craft than most men, they will consider it only work. We must instill that pride, but be careful; a little praise is enough. If we overuse it, it will lose its value. The same is true of punishment. I am a stranger here, so I count on you to choose captains and petty-captains who spare both the praise and the lashings."

* * *

For nearly three months the Warrior trained the men. Two-day marches became common and some companies became capable of marching for three or four days, then fall into their formations for training.

The buildings grew and the tents disappeared, furled and folded and stowed in wagons. The brothel had been finished first, along with the kitchen and dining hall. The infirmary was placed beside the temple and barracks became available. With less building to do, more men were trained as soldiers. Many of them seemed astonished at what they were able to achieve and now strove with a sense of purpose.

The Warrior had attended the Council meetings. Unless some matter of importance required the Council to gather, they gathered every fortnight, and the Warrior watched as the staff of office was handed to the Matron, then to the Farmer.

As soon as that meeting was finished he returned to the camp and, the next day, left Hondros in command while he rode out with a captain and a petty-captain of cavalry.

The most likely source of danger was from the north, so they rode toward Shicassa, the Warrior noting the best and fastest routes for marching men. He still wanted to limit the damage done by a passing army but, if war came, speed was more important than crops. His eyes sought out the few landmarks and he pointed them out to his companions. They stopped at each farmstead and the Warrior met the farmers. Sometimes they were offered meals, which were usually accepted, and most nights were spent on a pallet in a farmer's hut or in a bed of straw in a barn. At each place the Warrior asked about younger sons skilled with bows or slings and, in each place, he made sure the farmer had a way to warn his neighbors and the army should there be an invasion.

By the time he'd acquainted himself and the cavalrymen with the country and the people, it was time to return to the residence for the meeting at which the staff would be handed to the Fool.

* * *

As he handed the reins of his horse to the stableman, the Warrior wondered if he should look forward to the Month of the Fool as a form of entertainment or whether he should prepare himself for some disaster.

After eating a light meal, he used one of the bath houses behind the residence to scrub away the sweat and grime of a fortnight in the saddle. After returning to his rooms he sat on the bed and removed boots and jerkin. As he stripped off his shirt and breeches, he marveled at the bed. He'd never seen the like until he'd come to Valtierra. It consisted of a wooden frame with hardwood knobs that secured a web of ropes, on top of which lay a pallet. Sighing, he laid down on the pallet, wondering at how quickly one accepted luxuries, and drifted into slumber.

* * *

In the habit of rising early, the Warrior strode to the dining hall where he found only the Farmer, almost finished with his platter. They exchanged a few words then the Farmer left to see to the garden. The Warrior enjoyed a leisurely breakfast as the other members filed into the hall, chose food from the kitchen, and ate.

By midmorning the Fool still hadn't appeared in the dining hall but the Farmer had returned and, after murmuring to one of the women who worked in the kitchen, had trudged to the Chamber of the Twelve, the other members of the Council following.

After letting his irritation grow another sixth of an hour, the Farmer finally tapped the staff three times on the floor. "If we wait for the Fool until it's time to hand over the staff to the next leader of the Council, we will have done nothing," the Farmer growled.

Suddenly the Fool dashed into the chamber, managed to slide to his seat, and dropped into it.

"It's poor form for the next leader of the Council to show such insolence and indolence," the Farmer's voice grated.

The Fool leaned forward. "I was just hoping we could forget this foolishness entirely," the Fool said, "then I realized there might actually be matters of substance that would require my inattention. Please, continue."

Clearing his throat with a rasping sound, the Wise Old Man said, "I'd like to call for a vote to dismiss two magistrates and half a dozen constables."

The Merchant stared at him."For what reason?"

"Because the constables either accepted bribes or abused their authority—or both. It's disheartening to see how often abuse and corruption are kindred." The Wise Old Man's voice trembled with outrage. "And the magistrates abused their discretion. I'd heard claims of injustice from citizens and I asked three men of good reputation to watch the constables and magistrates. I want them not only to be dismissed but to be charged by the Council for their crimes and punished."

"Sounds like a good beginning," the Rash Youth said. "I'd vote to flay them alive if I thought the Council would support it."

The Warrior studied the Old Man, impressed he had taken such initiative. Apparently, the man understood what was most important about traditions were the ideals that had made them traditions in the first place. When the Farmer called for votes, he raised his right hand, and the Farmer announced the proposal had been accepted.

"Does anyone have anything else to discuss?" After a moment's silence, the Farmer stood and held out the staff to the Fool.

The Fool accepted the staff and, as the members stood and changed chairs until each occupied his or her seat for the Month of the Fool, twirled the stick, finally stopping to tap the end three times against the floor. "Meeting ended."

THE FOOL

Some might've relished being head of the Council but the Fool saw it as a disadvantage. He'd admired the Youth's fortitude and restraint, but he'd hang himself before he'd do the same. He'd have to work harder at the others to help them see things as he saw them, have them then propose the solutions he'd anticipated, all the while letting them think they had originated the ideas. Then it became only a matter of coaxing them to make their proposals at the proper time.

One or two of the Council could be played easier than a small harp but most of them were canny enough to make the game more interesting and require him to take more pains. Ironically, the easiest to manipulate was a manipulator himself. He'd long since learned where the Merchant's soft parts were and just what verbal barbs would sting the most. The man had too much of a temper to ever be a really capable schemer.

The Harlot was much more difficult to gull and he suspected the Crone was almost impossible to fool. This was not a problem—they were two of the people on the Council he most respected.

Council leadership was just another cell inside the prison, to the Fool. He hadn't visited the city since the Festival when he'd been given the mask and had no desire to go there until the next Festival when he could relinquish it. They'd expect him to act the fool in the city, a notion he found tiresome. He preferred to stay at the residence and let their expectations do all the work. Taking the sandbags from their bowl, he began to juggle. Fortunately, his apartment had a high ceiling and he was able to juggle all eleven.

A tapping at his door almost caused him to miss one of the bags but he managed to catch them all and tossed them into their bowl. "A moment," he said, as he drew on his mask and tied the laces then he stepped to the door and opened it.

He hadn't been expecting anyone, and the man he least expected stood waiting, leaning on his staff.

"I hope I'm not disturbing you," the Wise Old Man said.

"Not at all." The Fool gestured for his visitor to enter and motioned toward the chairs, now facing the fireplace. The small fire danced across charred wood and the Fool added a log, since the Old Man would probably need the warmth. "Would you care for a cup of wine?"

Lowering himself into the nearer chair, the Wise Old Man shook his head. The way he handled his staff, the very deliberate way he leaned it against the wall, showed he was trying to compose his thoughts into words and feared they'd be misunderstood or, perhaps, understood too well.

The Fool sat, crossed his legs and waited.

Finally the Old Man said, "I believe I would appreciate a cup of wine, but watered."

The Fool poured wine and water into a cup, poured only wine into his own goblet, and offered the Old Man the watered wine.

"You were very flippant at the Council meeting this morning," the Old Man said. "The People expect much of the Council, and we should respect that."

"As a matter of fact," the Fool replied, "I do, but I think they have rather different expectations of the Fool. I'll join you in hoping nothing of importance happens during my month."

The Old Man studied what he could see of the Fool's face and the Fool smiled. "I wasn't mocking you, if that's what you're wondering."

With a cautious smile, the Wise Old Man replied, "You do have a talent for flaying people with your tongue."

The Fool shrugged. "It's my role. It's nothing personal—well, with the Merchant it's personal, but he's special."

"Why do you dislike him so?"

Shifting into a more comfortable posture in the chair and with a sip of wine, the Fool said, "Commerce is necessary. A farmer hasn't the time or temperament to sell his own products. If the Artisan wants to sell an item to someone in a different city, he hasn't the time to look for the customer. But if commerce is necessary, most merchants are, at best, necessary evils. They often make more from the sale than either the farmer or the artisan, all without ever laboring over a crop or working in a forge."

The Old Man's smile turned rueful. "I wish I could say there was only one member of the Council I disliked. To be honest, there were times when, had I been a younger man, I'd have given you a beating."

"If you'd been a younger man," the Fool said, grinning broadly, "you wouldn't be on the Council and I probably would've been more diplomatic. Who else do you dislike?"

"I once disliked the Warrior," the Old Man admitted. He took a sip of the wine and appeared to savor it. "I was wrong about that. I don't really dislike the Harlot but I don't respect her profession. The Crone and I have bickered—much of it my fault, I suppose." He lowered his voice. "The Matron and her friends remind me of a flock of chickens, all clucking and pecking at those below them. And, again being honest, I don't care for the Merchant. His false heartiness and solicitude grate on me like your giggle."

"You see," the Fool said, "that's why I can't dislike you. Whatever I see as your flaws, you're an honest man." The Fool took a drink of his wine. "And I think you'd like the Harlot if you spoke with her."

"You may well be right." The Old Man's tone said he was not convinced. He finished the rest of the wine in his cup. "That was a good wine—and this has been a surprisingly good conversation. I'll join you in hoping nothing eventful happens in your month and I'd appreciate your hope that the same is true of mine. I suppose I've become a creature of inertia; I do prefer routine to crises or adventure." He reached for his staff and levered himself out of the chair. "Thank you."

The Fool rose quickly and opened the door, closing it when the Old Man had gone. Returning to his chair, he sipped at his wine. The old man was growing in self-knowledge, which was the first step to wisdom; he was truly becoming the Wise Old Man.

THE WARRIOR

The ride to the camp had become tedious. The vineyards were bare of grapes, the olives were gone from their groves, and even the last gourds had been picked. The country remained green—he doubted it ever became as withered as the sere land in the south—but he could find patches of gray-brown, and even the green had faded.

Topping the crest of a hill, he stood in the stirrups and looked back at the city. The gray stone walls were higher than those of the camp had been by at least the height of a man and he could see only a few spires above the walls. Those would be in what the Youth called the first quarter, the part of the city made up of temples and palaces, where the wealthiest citizens lived. The second quarter was the part of the city he'd visited, made up of shops and inns. The third quarter was given to the major courts and the open fields where the Festival was held. The fourth quarter was, he'd been told, slaughterhouses and workshops and the homes of the poorest in the city. He shook his head at the waste. Valtierra was wealthy enough no one who wanted to work should be truly poor. Still, that problem would have to be dealt with by the others on the Council. His first task was to improve the lot of his soldiers and forge them into an army, although he doubted even the Artisan with his remarkable skills, could advise him.

One specter that haunted him was the possibility of a revolt in Valtierra. If it came to that, he wondered whether the army would be called upon to help quell the rebellion. That would create new problems in the army. Most of the recruits were younger sons of farmers, who had no other trade, and the poor who could only improve their lot by protecting the city. If they were called upon to battle the poor people of the city, he wasn't sure they would follow their orders to fight. For that matter, he wasn't sure he could give such orders.

He was no closer to finding the spy, and he wondered if Khaimon had been wrong. While there were arguments among the members of the Council but with, as the Crone had said, twelve strong-minded men and women, some dissention was inevitable. Other people than Council members might be able to ferret out secrets. The stableman seemed a friendly man, if slow. He was almost as strong as a carthorse and seemed only a little more intelligent, but that could be an act. Still, if it was a charade, it was largely wasted, as the man seldom entered the residence.

Three or four women worked in the kitchen and cleaned, and any of them could be privy to conversations among the Council members. A spy needed only eyes and ears; they wouldn't necessarily need a voice on the Council.

He nudged his horse into a canter. Too many possibilities left his mind reeling, and he found himself looking forward to the simpler problems at the camp, matters he felt capable of handling.

A flash of movement and a loud, shrill squeal snatched his attention and he watched a hawk, a kill in its talons, labor upward. It'd caught a rabbit or, perhaps, a field rat. He'd seen almost exactly the same thing years ago, the day before his first battle. He'd believed enough in omens then to try to decide whether it augured good or ill.

He was no longer sure about omens and even less certain how they should be read. Was he the rat or the hawk? To believe in omens, a man had to believe he was only a marker in a game, and the Warrior rejected that part of the superstition.

If he were to take it as an omen, it was his duty to not only be the hawk but to make hawks of all his men.

THE ARTISAN

Shivering in the late fall morning despite his cloak, the Artisan rapped at the Warrior's doorpost. "A moment," the Warrior's voice said, then, in the time it took to don a mask and tie it in place, "Enter."

His gift to the Warrior in his left hand, the Artisan pushed open the door. In the last two months he'd had occasion to visit these rooms only twice, and he was struck again by how sparsely furnished the quarters were. Only a map on the wall opposite the bed and a wooden stand for the man's armor flanking the map made the room different from when it had been vacant.

"Remember when we first talked at my forge and you wondered what I was crafting?"

"I remember. You said it was something with which to amuse yourself."

The Artisan handed the long, thin package, wrapped in soft leather, to the other man.

The Warrior unwrapped the leather to see a sheathed sword. Drawing it, his eyes widened at the highly polished tapering blade. The crossguard was also polished steel but the Artisan had given it a short, curved section overhanging the mouth of the scabbard and had faced the guard itself with brass. Either the overhang, used as a hook, or the softer brass, could be used to capture an opponent's blade. The grip was wood covered with black leather, bound with silver wire, but the Artisan's greatest pride was in the pommel, a perfectly formed rose crafted of steel.

He smiled as he watched the Warrior handle it almost reverently, obviously awed by the workmanship. "It's yours."

The Warrior opened his mouth then closed it without speaking. Apparently, words seemed too poor, and he nodded, then removed his sword belt, laid his old sword on the chest, bound the scabbard to his belt, and buckled the belt around his waist.

"Sometimes," the Artisan said, "a smith's greatest reward is knowing something he's crafted is being used by a man who appreciates fine work."

"I will be honored to wear it."

"You're not wearing your armor," the Artisan observed. "I thought we were riding out to the camp today with Stemos."

"We are. I have not worn the armor except for leading marches for almost a month. The men are beginning to show some pride, so I have to begin to show some trust in them. Have you eaten yet?"

"Not yet. Getting out of bed was a challenge. It's turned cold earlier this year than I remember. According to the Farmer, this is going to be a long, cold winter." The Warrior closed his door behind them and together they walked to the dining hall, where the Artisan basked in the warmth of the kitchen. "You're from a colder place than this, aren't you?"

With a nod, the Warrior selected bread, cheese, and fruit. The Artisan had the same but added a couple of boiled eggs. As they sat at the table, the Warrior glanced around the room and the Artisan did the same, noticing only the Priest and Farmer had risen as early.

They ate quickly and, drawing their cloaks closer, stepped out of the residence. Stemos was already at the stable, chatting with the stableman, who was throwing the saddle onto the Warrior's horse.

Riding away from the residence, they let their horses have their heads. The Warrior's charger set a brisk pace and the other two ranged beside him.

They'd topped the rise before the gates and ridden into the valley when the Artisan caught the smell, and it wasn't as noxious as that of the city. The walls now stood no higher than a man's chest and were still being pulled apart.

"When you're done with this, perhaps you could turn your hand to making gold of dross," the Artisan said, grinning.

"Stemos and the Merchant are the ones to thank," the Warrior said. "And everyone has helped. The Merchant provides foodstuffs at a lower price."

Around the square, the buildings were drawn into ranks, straight streets between the rows of stone barracks. Men drilled in the square, using their heavy shields to force their way forward, stabbing the air with wooden practice swords. Other men sparred with shields and wooden swords.

"There are still some who grumble," the Warrior said. "But I would worry if they did not grumble. An army that does not grumble or complain a little is an army with no spirit at all."

Hondros strode to meet them, his face grim as usual. "It's becoming harder to get them out for drilling and marching. They're only soldiers three seasons out of four, at best."

The Warrior swung down out of the saddle. "I will try to find some woods where they can chop firewood. You have enough oxen to drag it back." The Warrior nodded toward the few dwindling piles of wood from the destruction of the old camp. "Once they have run out of wood, they will have more enthusiasm for the task."

"I've talked to some local farmers who'd be more than happy to have some fields cleared of trees," Hondros said.

"Very good. Have you had any other trouble?"

Hondros stared down at his right hand as he rubbed his fingers together, as though trying to wipe away something. "One of the men permitted to visit the city was caught drunk. While he was working off his punishment in the city, he recognized a deserter in the same work party. A constable brought them both back to the camp."

"Was the one caught drunk a good soldier?"

"Better than most."

"Then give him his stripes, but do it lightly, and cut off his wine ration for a fortnight. As for the deserter, give him his stripes and a choice to either work his way back into the army or have his right ear cropped."

Hondros' heavy eyebrows rose in surprise. "You know, of course, that would be like castrating him. Without an ear to wear a partner's ring in, he won't be able to find a partner."

"That was my intention. I would wager he is no better a man out of the army than he is in it. I would as soon someone like that did not breed."

The Artisan kept his face composed during the exchange, saving his concerns until he could find a chance to talk to the Warrior alone.

Together with Stemos and Hondros, they strolled through the camp. The kitchen had been built at one corner of the central square, the temple opposite it, and the infirmary beside the temple. The brothel stood at the northeastern corner of the camp. They visited each, in turn. At the brothel, they noticed a harlot with a split lip and a bruise that made her face look lopsided. The sight angered the Artisan and he clenched his fists until his nails, short as they were trimmed, pressed into his palms, but the Warrior turned to Hondros. "Do you know who did this?" His voice was soft.

"One of the lieutenants."

"Strip him in front of the men and give him twenty-five lashes with a saltwater soaked whip. He is not to visit the city or the brothel for a year, and he will lose his station. I want him to have less power than the rawest recruit. The men must remember they are supposed to be protectors, not persecutors. He may earn his station again, but he has to earn it, not have it given to him."

Hondros simply nodded.

They ate the noon meal with Hondros and his former company and, after an uncomfortable silence, finally broken by the Warrior telling a bawdy tale, they fell to eating with a will. The Artisan noted the men were all armed and armored, and at least this company seemed to know how to care for their weapons and armor. Stemos radiated pride that his plans had been executed so well, and the Artisan agreed this camp was Stemos' city, plans brought to reality.

After the meal they walked to the stables, saddled their horses, and rode back to the residence. As they topped the rise outside the camp, the Artisan signed to Stemos to fall back, then nudged his horse into a quicker pace, riding stirrup-to-stirrup beside the Warrior. "Your punishment for the deserter seems harsh," he said.

The Warrior stared at the Artisan a moment before he replied. "You do not understand. The greatest part of being a warrior is not battle, or killing the enemy, or even victory. It is standing with your brothers. It is essential to a warrior, or even a soldier. You and your brothers are standing together, relying upon each other. That man, the deserter, spat on that sacred bond. In the city, that counts for little, but he chose to be a soldier, then he chose to break faith. There must be a penalty appropriate to the offense."

"But to geld him—you know, of course, that cropping his right ear means he will not be able to find a partner?"

"I am just glad he betrayed us all in a time of peace, and not when he might have gotten other, better men killed." The Warrior shot him another glance. "Are you reconsidering your vote?"

"No," the Artisan replied. "I'd just realized how ruthless you can be—have to be, I suppose."

"It is necessary. I appreciate the freedoms you enjoy in your city, but those freedoms must be paid for. The army pays that debt by giving up many of those same freedoms. On the other hand," he smiled at the Artisan, "I want the rawest recruit, through his dedication and initiative, to be able to become first captain."

THE WARRIOR

They rode back to the residence in silence, but not an awkward one, although the Warrior used the time for dark thoughts.

He'd felt guilty accepting the sword, but refusing it would've been an insult, just as he'd felt guilty accepting the Youth's gift of a keg of ale. The gift from the Artisan had been more than a simple gift from the heart. Besides the skill and labor required to craft a piece of steel into a perfect rose, he knew the rose was the symbol of Valtierra. The Artisan had made him welcome, had, in a sense, called him the sword of Valtierra. As for the ale; the Youth was also welcoming him, giving him something fine from what had been his home. He didn't believe either the Artisan or the Youth was the spy, but he still couldn't completely trust them and to accept a gift from them seemed a sort of betrayal.

After he'd handed the reins of his horse to the stableman the Warrior thanked Stemos again for his assistance. It was easier to reform the army in the setting the man had provided. He supposed the Farmer would understand. One had to plow the land, tearing up the remains of the old crop to plant the new one.

He felt as though he'd been trying to ride a runaway horse for the last few months and he wanted time alone to sort out some of his impressions and try to grasp the situation. It was a little like gripping a snake—you wanted to be sure it wasn't going to bite you. Since he'd become the Warrior, the only time he'd had alone he'd been so tired he'd fallen asleep almost immediately. Now he wanted the luxury of a little forethought.

In his rooms he took off his mask, which seemed to grow heavier each time he'd had to wear it.

He'd accomplished much with the army. He'd match his best three companies with a like number of any soldiers he'd seen and three times their number of most he'd seen. But he'd come no closer to finding the spy—if, indeed, there was one. Even Khaimon hadn't seemed to be certain.

He was probably in no danger of assassination from the spy. A single death, even that of the head of the army, would be a bad trade if it cost the loss of a spy. On the other hand, Prince Tatros would probably consider it a bargain paying some cutthroat a handful of silver to do the deed, which is why the Warrior was always armed.

Drawing up each member of the Council in his mind, he assessed each, trying to guess the weakness of each. Everyone had weaknesses, but what flaw could make someone betray his or her city? The Harlot was a cynic. She'd called herself a realist, but that was the term most cynics preferred for themselves. The

Merchant commonly sold objects. Was he, too, for sale? The Fool was unpredictable. Who knew what sort of secrets hid behind that grin?

Arguments just as powerful could be made for none of them being the spy.

Even among the least likely—the Wise Old Man, the Crone, the Priest, and the Farmer, the gaps in his knowledge of them might be big enough to hide treason. He had no one he could turn to, no one on whom he could rely, no one he could, with certainty, accuse. Until he could find a way to solve the puzzle, he would simply have to tread warily.

He couldn't simply wait for the spy to make a mistake, he'd have to push the traitor into revealing himself or herself, but the time had to be right. For the present, he'd have to exercise patience and remain watchful.

He wished he knew the man who'd replaced him as head of Tatros' army. He'd give everything, including his new sword and what was left of the tun of ale, to know how that army was being led. Ironically, his best ally was probably Tatros himself. The prince wasn't likely to let another man make the army as strong as Anton had wanted it.

The thought brought with it another shock. It seemed that Anton was another man, someone he'd once known reasonably well.

Other matters required his more immediate attention. He'd need to ask the Farmer and the Merchant to use their resources to find out what sort of fortress the Shicassans had built in Sweetwater Valley and how strongly they'd garrisoned it.

The Merchant also traded with merchants in Benett and Shielba. The Prince of Shielba wasted his country's substance on the baubles created by Valtierra's artisans; the princedom was the source of superior iron. The Artisan would know more about Ravanna, and the Matron, the Crone, or the Mother would have friends in Lancar. He'd need to know if any of them represented as great a threat as Shicassa.

Knowing Tatros and his ambitions, he suspected the man had designs not only on Valtierra but on Benett as well. The port city was wealthy and provided an opening to the great sea.

He shook his head. One reason for the continued existence of all the little city-states was none of them had a really good army. He could think of half a dozen families in the south who could gobble up the lot of them like ripe grapes and not bother to spit out the seeds.

Again he shook his head. Too many ifs, guesses, and suppositions. One couldn't lead an army into strange country without scouts. Which reminded him; it was time to start training his cavalry in different tactics.

He'd done all he could for the day and the weariness was catching up with him. He'd earned a nap. Taking off his boots and jerkin, he laid on the bed and was asleep almost before his eyes had closed.

THE PRIEST

After giving thanks to the Trinity, he sat on his bench beside the pond, reflecting on the limits of prayer and meditation. Late fall and winter were always the time of the Destroyer. Dead plants and dead leaves were the marks of His passing. He hoped it wasn't also the late fall of the Faith as well. What happened to the gods when They were no longer remembered? It seemed blasphemous to think of the Trinity as dying or fading away, like the grass. Perhaps They died and were reborn in new forms, with new names, but life, death, and sustenance were all around and he couldn't imagine a world without them.

The Faith might be receiving fresh life from unexpected places. The priest who'd volunteered to serve the temple in the army camp had told him that, while the numbers were still small, more soldiers and even the harlots were beginning to come to the services. He suspected some of them were coming because the Warrior granted each man time to attend the Sabbath rites instead of working or drilling, but the priest seemed to believe he was gaining believers.

The other unexpected revitalization was as much a danger as a blessing, because it was also dividing the priesthood. A priestess had developed a following among the poor. She preached much the same message as the other priests and the few priestesses, but she accused some priests of favoring the wealthy.

Several of the priests had approached him to denounce her as a heretic, but he'd heard her speak and he found himself agreeing with much of what she said. He was afraid the faithful would be divided but perhaps conflict would be preferable to the slow death of the Faith he'd been fearing. And she was right that some of the priests seemed to believe the priesthood was the Faith. If he were looking for heretics to denounce…

He slowly stood and stretched. Perhaps the priestess would be the next Priest and he wondered if that would be a good thing. She might very well lose her voice and power if she became another cloistered member of the Council.

That was for the Sustainer to think on and worry about. The Priest drew his cloak tighter about himself and paced back to the residence and the evening meal. Yes, prayer and meditation had their limits. He accepted the fact he was not a person of action, like the Warrior or the priestess, but he prayed to the Trinity he had the courage to stand firm for what was right.

THE WARRIOR

He'd just sat down with his platter and cup when the Youth entered the hall. The Warrior smiled when he remembered the Youth's pride at giving him a keg of ale—and a good ale it was, too—and the face the Youth had drawn at his first tentative sip. When the Youth had said it tasted like horse piss, the Warrior hadn't been able to resist asking him how he'd recognized the flavor.

He'd become friendly enough with most of the members of the Council to be able to engage in such banter, confident the others wouldn't take offence.

Carrying his platter and cup, the Youth strolled out of the kitchen and sat down at the Warrior's table. "Are you still thinking of visiting the city this evening?" the Youth asked.

"I am. Would you care to join me?"

"I'd like that. I haven't seen much of you lately."

"I have been spending more time at the camp and learning the country. The best maps are the ones behind the eyes that have seen the land. The last week I have been exploring the northern and western borders. I have also been visiting farmers and herdsmen. They can give better warning than the watchtowers, and they are the best recruits for archers and slingers."

He finished the last of his bread, washing it down with the last sip of ale in his cup. "What sort of excitement are you expecting to find in the city?"

"Music. Some of the musicians are going to gather. What sort of music did you have in the south?"

"Horns and drums, for the most part." He stood and carried his platter and cup to the kitchen, washed them, and returned to the table. "What can I expect to hear tonight?"

"Tambours, tambourines, flutes, the smallharp, and a voice as hauntingly lovely as a view of the hills in mist."

The Warrior chuckled. "When you become so lyrical I have to wonder if it is about the voice or the woman."

The Youth grinned. "She does appeal to the eyes as well as the ears."

"Are you celebrating some sort of festival?"

"The end of autumn." The Youth finished his meal and gulped the last of his wine. "Are you ready? You might want to fetch your cloak."

"It is still pleasant. The breeze is mild and it does not smell like rain."

They set out for the city, walking briskly. To the Warrior, the light chill in the air was invigorating and as they neared the city he realized the stench he'd noticed before was less unpleasant and tried to decide whether it was because of the slightly colder weather or because the Wise Old Man's reforms had made the place cleaner, or if he'd simply become used to it.

As they passed through the gate he observed the streets and alleys seemed to be cleaner. Too many people still roamed the streets for his taste, but he saw fewer than before and most of those he saw seemed in a hurry to be somewhere else, probably someplace warmer. Most of them also seemed to be hurrying in the same direction the Youth was leading him.

Within a hundred paces he could smell wood smoke and in the next hundred could see the bonfire ahead. At nearly the same time, he heard the music; some sort of high-pitched pipe, a soft drum that sounded like a rapidly-beating heart, and another instrument he couldn't identify. The music, its tempo stately, soothed rather than excited. He listened as he approached and, as the song ended, peddlers hawked their wares for a few moments, then he was near enough to the raised dais that he could see the performers. Four men held instruments and he could see the instrument he hadn't recognized was stringed, probably the smallharp the Youth had mentioned.

A young woman joined the men on the dais and the Warrior almost held his breath as she began to sing. The words were hard to make out as they were drawn out in song, and the lilting language, from her mouth, seemed almost liquid. The Youth's praise for her voice was, if anything, understated. Her voice was pure and sweet as the best water he'd ever drunk. It soared, rising higher, then dropped and, although he didn't recognize the words, he experienced an intense longing mixed with peaceful contentment.

In the light of the torches her face was a thin oval framed by lank hair so pale a blonde it was almost white, and he understood why the Youth was so excited. She was, to him, too thin, and he marveled that such a powerful voice could issue from such a small body.

She finished the song and only waited for the shrill ululation of the crowd to still before she started another.

For perhaps an hour the Warrior enjoyed the music. The woman was followed by a man with a voice that made up in power what it lacked in range, and musicians played several pieces without vocal accompaniment. The tunes were alternately sentimental and rousing, and he enjoyed it all.

As the last song ended, the musicians threw water on the fires, leaving only the torches and he and the Youth joined the line to throw coins onto a blanket. When the Warrior's turn came, he tossed a silver coin and a handful of coppers onto the heap.

The Youth tossed a couple of coins and said, "That was a rich payment."

"It was rich entertainment," the Warrior replied. "Thank you for suggesting it."

"Do you think we have time to visit a tavern?" The Youth adjusted his cloak against the cold.

After raising his eyebrows the Warrior realized the Youth couldn't see the expression, but said, "Are you sure you want to have me in a tavern after the other time we visited one?"

One side of the Youth's mouth twitched into a half-smile. "The story of that night's been told enough that you're likely to receive only respect."

The Warrior suspected the Youth had meant fear rather than respect, but as long as he didn't have to kill some drunkard, he was willing to accept either. The crowd had thinned after they left the square, and his mood had evaporated, leaving him with his usual wariness, so he eyed the large, balding man walking toward him. The stranger's face was grim and determined and his right hand could be concealing a blade.

"That is close enough," he snapped at the man, and his own knife was in his hand.

At a warning shout from the Youth, the Warrior spun forward and to his left, spoiling the other man's attack, noticing something flashing in the air past him.

As the other man slashed upward, the Warrior brought his own knife down, gashing the arm. The other man stumbled, the Warrior punched him in the side of the head and the man fell, sprawling, to the street, his knife skittering across the stones.

Glancing toward the Youth, he saw him thrust his sword into the side of another man who'd been too slow making his escape.

The Warrior threw himself on the man he'd felled, driving his knee into the other's spine. He reversed the knife in his hand with a flick. "Who paid you?"

The downed man simply set his jaw and snarled.

Catching the man's right ear in his left hand, the Warrior moved the blade just below the ear, barely drawing blood. "Tell me," he demanded, "or I will carve off both ears, then geld you properly."

The man grimaced at the threat, then screamed as the blade swept upward. The Warrior tossed the ear into the street. "You had better tell me quickly, or you will not be able to hear the questions."

"I don't know his name," the man rasped. "He was an outland merchant."

The Warrior paused a moment. Either the man knew nothing or he was going to tell nothing. A quick slash cut the lobe off the left ear. "Move and I will nail you to the street."

He looked to where the Youth stood over a body, wiping his blade clean on the corpse's shirt. "Are you hurt?"

The Youth shook his head and looked past the Warrior to a middle-aged man with a ginger-colored beard, who held his arm, blood staining his fingers and the sleeve of his shirt.

"Apparently," the Youth said, "that one you're kneeling on was to distract you and maybe finish you off after this one wounded or killed you with a thrown knife. Our friend, here," he nodded at the wounded man, "seems to have caught the knife." He pulled the cloak off the body, strode to the injured man, and, using strips torn from the cloak, helped bind the cut on his arm. After he'd finished, he searched for and found the knife.

The man under the Warrior tried to move his arms closer to his body and the Warrior drove his knee harder into the man's back, wringing a grunt out of him.

Constables rushed toward them, short swords drawn. One of them tied the legs of the man under the Warrior with a length of short rope so he could hobble but not run, then two others hauled him roughly to his feet. Two more caught up the corpse by his arms and began to drag him away. The leader of the group strode toward the Youth and the Warrior. "Will you come with me?" His tone suggested they would come.

"In a moment," the Warrior said, and retrieved the ear and the earlobe. "You have done good work making the city clean, and I hate to leave a mess."

"Leave them," the constable said. "You'd be robbing some stray dog or cat of its dinner."

With a shrug, the Warrior tossed them back into the street.

Most of the constables wore red brigantine jacks while the leader wore a red tunic and breast and back plates, and all wore light helmets and red cloaks with the Valtierran rose embroidered or painted on them.

The leader of the constables strode perhaps two hundred long paces before leading them into an imposing guardhouse. A handful of constables lounged about, perhaps the same number of persons sat chained to the wall. The stench was worse here than outside, most of it probably coming from the buckets beside the prisoners. Beside a fire pit sat an elderly man with thin features set in an expression of profound boredom, although his features became animated as soon as he saw the masks.

Within moments the other constables followed them in with the prisoner, the corpse, and the wounded man.

The elderly man smoothed his red robes and leaned forward, resting his arms on the table. As the constables drew nearer, still keeping a respectful distance, the man said, "This looks interesting. What happened?"

The chief constable reported a boy had run to his patrol, shouting about fights and knives and when they'd arrived he'd found one man dead and two wounded, with the Youth binding the wound of a man with a gash on the arm and the Warrior holding another man down.

The gray eyes under shaggy brows turned to the bystander who told how he'd been cut by a thrown knife and turned to see two men struggling and the Warrior knocking down the man with the missing ear, then he'd seen the Youth thrusting his sword into the other man. As soon as he finished his story, one of the constables led him away. To a physician, the Warrior presumed.

"What have you to say, Warrior?" For an old man, the magistrate had a strong voice.

"I saw this one approach me," the Warrior indicated the bleeding man with a nod. "He seemed to be holding his knife up his arm and I told him to halt. The Youth shouted a warning and I moved. He tried to stab me and I saw a blade flash past. I took him down and held him for the constables."

The magistrate turned his gaze on the Youth.

"It's as the Warrior says. I saw the man approach, too, then saw a sudden movement and shouted a warning as I saw the dead man raise his arm to throw his knife. He was turning to run when I got my sword out and I lunged at him."

"What have you to say for yourself?" the magistrate demanded of the man being held by the constables.

"My friend and I were just going to a tavern when we were set upon by these two."

The magistrate turned and spat into the fire. "I should have you hanged just for being such an inept liar. As it is, you'll hang in the morning anyway." Facing one of the constables, he asked, "Why did you drag that carrion in here? It's leaving a mess of blood on the floor. Throw it into an offal pit."

As the body was hauled out, the magistrate gestured to the wall. "Chain this one up and hang him first thing in the morning. And toss his corpse in the same pit as his friend."

"Now that the business is concluded," the magistrate continued. "Would either of you care for a cup of mulled wine?"

"Perhaps a cup against the night's chill," the Youth said.

The Warrior shook his head. The excitement of the battle had died, leaving the taste of ashes in his mouth, and no amount of wine could wash that out. He watched three constables chain the man he'd fought to the wall, his wrists as well as his ankles, and take off the rope hobble.

"I'd have hanged him for stupidity," the magistrate said conversationally. "Any fool who'd attack a man who doesn't need a cloak in this weather is criminally addled."

"Is there always a magistrate at the prison?" the Warrior asked.

"Of course," the man replied, "and we're busier at night but I've noticed law-breaking becomes less frequent with the coming of cold weather. Do you need to hurry? The constables haven't had anything new in the way of conversation for months. Not since you were voted onto the Council." He nodded to the Warrior.

The Warrior's smile was wry. "At least that inspired something to talk about."

After taking another drink from his cup, the magistrate nodded again. "That, and the Wise Old Man deciding to make the city less of a sty. We haven't had so much change in years."

The Youth emptied his cup in a long draught and set it on the table. "I'm afraid we must return to the residence. We have a matter for the Council to discuss."

The magistrate cocked his head. "Isn't this the Month of the Fool?"

"Yes," the Youth admitted.

"Then the Trinity help you and all of us. Any day I expect to hear of a decree that everyone is to wear his tunic front-to-back."

Drawing his cloak about himself, the Youth said, "I've managed to talk him out of it so far."

The magistrate turned his chair to again bask in the warmth of the fire.

As they walked out of the guardhouse, the Warrior asked, "Are you all right?"

"As right as rain in spring. Why do you ask?"

"Because," the Warrior said, "after I had killed my first man I almost puked my guts up."

The Youth glanced at him then stared ahead. "I didn't have time for thought. He'd thrown a knife at you and I couldn't tell, at first, whether you were wounded or not. I just ran him through. Now I feel very good. The mulled wine tasted better than I'd remembered, and the harlots look even more appealing."

"Interesting," the Warrior said. "You have the makings of a greater Warrior than I, because you don't hesitate to strike or ponder it after. Just take care you don't become too fond of it. That has been the ruin of many a good man."

The Youth seemed to consider the thought before he said, "I'll be careful." After another long pause, he said, "And you're right, they were paid to kill you. Tatros, you suppose?"

"I have no proof," the Warrior replied, "but I know it the way I know my own boots."

"I'll tell the Fool. As I said, this is a matter for the Council to discuss."

THE FOOL

The Fool groaned to himself when the Youth told him of the attack on the Warrior, but all he said was, "Tell the others the Council will meet in the second hour after dawn."

After the Youth had gone he took off the mask he'd just donned and set it on its stand, then returned to bed, where he fought to get back to sleep, but his mind was too noisy, rehearsing arguments.

Finally, with a muttered curse, he sat up, then rose and found flint, steel, tinder, and a candle. When the candle flickered to life, he sat in the chair. The residence was a prison, as was a seat on the Council, and the damned mask was the worst prison of all. One barred wall was the leadership of the Council, which made his usual manipulations impossible. He found it far easier to play the Fool as just another member, particularly when truly important issues were at stake. As the leader of the Council, he was under too much scrutiny to be able to play his usual games.

He considered visiting the Harlot. They'd become good friends, but he couldn't bring himself to strain the friendship by asking her to share his burden. The load was his, and he'd have to carry it.

Still, he had other friends to turn to. He took the sandbags out of the bowl and began to juggle them. Too tired for proper coordination, he kept dropping them, never able to keep five in the air at the same time. So much for some friends, he thought, and returned them to the bowl.

If he were going to be restless, he might as well be restless in relative comfort, he decided, and snuffed the candle and crawled back into bed.

Plans were a useless exercise. His intuition had stood him in good stead before; best to rely upon it now. With that decision made, he quickly fell asleep.

* * *

The morning meal, seldom a lively affair and never on mornings when the Council met, dragged on in silence, each member of the Council eating alone except the Youth, who sat with the Warrior, talking in undertones. The Warrior remained almost as silent as the others.

Following custom, the Fool stood first and the rest of the Council followed him to the chamber. With the staff of office he rapped three times on the floor. "The reason for this meeting will become clear if the Youth will tell us what happened last night."

He was sure the Youth had told each member of the Council the story when he notified them of the meeting, but he found it useful to remind them. As the Youth retold the story, he glanced around the table. Its curved design made it possible for every member to see every other member, and the Fool was grateful his chair was no higher than any other. All the mouths below the masks were grim and set.

When the Youth had finished his recitation, the Fool asked, "Has anyone any questions?" The only answer was silence.

Turning to the Merchant, he asked, "What is the state of the city's food supply?"

"Only fair," he admitted. The Merchant spread his hands. "Winter's come early this year, and the Farmer says it looks to be colder and longer than in any year he remembers. We may have to take measures so everyone has enough to eat. No one will starve, but no one will get fat this winter."

Nodding, the Farmer added, "We'd mostly finished the harvest in Sweetwater Valley before it was taken from us, and the city got most of the crops, either in taxes or paid for. Without that food, we'd be facing famine. And if, next year, the weather is as bitter, some in the city will starve."

Just as the Fool was wondering if any of them had the wit to see the problems having a single cause, the Wise Old Man raised his reedy voice. "Shicassa and, most especially, Tatros is our enemy. Even if next year is milder, we'll have no surplus to sell. He'll grow stronger as we grow weaker."

The Mother's soft voice carried a hard edge. "If the city must lose its children, let it be by quick death in battle rather than slow starvation. Tatros has struck at us twice. Do we wait for a third provocation? I propose war with Shicassa."

"This seems truly to be the time of the Destroyer," the Priest said. "I'd hope for a peaceful resolution, but perhaps the Destroyer is already honing His blade."

The Warrior slowly stood, paced around the table, and stood within the arc. The Fool admired the man's canniness. If he hadn't calculated the move, he had excellent instincts. The Warrior paused, then said, "If we are to vote on war with Shicassa, I must abstain. Some might claim I voted for war because of my detestation of Tatros, and if I vote against it, some may see it as cowardice, a charge no warrior can bear and no commander can ever be accused of if he wants to lead men in battle.

"The decision is yours to make." He gazed at each member of the Council in turn. "But I must remind you of the consequences. War is a gamble. Valtierra may lose, and what will become of the city then?" He stared again at the Old Man. "You have begun making reforms to improve the city, but war brings chaos." To the Mother he said, "You spoke of a quick death. While it may be quicker than starvation, to those dying in agony, time passes with a painful slowness." To the Merchant and the Artisan; "War disrupts trade and cheapens everything. Will you be prepared to stop making fine tools and weapons to make more tools and weapons of lesser quality? Will you be ready to bring more smiths into the guild to help make the difference?"

Taking two steps into the arc, he continued, his voice rising. "And winning the war may be as big a catastrophe as losing it.

"Some have suggested alliances could be the salvation of Valtierra. I fear they could mean the opposite. If we were to conquer Shicassa, we would have new neighbors who would fear they would be next. Is it so hard to imagine them forming alliances to end a danger and gain some of the wealth of this city?" He paced slowly back to his seat and sat down.

"Does that mean," the Merchant asked, "that you wouldn't lead an army against Shicassa?"

"No," the Warrior replied. "If you choose to go to war, it is my duty to lead, and I will do it as best I can. In some ways, it is a bad idea to have a Warrior on the Council. The decision must be yours. I simply carry out that decision."

The Matron had been staring down at the table before her as though trying to read an answer in the grain of the wood. "At least we should warn Tatros that another provocation means war."

The Artisan shook his head. "To a man like Tatros, that's inviting another provocation. If pressed, he'll start the war; if he meets no resistance, he'll continue to push."

"Even a man like Tatros has his price," the Merchant said. "Perhaps we could buy him off. Or, at least, buy time."

"Never!" The Rash Youth pounded the table. "What have we to give him? And what will he take after that? And every concession weakens us and strengthens him. I'd rather fight a losing war against such a mad dog than feed him."

The Priest had seemed to be musing, listening to the arguments and gathering his thoughts. When he spoke, his voice was soft, so that the others had to listen closely to hear him, and he spoke slowly. "I find it interesting that the one man on the Council who speaks most persuasively against war is the Warrior."

The Warrior's reply was equally soft and slow. "That is because I am the one most intimately familiar with war and the losses from war. And I speak neither for nor against war. I just want you to know, and the people of the city to know, what choices you are making."

The Fool chortled. "Unless you're hoping the wind from this discussion will blow Tatros off his throne, we're accomplishing nothing. Has anyone a proposal to offer?"

The Old Man's high-pitched voice rose even more in indignation. "We're here to arrive at decisions, but choices made with too little forethought will likely lead to too much regret. If you have nothing to add or propose, then keep silent until a proposal can be formed."

"Actually," the Fool replied, "I do have a proposal. I propose we charge the Warrior with winning back Sweetwater Valley. Whether he does it by invasion or diplomacy will be his choice. He's already shown he's not eager to take us to war. He is also to deal with the consequences, and to notify the Council as soon as events permit."

The Merchant glowered at the Fool. "That gives too much power to one man. While I'm second to none in my respect for the Warrior, power has often corrupted good men."

The Artisan hardly waited for the Merchant to finish before he said, "I don't like giving so much power to one man either, but since the Council can take its authority back at any time, and since I have found I can trust the outlander more than many born in the city, I favor the plan. If events move too rapidly, the Council will never be able to decide as quickly as one man, and the Warrior is the man I believe is the most capable of making those decisions."

The Fool was delighted to see them arguing the proposal while forgetting who had advanced it, although the Harlot caught his eye and smiled.

"We trusted him enough to ask him to join us," the Crone observed. "I believe we can trust him in this, unless anyone has a good reason to oppose it. I call for the proposal to be put to the vote."

"I must abstain from voting," the Warrior said.

"All in favor," the Fool said, "raise your right hands." All but the Fool and the Warrior raised their hands, although the Mother and the Merchant hesitated. "All opposed, raise your right hands." No one moved. "The right hands have it, and the proposal is accepted."

The Artisan chuckled, then the Harlot and the Wise Old Man laughed. The buffoonery had served its purpose.

"Unless someone else has something to bring to the Council…" After a long, silent moment the Fool rapped three times on the floor with the staff. "This meeting is ended."

Slowly the Fool exhaled, relieved he hadn't needed drop his mask to gain the ends he'd wanted. Most would forget the source of the proposal, if they hadn't already, and he'd be handing the staff to the Wise Old Man in four more days, again free to simply play the Fool.

As he stood, the Harlot touched his arm and murmured, "Well done."

"May I see you this evening?" he asked, hoping she'd agree. He'd come to treasure their conversations, one of the things he'd miss when their terms on the Council ended.

"If we keep meeting like this, people will gossip." She paused, and he prepared himself for a lonely evening. "Fortunately," she said, "neither Fools nor Harlots care much about the opinions of others."

He laughed then, and had to fight down the urge to hug her.

THE CRONE

As she left the Council chamber the Crone touched the Matron's arm. "Would you ask Minea to bring me the noon meal in my rooms?"

The Matron's eyes widened in concern. "Are you ill?"

"No," the Crone replied, "merely tired."

"Very well, I'll ask her."

The Crone smiled to herself. The Matron, who tried to hide her trivial machinations, was so gullible herself. Ignoring the others, she hobbled to her room and sat on her couch. Picking up her knitting, she began another row.

She'd always been aware of the Fool's cleverness but he had been magnificent in the Council; letting the Rash Youth stir the members' passions—the Youth had already told everyone the story as he'd announced the meeting, but hearing it again had made it more immediate. Then, by using the Merchant and the Farmer, he'd made plain the threat posed by Tatros. He'd had to step out of the shadows with his proposal but he'd let the others argue it.

The Warrior was another matter. He seemed almost too deep for cleverness and his honesty, though reassuring, was sometimes irritating. He'd almost cut one of his own legs off with his speech.

Like the Matron, the Merchant was another schemer with no finesse. She was sure he had designs she hadn't found out yet but she'd caught enough of them to know he wasn't even a promising beginner. Both the plots and his clumsiness were probably the result of his being a Merchant.

Despite his flaws and, perhaps, because of them, the Warrior had been the Council member best able to deal with crises. Most of the rest of them lacked imagination. The two with the most imagination were crippled by other weaknesses; the Rash Youth let himself be ruled by imagination and emotion, while the Fool was widely misperceived as an empty-headed trickster. She supposed that, in the Fool's darker moments, the prejudices against him rankled him, but he often used those misperceptions himself.

She hadn't anticipated the form of the threat or the opportunity to Valtierra but she'd seen it coming and she was confident the steps she'd taken would lead to the best conclusion.

She was almost startled by the soft sound of someone gently kicking the bottom of her doorpost. After making sure her mask was in place, she said, "Enter."

After a moment Minea shoved open the door, bearing a tray of hummus, bread, olives, grapes, with a steaming cup of honey-and-lemon flavored tea. She set them on the low table before the couch and closed the door.

Ignoring the food, the Crone motioned for Minea to join her on the couch. In undertones, she asked, "Have you learned anything more?"

"Nothing of note. The Matron asked me to deliver a message to the matriarchy. It was written in the women's scrawl. She wanted them to know the Warrior is now our war leader but that Lancar has nothing to fear from us."

The Crone sipped at the tart-sweet drink. "Lose the message. No. Better, let me write another message. If the matriarchy wishes to punish, it shouldn't be you, it should be that stupid cow who believes the matriarchy actually cares about women." It hadn't taken the Crone long to realize the matriarchy served only themselves. If they could see a momentary advantage or profit in it, they'd pass the news to Tatros by the fastest courier. And there was always the chance that if Valtierra was attacked by Shicassa, the matriarchs might decide to try to seize Valtierran land in the south. "Anything else?"

"The Merchant sat with the Farmer in the dining hall. I couldn't hear what they were talking about."

"Not important." The Crone waved away the matter. "The Farmer will tell me if I only ask. He has no talent for lying."

Minea had warmed to the report. "As usual, the Mother eats alone, and the Fool and the Harlot are sharing a meal."

"Now there's a couple worth watching." As Minea only stared at her and she continued. "The Fool is remarkably clever and, if she lives long enough in her trade, the Harlot would be a great Crone. She has the qualities needed, and she's just found a cause that will force her to develop them. She's obviously intelligent enough to ally herself with the Fool and still not alienate the others on the Council."

"But the Fool has no power," Minea objected.

"I suppose if you never see him in Council you might believe that. He can use humor to either create or dissipate tension, then use it to persuade. The Month of the Fool is his greatest challenge, but he's met it. If you're to become the Crone, you need to learn to look past appearances."

Minea sighed. "The more I see of the workings of the Council, the less I want to become a member."

"That's not an uncommon observation," the Crone replied, "and sometimes the ambition that drives some to strive for a seat on the Council is the strongest reason for not choosing them."

THE MOTHER

The anxiety she'd felt at the meeting remained with her. She'd shocked herself with her proposal for war—she was supposed to be nurturing and favor life. When she reached her apartment, she accepted her son from the kitchen woman she'd left him with but he continued to fuss.

Opening her robe, she tried to nurse him but he had no interest in suckling. She wondered if he felt her mood and reflected it. She took a deep breath, and two more, then began to sing to him. At first, it seemed a pointless attempt but he gradually began to relax. Putting everything else out of her mind, she continued to croon to him until his eyelids drooped and his head nodded.

When he'd finally gone to sleep, she stared at his face again. Whatever came, she would not, could not watch him starve or die by an invader's hand. As soon as she realized what she was thinking she threw the thought away as though it were a stick that had turned to a snake in her hand. It'd only make her upset again and disturb her son.

Where, she wondered, was the father of her son? It was idle rumination. Some mistakes were more embarrassing than most. Kapaneus had made a fool of her but, looking at her sleeping son, she could almost forgive him. Almost. He had plied her with sweetened words, a soft voice, and a pretty face. Once he'd learned she was pregnant he'd taken his pretty face and honeyed words to some other woman—or several.

Perhaps that was why she was so wary of men, including those on the Council. The Rash Youth reminded her of Kapaneus while the Fool was unpredictable and, to her, that hinted of danger. The older men reminded her of her father, who'd made his disapproval clear. His glances had been poisoned with contempt and he pointedly ignored his grandson. It was safer to ignore the men and, if they thought her shy, so much the better.

The Matron, if she didn't disapprove, was too involved with other things— her friends, her painting, and ruling her family through messengers—to offer support.

The Harlot greeted her politely and sometimes visited to entertain her son with shiny baubles but she had her own wall of disapproval to face each day. The Mother sometimes thought that might have somehow soured the Harlot's soul.

Still, she needed to speak with someone. Humming softly to her infant, she closed her robe and walked carefully to the dining hall. She'd planned to arrive late, with some of the others already gone and most of the others preparing to leave. She was a little surprised to see the Fool and the Harlot dining together.

Both had finished their meals and were obviously enjoying their wine and murmured conversation.

Walking to the kitchen, she asked Minea to bring her a platter with fruit, cheese, flatbread, and hummus, with a cup of milk, then returned to the hall and carefully seated herself at an empty table.

Minea brought the food and milk, returned to the kitchen, then walked through the hall with another tray of food. It looked to be a light meal and the Mother realized the Crone wasn't in the hall. Usually, the old woman ate slowly and she and the Wise Old Man were the last to finish a meal. The food on the tray was probably for the Crone.

The Artisan and the Warrior both stood and left the hall, the Artisan probably bound for his forge and the Warrior for his army.

She ate slowly, both to savor the food and to avoid disturbing her sleeping son, and the others had left by the time she'd finished eating.

The need to speak to someone seemed more urgent and she worked her way to her feet and took the corridor to the Crone's apartment. She paused at the doorway, her reluctance at odds with her need. Finally, she took a deep breath and rapped gently at the doorpost.

"Come in."

Taking another deep breath, she walked into the Crone's quarters. Minea had just lifted the tray from a low table before the couch.

"I hadn't meant to intrude…" the Mother said.

"You aren't intruding," the Crone replied. "I invited you in." She gestured toward a place beside her on the couch. "I'd been hoping for a chance to talk with you."

With a pin-prick of wariness, the Mother sat carefully on the couch, as she wondered if she were about to be scolded.

The Mother shook her head. "I felt I needed speak with someone and could think of no one else I felt I could really trust. I find it hard to trust the men and feel…unwelcome among the women."

"There's trust and then there's trust," the Crone said. "Have any of the men done anything to make you doubt their intentions?"

For several moments the Mother searched her memory before shaking her head again "No. Perhaps, as I said, it's a flaw of my own."

The Crone's smile was warm. "It may not be a flaw, but it should probably be overcome. Power on the Council has little to do with who holds the staff. It lies much more in your ability to persuade others. Because you're young, you haven't had the experiences of some of the other members, but some of us have forgotten what it is to be young, which is why you and the Rash Youth are on the Council."

Absorbing this fresh perspective would take time and reflection, the Mother realized, and she had more immediate concerns. "I also feel as though

I'm changing. Today I proposed war with Shicassa without concern for the mothers of both cities who would lose their children."

"Perhaps." The Crone cleared her throat, took the cup from the low table, sipped at it, and said, "But I think you felt fear for your own child. Tatros threatens us all, and nothing is as fierce as a mother defending her child. I don't agree with your vote but I do understand it."

"What do you think I should do?"

The Crone studied her and the Mother couldn't tell if the old woman was pleased or not with what she saw, then the Crone said, "That is for you to decide. Remember, you should seek the advice of people who understand the matters we face, but advice and guidance are two very different things. For better or worse, you must be your own guide."

While the Mother considered what she'd been told, the Crone rummaged on a table beside the couch, finally holding up a small knitted robe. "I'd been meaning to give you this. The nights are becoming colder." She pawed through the pile of fabric again and handed the Mother a small cap to match the robe. "I'd been meaning to give these to you for your son."

Blinking rapidly at the stinging in her eyes, the Mother accepted the gifts. Somehow, it seemed disapproval was easier to deal with than acceptance, or perhaps it was the relief she felt that moistened her eyes, as the sudden warmth reminded her of the isolation she'd felt.

"On another matter," the Crone said, "are you familiar with the women's scrawl?"

"No, I've never heard of it."

"Then it's time you learned," the Crone said. She apparently noticed the infant begin to stir. "When we can be alone, I'll teach you. Some men can write and they consider themselves educated, but most women can use the women's scrawl. It's something no man can be allowed to see, it can only be handled by and read by women, and it's very useful. We'll begin tomorrow."

Clutching the gown and the cap, the Mother carefully levered herself to her feet. The Crone stood and opened the door for her, the Mother nodded her thanks, then walked down the corridor to her room as rapidly as possible without jarring her son.

In her own rooms again, she removed her mask before she changed the cloths in which her baby was wrapped. Even her mask, the least fearsome of all, frightened her son, so she wanted her face to be the one he saw when he woke. Opening her robe again, she prepared to nurse him while she tried to sort out her new discoveries.

THE WISE OLD MAN

Hearing a rapping at his doorpost, the Old Man hobbled to the door, opened it, and stared at the mask of the Crone, as wrinkled as his own. Without a word, he stepped aside and allowed her to enter the room.

"I'd like to ask your help," she said.

"What do you need of me?"

"Actually, nothing." The Crone sat it the chair facing the fireplace. "I thought you might help the Mother be more at ease with the Council. She seems to feel most of us hold her in comtempt."

The Old Man took a seat in the other chair. "How did she get such a ridiculous notion?"

The Crone glanced around at the pale tan walls devoid of decoration and the sparse furnishings. "It matters less how she became mistaken than how we can change her mind."

The Old Man grunted assent and absently stroked at his beard. "I was only thinking," he finally said, "that we'd have a better idea how to change her mind if we knew how she'd made it up in the first place."

"It doesn't matter," the Crone repeated. "One thing; it's best not to approach her when her son is awake. The masks frighten him."

The Old Man grinned. "Then he and I have something in common, at least part of the time." He leaned over to the stone base of the fireplace and picked up a glazed clay pitcher and a cup. After filling the cup, he offered it to the Crone and, after a shake of her head, sipped at the tea in the cup. "My granddaughter made me these cups for me—with some help from her mother."

He sipped again, then said, "I admit to being surprised the Youth was so capable in his leadership of the Council. And the Fool surprised me even more"

"I wasn't surprised by either. Both of them are very aware of what's needed of them."

He nodded. For a time they sat silently until he noticed she was preparing to leave, and he felt he needed to make an admission. It was almost painful to admit an error, but he finally said, "I think you made a good choice with the Warrior."

Instead of the barbed reply he'd expected, the Crone simply said, "Thank you."

"We should talk more," he said. "I wonder how many times we've opposed each other in Council when a conversation could've brought agreement."

"Yes," she agreed, "let's do that." Using her staff, she worked her way out of the chair and hobbled to the door.

As she closed the door behind her, the Wise Old Man took another sip of tea and ruefully smiled to himself. Admitting he'd been wrong hadn't been easy but it hadn't left any welts. He'd have to overcome his habit of reflexively opposing change and consider matters from several sides before making decisions which were difficult to change. Suddenly, he realized he and the Rash Youth were two sides of the same coin.

THE FARMER

Almost his only work in winter was to feed and milk the goats and, perhaps, make cheese, and the Farmer always felt somewhat ill at ease when his hands were idle. Winter was the time to sit by the fire and plan next year's crops, but it was also a time of chafing, waiting for the chance to start the work.

Thank the Trinity, he thought, the Warrior, not he, was having to plan some way to recover Sweetwater Valley. When he looked up from the crops he grew and the animals he tended, he felt lost. Comfort came in living in accordance with the seasons and raising crops and animals.

He hoped his son was taking care of their two precious cows. Winter was a hard time, when the wolves ranged far, hunger making them bold. The Warrior had assured him Valtierra's cavalry would spend much of their winter hunting and killing wolves.

He was gazing at the pond, not really seeing it, when he heard the Warrior's voice. "Can you tell me what the Shicassans have done in Sweetwater Valley? How they are treating the people?"

The Farmer looked up as the man approached. "They expelled the farmers and moved in their own people."

"Do you know where I can find some of those farmers to speak with?"

"We'll ride to my farm tomorrow. My eldest daughter's husband was one of them. They're staying with my family until he can either return to the valley or find other land." After a moment's silence he added, "He told me they've garrisoned the place with over a hundred men. The man who commands them is called Khaimon."

"That will make my task more difficult. I have served with Khaimon and he is an able commander."

To the Farmer, the comment smacked of admiring the weeds that could choke your crop. "You sound as though you think highly of him."

"I do." After reading something in the Farmer's eyes, the Warrior continued, "I suppose we warriors have our own guild, rather like the artisans. Do not worry. It will not keep me from fighting him if I must, but I respect the man and, more to the point, I respect his abilities."

The Warrior sat on the nearest bench. "Did your son-in-law mention who might be commanding the whole Shicassan army?"

"At least for the time being, Tatros himself." The Farmer chose a pebble, tossed it into the pool, and watched the rings of ripples spread. "I don't know whether that's good news or bad."

The Warrior spoke slowly. "A bit of both, I suspect. Tatros is not a particularly able tactician but he is likely to make up in aggressiveness what he lacks in skill, and he does not care how many of his own men die as long as he gets what he wants." He seemed to be thinking of things the Farmer couldn't even guess at. After a pause, he remarked, "What makes him most dangerous is that he knows so little about tactics he might do something totally unexpected simply because he does not understand or care about the consequences."

"I don't understand," the Farmer admitted.

The Warrior shifted on the bench to easier face the Farmer. "Let us say I wanted to attack Valtierra. Only a month ago, I would have sent a small force, mostly archers and slingers, to hold down the soldiers in their camp, and sent most of my army against the city. And let us say I have decided to do it on cheese parings, so the men are only supplied for two or three days in the field. Whether the battle went for or against me, there would still be starving men besieging a city and the death toll on both sides would be immense, not to mention farmers left to starve or simply killed for their stores. No competent soldier would propose such an attack, but a fool or a madman would not only propose it but find leaders under him to carry it out."

The Farmer managed a bitter chuckle. "If you're trying to reassure me, you're not doing a very good job of it."

THE WARRIOR

So much to do and so little time in which to do it, nor did the weather give any help. He'd needed the aid of the artisans to obtain two hundred lances, each nearly three times the length of a man, and now he had to train the three companies of cavalry to use them between wolf-hunts. The men had begun charging hoops hanging from frames. The hoops had become successively smaller until, at a full gallop, many of them could drive the tips of their lances through a hoop no larger than a man's hand from tip of thumb to tip of middle finger.

Mounts were also found for the two best companies of foot soldiers. Besides learning to ride almost as well as the cavalry, they practiced scaling the granaries. Those unable to scale a wall learned to climb a rope hanging from the lip of the granary. They were also taught to move quietly and kill silently, using sword or knife. A few more mounts were gathered for half a company of archers. He didn't expect them to launch their arrows from horseback, like some of the wild tribes of the southwest, but riding instead of marching could get them into battle sooner and with steadier hands.

If the men could perform their duties when they were shivering and their teeth chattering, they should be able to do them that much better in more pleasant weather.

The Farmer's son-in-law had been able to add little to what the Farmer had already told him except that the watchtower had been fortified in Sweetwater Valley, although work had stopped on the wall Anton had started.

After a brisk walk to Hondros' quarters, he rapped at the frame, waiting until the captain invited him in. Hondros' wife answered the door but Hondros appeared almost immediately, buckling on his sword. "I am leaving you in charge for the next fortnight. I have a Council meeting to attend tomorrow, then I will finish my tour of the borders."

"Are you expecting trouble from anyone other than Tatros?"

The Warrior shook his head. "No, but trouble comes most often from unexpected sources. I would rather know more than I need than less. When spring finally comes, I want our men ready."

Hondros raised his eyebrows. "Around here, wars are usually fought in early summer or midsummer, when the crops are in the fields. Spring is a time of planting, and I don't mean bodies." The last remark was accompanied by a half-grin. "I suppose that was one of the reasons you took the valley from us—we weren't expecting an attack after the crops had been harvested."

"That was one of the reasons," the Warrior said dryly. "I do not intend to make a major attack in the spring, but I want the men ready, and I expect them to be ready to defend the city at any time. With Tatros, we are dealing with a left-handed swordsman. He may not be very good, but he will attack from unexpected angles."

"When are you leaving?"

"After the noon meal."

Hondros grinned. "You know, of course, one thing that's made you popular with the men is the way you're feeding them."

"No one should have to eat slop. Whether they are grateful or not, they are beginning to show pride in themselves, and that is most important." The Warrior gestured at the camp. "I am hoping more men are trying to be transferred to the first three companies."

"They are, and we've already placed twenty of them. The captains appreciate being able to replace good men with better ones. Soon, we'll have five companies better than the best was on that first march, and the worst of the fighting companies will be almost as good as the best was then."

The Warrior clapped Hondros on the shoulder. "The credit goes mostly to you and your captains. Good leaders might not make a good army, but you cannot have a good army without them."

Hondros shrugged. "But you're the one who started it."

The Warrior grinned. "But I had the advantage of being an outsider. I did not know anyone so I only needed to look for the best men for the work." After a moment he added, "Speaking of work, I have not drilled with the sword recently. Would you spar with me?"

"I suppose that's one of my duties."

Together they strode to the drill field where both removed their cloaks and donned the heavy leather practice armor and Hondros put on a helmet. Both took a light cavalry shield and a wooden practice sword, and they began the swordsmen's dance, side-stepping, covering with their shields, and taking tentative strokes, both men maneuvering to try to force the other into facing the morning sun. Hondros was good, perhaps the best swordsman in Valtierra, and very quick. Some of the other men at practice stopped to watch them and the Warrior continued to spar until he was sweating despite the chill.

They'd performed their warriors' dance for over an hour and the Warrior began to wonder whether he'd be able to outlast Hondros when the man finally stepped back and raised his sword. Then the Warrior wondered whether the man was as tired as he was or whether he was simply giving his commander a way to gracefully retire.

After taking off their practice armor and putting on their cloaks again, they watched the other men practice until the time of the noon meal.

The camp's rations had been pared down but no one went hungry. The meal consisted mostly of flatbread and hummus, supplemented by tubers, cheese and bits of meat from small game. After finishing their meal, the Warrior and Hondros sauntered to the stable.

Though larger than most of the horses from the south, his mount still detested the cold and dampness but eventually allowed himself to be saddled and only fought the bit as a token protest.

The ride back to the residence was chilly, even for the Warrior, and when they arrived at the stable he made sure his animal was well-fed, rubbed him down himself, and covered him with a blanket.

In the south, they'd have been breaking ice so the animals could drink and staying in their leather tents by dung-chip fires, only venturing out to feed hay and grain to the flocks and herds or to hunt, eating whatever they could kill. He supposed, to the northerners, the weather seemed just as inclement, although he'd seen no ice and what little snow had fallen had melted almost before it had touched the ground.

Entering the residence, he stopped by the kitchen for an urn of warm water, which he carried to his quarters. He'd spent almost a fortnight without washing except his face and hands. After washing himself as best he could, he dressed in fresh clothing and walked to the dining hall. The Rash Youth waved him to his table and he signaled he would return. In the kitchen he noticed the shortages were shared by the Council. Putting a few small portions on his platter, he added a cup of ale. A tap or three on the keg let him know it was still over half full.

After setting his tray and cup across the table from the Youth, he sat down.

"You've been spending most of your time away from the residence," the Youth said.

The Warrior chased down a bite of hummus and flatbread with a sip of ale. "I have had many things to do. It is not easy to teach soldiers to fight like cattle thieves, among other things. Has anything of importance happened here?"

"Just more of the usual." The Youth had finished his light meal and was tarrying over his wine. "Very apt that the Month of the Wise Old Man should be in the dead of winter."

"What do you suppose the meeting is about?" the Warrior asked, then finished his own dinner.

"You haven't been keeping track of the days. Tomorrow marks the end of the month and the Wise Old Man turns over the staff of office to the Artisan. Will you be staying at the residence for a while?"

"I am sorry. I will be leaving after the meeting. I have not seen all of Valtierra's borders yet."

"Why wear out your horse? The borders to north and south are rivers. To the east, the only indication of a boundary are the watchtowers, while to the west the country becomes more hilly, again with watchtowers."

"I still need to see them, to look to the defenses."

"They're your saddlesores," the Youth replied. He lowered his voice. "Have you yet come up with a plan to pry loose the valley from Tatros?"

Instantly the Warrior was on his guard. It might only be a friendly question, but the answer would be worth much to Tatros. "Nothing yet, just still playing with some ideas."

"I wish I could be of help," the Youth said, "but I couldn't find an idea that didn't fit worse than bad boots."

"What I would like to know is if Tatros has found a new leader for his army."

With a grin, the Youth said, "You haven't been asking the right people. The new commander is another outlander, called Yanush. It's said he wears a bearskin as a cloak with the head as a hood and clasped near the clawed paws. They also say he's as big as a bear, and as fierce." After a momentary pause, he added, "He's supposed to be a brutal man. Of course, much the same was said about you."

The Warrior chuckled. "I hope I have not disappointed anyone. But where did you learn this?"

"The mummers who stage the shadow-plays are almost as great vagabonds as the singers and musicians. I enjoy learning from them what's going on outside Valtierra's borders. I suppose the Merchant might also know of it through his fellow merchants."

Finishing his ale with a long final draught, the Warrior wiped his mouth with the back of his hand. "Remind me to spend more time in the city with you. I have been trying to get that information for over a month."

"I'm becoming a bit nervous about taking you into the city. It seems every time we go, someone gets a blade wet or is beaten."

"There is that." The Warrior stood. "I need to speak with the others, but thank you for your information. I will try to repay you in wine, although I am afraid my purse will not be able to match either my gratitude or your thirst."

After taking his tray and cup back to the kitchen he stopped at each table and exchanged a few words with each of the other members of the Council.

The Fool grinned up at him. "I hope you don't carry a grudge."

"Too heavy a load for me. And for what?"

The Fool grimaced comically. "If you don't remember, I'm not sure I should remind you, but I'm the one responsible for giving you an impossible task."

"That was the decision of the Council, and it was a logical decision, and it is not impossible, merely difficult."

The Wise Old Man was subdued, as though harboring a secret, one that wore at him. After a few words with him and each of the others, the Warrior made his way to his quarters. He felt drunk, decided it was the weariness more than the ale that turned his feet to leaden blocks and left him as unbalanced as he'd been on the ship that had carried him south.

He'd almost reached his door when he stumbled, over-balanced, and fell against the wall and slid to the floor. From very far away, it seemed, he heard a voice shouting and, within moments, someone had poured a foul-tasting concoction into his mouth.

His stomach cramped, revolted, and his throat burned with vomit. For what seemed hours his stomach continued to churn and he hardly had time to breathe between spasms of vomiting.

He was finally given another cup to drink, this one less foul but still unpleasant, and he threw up little but water. Again, from far away, he heard a voice say, "He'll recover but he needs rest. Help him to his bed and post guards at his door."

Strong hands and arms lifted him and carried him to his bed. His boots were pulled off and he was covered with a heavy blanket, just before he became lost in the heavier blanket of sleep.

THE FOOL

He'd noticed the Warrior becoming unsteady as he'd moved from table to table. Worried, he'd followed the man into the corridor and seen him fall. Immediately, he'd cried for help.

Moving surprisingly quickly for her age, the Crone had mixed an emetic from items in the kitchen and ordered the Artisan to administer it.

They all watched as the Warrior spewed vomit and the Fool seemed to smell an odd sweetness in the odor. After the Warrior had voided himself of what seemed every meal he'd eaten in the last week, the Crone put together another mixture which she again had the Artisan give the Warrior.

The vomiting slowed and was mostly water, then the Crone had the men carry the Warrior to his bed and the Wise Old Man sent the stableman to the city for two constables to watch outside the man's door.

The Crone seemed almost as exhausted as the Warrior but, after directing some of the women from the kitchen to clean up the vomit, she approached the Fool. "We need to talk."

The Fool nodded. "Let's talk in the kitchen. And be sure to have some more of those potions ready."

"What are you going to do?"

"Be a fool, of course." Most of the others had gone to their apartments and the Fool had to walk slowly to let the Crone keep up with him. In undertones, he said, "There's only one thing the Warrior eats or drinks that we don't all consume." He stopped at the keg and poured a little ale into a cup.

Like most of the others, the Fool had sampled the ale when the keg was new. He'd only had the one drink, finding it not to his taste. Now he took a sip from the cup, rolled it around in his mouth, then spat it into the drain hole in the corner of the kitchen. He tried to exactly remember the taste then, and this sip did seem different.

"I hope you're wrong," the Crone said. "I've noticed your perception and cleverness, and those are qualities we can ill-afford to lose. If you hadn't followed the Warrior out of the room, he might be nearly dead now. Or already paying the debt to the Destroyer."

"I don't think I took enough to poison myself," the Fool replied. "The Warrior drank an entire cup and it still took some time to fell him. But if he hadn't stopped to speak to each of us and had gone immediately to his rooms, he might've died and we wouldn't have known till the morning,"

They waited for perhaps half an hour before the Crone asked, "How do you feel?"

"I seem to have a flock of butterflies in my stomach and the room seems to be shifting a bit. It's nothing I can't deal with."

"Drink this," the Crone said, and her voice held the iron edge of command.

The Fool stepped to the drain hole and swallowed the foul mixture, then puked into the drain. After losing his scanty dinner, he accepted the second cup and finished throwing up the meal and the water.

"I think it'd be best if you didn't eat or drink anything more until morning."

"Don't worry," the Fool said, with a grin, "I find my appetite greatly diminished." He walked on legs that seemed to want to bend in strange places, staggered to a chair and fell into it. "I watched the others after we found the Warrior. They all seemed concerned. We need to find the one who was concerned the poison didn't work."

"Do you have any ideas?"

He chuckled. "Thousands of them. I'm the Fool, remember? Unfortunately, none of them has to do with finding a traitor and a would-be murderer. I believe you and I can trust each other. I'm the one who found him and you were the one who saved him."

"And the others?"

"Hard to say. Before tonight, I'd have trusted all of them. Now, I just can't say. Some, I'll admit, I trust more than others, and I'd risk my life on my feelings, but I can't afford to risk someone else's life on my intuition." He stood. "We'll talk more about this after we've both had a chance to think on it."

His legs seemed to have steadied somewhat, and he wondered whether it was the poison or the vomiting that had weakened him more. He walked to the room of the Harlot. At his rap, he heard movement before she said, "Come in." Her voice had a rising inflection, almost like a question.

Her fingers still tying her mask in place, the Harlot nodded toward a nest of cushions. He noticed, below her mask, a pallor to her face. "You should be more careful who you invite into your room." He could see that she was just beginning to relax. "What's wrong?"

The Harlot's thin smile wavered. Moving a cushion aside, she displayed a dagger. "If it was someone I really didn't want to find at the door, I was hoping this would buy enough time to scream for help. We both know someone on the Council is a traitor, and that the Warrior was poisoned."

"How did you know, and how many of the others know?"

"I smelled it in the vomit. A harlot needs to know some odd things, and I recognized the scent. It's a slow poison made from berries. I don't know how many of the others have thought of poison. Some may simply think the ale's gone bad or the Warrior got some disease from his time in the camp." She leaned back in her own nest of pillows. "The only two I know I can trust are you and the Crone."

"I'm adding you to my list of those I can trust," the Fool said.

"Who would trust a Harlot?" Despite the smile, he detected a touch of bitterness in her voice.

"Perhaps only a Fool." He sank onto the cushions. "Have you noticed anyone acting strangely?"

"Only the Old Man. I thought he was simply calling the meeting to turn leadership of the Council over to the Artisan, but he received a message yesterday and he's been uncommonly silent and grim ever since."

"He's never been the most garrulous of souls but, now that you mention it, he's been even more reserved. He eats alone and I haven't even seen him speaking to the Priest."

"I saw you and the Crone walk off together. What was that about?"

He grinned. "Jealous? No need to be. I just wanted someone who knew the best emetic when I sampled the ale. I had the same suspicions you did but needed to be sure."

She stroked his cheek below the mask. "You dear, sweet Fool. No one can claim to be braver."

He felt his face flush, a curious mixture of pleasure and embarrassment, and her laughter was perhaps the sweetest sound he'd ever heard.

"You," she said, "may be the first man I've seen blush in a very long time."

"I wish …" His voice seemed to lose itself. He cleared his throat and tried again. "I'd like to still be friends with you when we can take off the masks."

Her smile turned winter into late spring, warming him. "Be sure of that."

Feeling awkward, he levered himself to his feet. "I'll see you tomorrow. Perhaps we'll learn more then. In the meanwhile, be careful."

"Obviously, more careful than you. I haven't taken any poison just to try the taste."

He'd become accustomed to going alone to an empty bed, but tonight he found it particularly painful.

THE PRIEST

Having performed his morning prayers and ablutions, the Priest padded to the kitchen, satisfying himself with a single piece of flatbread and a cup of tea. Fasting and bare rations had left him feeling hunger more often, of late, and left him with no reserves of energy. The Warrior sat nursing a cup and had either already eaten or was fasting, looking not too much the worse for last night's illness.

The others, as usual on a morning of a Council meeting, all sat alone and the silence was as thick as murky water. He seemed to hear a general sigh of relief when the Old Man worked himself to his feet and hobbled his way toward the Council chamber.

The Old Man waited until they were all seated before he tapped his staff three times. A cup of water sat before each place at the table, never a good sign because it suggested it was going to be a long meeting, and the Priest, who'd had his suspicions, was certain they were to learn of same major dilemma.

The Old Man sipped his water, strengthening his voice, then drew a scroll out of his robe. "Before I turn over this staff to the Artisan, I must tell you of a message I received from Shicassa. The gist of this message is that Tatros is willing to return Sweetwater Valley to us in return for our accepting his rule. He claims we'll be able to keep our Council, but it must be subject to him."

"Never!" the Rash Youth snarled, slamming the table with his fist so hard the cups danced. "I'll see the bastard dead and his head atop his own flagpole before I ever take an order from that scum."

"It's a solution to our problem," the Farmer said, "how to get the valley back without having to go to war."

"Not a good solution," the Merchant said.

"I didn't say it was a good solution," the Farmer snapped, "only that it was a solution."

The Old Man's fingers twisted in his beard. "I'd most like to hear what the Warrior has to say."

The Warrior paused for a sip of water, and his voice sounded tired but firm. "It is another provocation. He wants us to fight over this for the next four or five months. The man has no idea how to lead an army, but I doubt even he is fool enough to start a winter campaign. He wants to divide the Council, even divide the people of Valtierra so that when he does strike, he can face an enemy not fully prepared to resist him."

The Warrior had hardly finished before the Fool giggled. "I take umbrage at that. No self-respecting fool would do most of the things Tatros does daily. Even a fool wouldn't keep a flock of sheep for a harem."

Even the Priest found himself chuckling at the slur.

Before the laughter had died, the Crone's sharp voice rose. "The man has offered greater provocation than a cheap attempt to bribe us. Last night's attempt to poison one of us was more than enough to justify a vote for war."

Like the others, the Priest was shocked into silence as all the members stared at each other, all but one of them wondering what hid behind the masks. The Crone had also gone silent and, after a moment, sipped from her cup before continuing. "There is a traitor among us. Someone poisoned the ale. It was no fit of illness or an accident that almost killed him."

In the next leaden silence the Priest cast a glance at the Wise Old Man and felt a wave of pity for him. Even behind the mask, in the way he sat, the man looked weary beyond exhaustion. It was one thing to suspect a traitor, but it was devastating to have the evidence thrown in one's face.

"That man must be destroyed, and his slinking spy with him!" the Rash Youth raged. "They should be flayed alive and cooked on a griddle."

"I had been warned," the Warrior said softly. "At least, I had been told there was a spy."

"And why hadn't you warned us?" the Merchant demanded. "Who warned you?"

The Warrior's laugh was brittle. "In the first place, would you have trusted me, an outlander, over one of your own? I hope I have earned your trust by now, but I could not count on it before. As for who warned me, do you think I would be fool enough to tell everyone, including the spy, the name of someone to whom I probably owe my life? Tatros would have him killed as soon as possible."

"You've earned our trust, Warrior." The Artisan peered around the table as though daring anyone to disagree. "I've long since stopped seeing you as an outlander, despite your accent. And you're right. We need all the friends we can get against Tatros, whether we know their names or not."

"Perhaps," the Matron said, "the matriarchs might send us help, if we asked them."

"You might as well wish on a star," the Old Man said. "At least we have an honest Harlot. The matriarchs may not spread their legs for temporary advantage, but they're not likely to offer us help when they have none to give. They're too weak to even help themselves. They like having us between them and Tatros, but if we fell, they'd fall like a one-legged milking stool."

The Merchant's mouth twisted into a scowl. "As much as I hate to admit it, the Wise Old Man is correct. I followed the bright hope of an alliance but none of our neighbors can or will help us. Lancar is hopeless and Shielba's prince knows his princedom is likely next. He's probably scurrying to find the fastest horses for wagons to haul his expensive toys away. Ravanna is only beginning to build an army. The guilds have relied upon their militia for far too long. And Amarr, north of Shielba, is top-heavy with idiots on their Council."

Another glum silence followed, even the Rash Youth thinking instead of simply raging. At last the Priest spoke. "Do you hear that sound?" He paused to let them listen, then continued, "It's the Destroyer whetting His blade. We must decide what and who are to be reaped."

The Mother sighed. "I'd been re-thinking my vote on going to war, but it seems inevitable. Do we wait for war to come to us, or do we unleash it on Tatros?"

"I've hardly begun to decide how to win back your valley," the Warrior said. "I propose to leave our decisions as they stand."

"And I, of course, have to oppose such a commonsense move," the Fool stated. "Although I haven't decided whether it's more foolish to accept an insulting bribe or to throw ourselves into a war without consideration of the consequences."

The Priest stroked his chin and eyed the Fool, suddenly seeing his game. "I propose we table the matter until we can come to it with clearer heads."

The Youth snapped, "And I propose we march on Shicassa and display Tatros' head. And if we have to level the city to get it, we'll all be the happier."

"The Priest's proposal was offered first," the Wise Old Man said, his voice cracking. "We will vote on it first."

The Farmer, the Harlot, the Crone, the Wise Old Man, the Warrior, and, after a moment's pause, the Matron and the Merchant voted with the Priest, but when the Youth's proposal was put to the vote, only the Youth, the Artisan, and the Mother raised their right hands.

"Are there any other proposals on this matter?" After a pause, the Wise Old Man announced, "Then, until another meeting and another vote, our earlier decision stands." He turned his mask toward the Merchant. "Are the people getting enough to eat?"

"The constables told me they'd captured half a dozen men trying to break into a granary." He looked down at his hands. "One of them has a family and was afraid the rations would be cut again. The other five had intended to sell it."

The Rash Youth had been leaning on the table, a hand against his cheek. Without changing his position, he said, "I'd give the man with the family a month of cleaning the streets and hang the profiteers."

"That seems rather harsh," the Matron said.

"Not as harsh as stealing food that keeps others from starving," the Youth retorted.

After the suggestion had been restated as a proposal, all but the Matron voted in favor of the measure.

The Wise Old Man stared at the masked faces around the table. "Does anyone else have a question or a proposal?"

The Youth snapped, "Only that we nail Tatros' guts to a tree and walk him to death around it, but I don't suppose that could draw enough votes."

"Then I give this staff to the Artisan and hope his month is easier than mine has been." The Wise Old Man set the staff of office on the table and, using the table and the staff the Artisan had brought, managed to get to his feet and shuffle to his accustomed chair, letting the others move from one seat to the next until they were properly arranged for the Month of the Artisan.

"Since there are no other matters to discuss, I call this meeting of the Council ended." The Artisan tapped the staff against the floor three times.

As they left the table, the Fool tugged at the Priest's sleeve. "Thank you."

The Priest smiled. "I still don't quite understand your game, but I begin to see some of the rules. Why did you want me to make that proposal?"

"It wasn't personal. I just wanted anyone with wit enough to make the proposal." He leaned forward and lowered his voice. "Tatros believes our Council will wallow in indecision, and it's in Valtierra's interests that we don't disappoint him. If your proposal had been accepted, he'd have been warned we were still capable of making decisions."

The Fool flashed a grin, turned, and hurried out of the room, leaving the Priest to wonder why he'd ever considered the man daft.

To the Priest, the world seemed to have shifted until he could no longer be sure whether to look east or west for the morning sun. Deciding to fast, he returned to his room for his cloak and a pair of boots and walked to the city's poorest quarter.

The temple he sought was old but lovingly cleaned. Inside, after his eyes had adjusted to the dimness, he stared around at the plain seats and the shrine. The paint and gilt had been polished so often they were all but invisible, but the polished grain of the wood seemed even more elegant. He stopped at each of the three shrines and touched his forehead as a sign of submission to each of the Trinity.

A robed and cowled figure stepped out of a door almost hidden by the pulpit, stared at him for a moment, then motioned him to follow before going back through the door.

When he entered the room he observed it was small and bare, with a tiny stove, a chest, and a pallet on the floor. The priestess shoved back her cowl to reveal long, curly, auburn hair and eyes as green and slanted as a cat's. "Did you come here to accuse me of heresy?"

"Far from it. I came because I wondered if my office wouldn't be better served by a priestess. You give the people a message of hope, and hope is the midwife to change. I haven't decided, though, whether you might have more power to influence outside the Council rather than as a member."

She sank until she was sitting on the pallet, and the Priest sat on the chest. "I also thought it best to give you some information." He related the story of the two attempts on the Warrior's life and the attempt to extort the Council.

"And did you vote for war?" she asked.

"No, I was prepared to, but the Warrior and the Fool convinced me it would be a mistake."

The green eyes narrowed. "You seem to take your Faith lightly. It's ironic you were swayed by an idiot and a man of violence."

Studying her face, he noticed her lips were compressed into a hard line. "Let's just call it a theological difference. Your message of hope invokes the Creator and the Sustainer, but we respect the Trinity, and the Destroyer has His place, too. As for the Fool and the Warrior, you judge very quickly.

"I was as presumptuous, forgetting that some judgments are the concern of the Trinity. The Warrior has built far more than he's destroyed. As for the Fool, I'd dismissed him as someone who spoke before he thought—if he thought at all, but he's far deeper and much more clever than he seems. If we make the mistake of judging others, we must be prepared to admit we're sometimes wrong."

He'd watched her closely as he'd spoken and had seen her blink and her cheeks flush, as though he'd slapped her face.

Everything that needed be said, or could be, had already been said so he stood, nodded to her, and walked back through the temple, pausing to bow and touch his forehead before each shrine.

He doubted his support or opposition would make any difference at the next festival, a little over a year away, but he also doubted he would support the priestess unless she showed herself capable of change. She was too quick to judge and too unbending to admit mistakes, much less learn from them. And, like it or not, the Destroyer was one of the Trinity and He had his time, too. That had perhaps been the hardest lesson for him to learn, along with the differences between tending the needs of the people and governing them.

THE MATRON

The meeting had left her feeling utterly defeated and lost. She still believed in the matriarchs, but hadn't been able to marshal an argument in their defense, and she'd received no reply to her message.

The machinations of Tatros and even the Council had left her yearning for simpler times. The threat of war and a near-famine that might be worse next year had almost paralyzed her. She'd ignored the real and lost herself in illusion, and it was past time to set aside the comforting daydreams and deal with the dangers facing Valtierra.

First, she must make her peace with the Crone. She'd treated the old woman with more fear than respect, assuming her age had dulled her sharp mind. Now she must honestly listen, trying to learn, rather than pretending to learn while hiding her reservations. The humiliation she'd feel must be borne.

She wondered how some of the others dealt with change. The Wise Old Man usually resisted it until he could understand the need for it. The Priest was also wary of change, while the Youth reveled in it, but, of course, his were the wild passions of youth. She wondered if she'd forgotten those or whether she'd grown too old too quickly.

The Fool and the Warrior moved through changes without missing a step. The Fool was probably simply unaware of most of the world around him, but the Warrior seemed to have an almost equal affinity for tradition and for change.

She'd go to the dining hall and wait for the Crone to appear or, if Minea took a meal out of the room, she knew it would be for the Crone. Either way, she felt safer if the Crone were eating a meal. Perhaps because they'd both be eating, but, for the Matron, the meal would consist of her own words and her pride. She suspected both would need sweetening and would still be indigestible.

THE WISE OLD MAN

The fire's heat seemed to take longer to bring warmth to his chilly old bones, and the smoke from the fire seemed harsher each year. He sneezed and used a cloth to wipe his runny nose.

The constables and magistrates reported less trouble in the city than usual, a bit of good fortune he attributed primarily to the cold weather. Even drunkenness had become less common. Or at least less public.

A rap at his doorframe caused him to duck into his mask before saying, "Come in."

The Priest entered his apartment carrying his own cloth for wiping his nose. "I was just hoping to share your company and your fire."

"You're welcome to both. Even more welcome if you'll toss another log on."

The Priest picked up a split log and carefully shoved it into the fire, snatching his hands back as soon as it was in place. It reminded the Old Man of someone feeding a large animal of dubious disposition. After taking the other chair by the fire, the Priest asked, "Did it seem odd to you—the timing of the attack on the Warrior?"

The Old Man considered the question. He'd been shocked anyone would have the temerity to attack a member of the Council. "What time would have been appropriate for such an act?"

The Priest shrugged. "Perhaps news travels slowly. Or perhaps Tatros wasn't aware of how popular the man is with the soldiers."

The Old Man blew his nose. "Perhaps that was why he did it. Perhaps he wanted to provoke the army, or maybe to intimidate them."

"The first might be the more likely, but Tatros seems to enjoy playing with fire. According to the Artisan, our new army is three or four companies smaller but much more capable." The Priest held his hands out to cup the heat.

"Who can understand a bully like Tatros?" The Old Man gestured to a clay jar near the fire. "Would you care for some mulled wine?"

The Priest smiled. "I'm not feeling particularly abstemious in this weather." He dipped out two cups of the warm, spiced wine, handed one to the Old Man, and sat down again. "I find myself wondering whether Tatros has spies among us. Besides the Council itself there are a number of people who work intimately with us—everyone from the cooks to the stableman."

The Old Man lapsed into silence. If there were a spy in their midst, why hadn't he or she been more active? Why pay some back-alley thug to do something a spy could do with a pinch of poison? Although both attempts had failed, why hadn't the spy finished it, perhaps even killed some other member of the Council? After a sip of wine, the Old Man asked, "Do you think the Warrior has any chance to re-take the valley without starting a war?"

Shaking his head, the Priest replied, "I don't see how. Tatros isn't likely to lightly accept our taking back something he's stolen. I don't know that much about the people of Shicassa but I don't think any leader can let his subjects see him as weak."

The Priest looked into the fire as though scrying in the flames before he glanced at the Wise Old Man. "Yours was a very hard month."

After blowing his nose again, the Old Man almost smiled. "I remember a conversation with the Fool. We wished each other a dull month. It seems neither of our wishes were granted."

The Priest nodded. "Wishes are seldom granted. I'd wished you'd shared the burden you bore, if not with me, than with someone. That was too much for one man to bear. I was worried about you."

The Old Man grimaced and slowly shook his head. "It's why we were chosen—to bear the load." He sipped at his wine. "They don't really choose us, you know. They choose the archetypes. I think, in a way, they believe the masks have power. Perhaps they're right. I know that I've changed more in that last year than I had in the two decades before I was chosen. I feel as though I'm growing."

Dipping up another cup of wine, the Priest said, "But we're only people wearing masks."

"Sometimes I wonder," the Old Man replied. "Are we wearing the masks or are they wearing us? As we wear them, we strive to become what they represent. I don't believe in magic—spells and hexes and charms—but maybe we make our own magic, and it has nothing to do with trinkets."

"If the masks indeed have magic," the Priest observed, "it didn't seem to help the last dozen or so Councils. It's been at least that long since the Council has done anything of importance."

"The other Councils were never tried as this one has been." The Old Man wrapped his gnarled hands around his cup, drawing warmth from it. "You're too young to remember the easy times. Tatros' father was a decent man. His greatest fault was siring an adder then indulging him. His sudden illness is not a subject of conversation in Shicassa, at least not among people who want to live long. I'm not given to gambling but I'd wager my house the old man was poisoned. That was—what?—seven years ago. It took Tatros at least four of those years to consolidate his power. Until then, our border with Shicassa was as secure as any.

"We had more to worry about from the matriarchs. Their warrior women were, until the last decade or so, a potent force, although most of their battles were to their south and west. Eventually, though, their leaders became comfortable, even complacent, and that tree rotted from the top. Fewer women joined the army—it was an easier life outside the army. Now, a quarter of their forces are men, many of them resentful they're unable to become anything higher than petty-captains.

"Ramos, the Shielban prince, has always been a suspicious man and spent most of his time ferreting out conspiracies in his own court. Some of them might even have been genuine. He's sired no sons and it's said he plays the three commanders of his personal guard against each other, so each will protect him more loyally than the others. I wouldn't be surprised if one of them manages to gain enough power, while hiding it, to kill the prince. And, of course, his fellows. Then we'll have a different problem with Shielba."

The Priest carefully placed his empty cup on the floor. The Wise Old Man recognized the signs; on the Priest's empty stomach, even the watered wine was potent and he'd become cautious in his movements. "I wasn't aware you were so knowledgeable about the lands outside Valtierra."

The Old Man sneezed and blew his nose before he replied. "I wasn't always an old man. And old men share memories the way young men share a bottle of good wine. I'm aware of the differences between Valtierra and her neighbors, and I cherish those differences. Only Amarr has a government chosen by its people, and its Council is so large it's unweildy and often corrupt."

The Priest leaned back in his chair. "Have you given much thought to who the traitor might be?"

"I've thought about little else. I've even asked the stableman if anyone had asked him to give a message to anyone outside the Council. Just a thought. And I'd asked the Crone to question the women who cook and clean in the residence. She vouches for Minea, and Minea is sure of the loyalty of the others."

"So, it has to be someone on the Council. Who would you suspect?"

The Old Man shook his head. "My feelings can have nothing to do with it. It's very easy to suspect someone you don't like and trust those you do like. If I were Tatros and could have any member of the Council in my pay, I'd choose you, the Artisan, or the Farmer."

The Priest leaned forward again. "Why the three of us?"

"Because you're the last people anyone would suspect. The Farmer gives the impression he's a simple, honest man interested only in his crops and animals. The Artisan also seems a straightforward man, as simple and as blunt as one of his hammers. As for you, what better disguise for a traitor than sanctity?"

The Priest blinked owlishly. "And which one of us do you think it is?"

"None of you. That's the problem." The Old Man drained his cup. "If it were one of the three of you, I really wouldn't suspect you. As it stands, the only three I know are not the traitor are the Warrior, who's almost been killed twice, and the Crone and the Fool, who saved him."

"Perhaps it's only because the wine has made me dizzy, but one could still suspect the three of them." The Priest stretched his arms and legs, apparently trying to fight drowsiness. "The Warrior is unlikely, but if he had only seemed to have been threatened, it could be an elaborate plan to get us to trust him and suspect each other. As for the Fool and the Crone, what better way to convince others of your innocence than to save someone you'd poisoned yourself?"

"I'd thought of that." The Wise Old Man ran his fingers through his beard. "But it's too elaborate by half. By threatening and then saving the Warrior, they'd have accomplished nothing except to warn us there's a traitor among us. It wouldn't be worth the risk." He was seized by a racking cough until his entire body shuddered.

The Priest leaned forward, almost coming out of his chair. "Do you need a physician?"

The Old Man shook his head as he dipped up just a sip of wine and drank it. "No, it's just age and this weather. I'll live to serve my term on the Council." He hoped his determination would make it true. "Too much of my work is unfinished."

"I'll pray to the Sustainer that you're right," the Priest said. He worked himself out of the chair and to his feet. Still moving with the caution of a man who can't trust his body or his balance, he walked to the door. "I very much hope you're right." He opened the door and closed it carefully behind him.

The Wise Old Man stared at the ruddy, glowing shapes on the black and gray logs.

THE MERCHANT

The numbers and lists, which usually absorbed his whole attention, all seemed to flow together. The evening meal had been adequate, if not filling, and had been taken alone. The Youth was still fuming, as though rejection of war had been a personal affront. The Artisan had come in, devoured his skimpy meal, and gone out again, apparently keeping his hands busy. The Matron and the Crone had eaten together, murmuring their conversation, as had the Fool and the Harlot. The Mother, always a bit aloof, had concentrated on her son. The Farmer, a stolid block of a man, had concentrated on his meal and the Priest and the Wise Old Man had eaten together but in silence.

The Warrior had ridden away after the noon meal and hadn't returned. He'd probably ridden to the camp. If he had any sense, the man might be leaving to offer his sword to some other employer. After two attempts on his life, he could be excused for seeking a safer line of work or, at least, a safer place to practice his trade.

Rubbing burning eyes with the heels of his hands, the Merchant decided to set the scrolls aside. The comfort they usually gave him was absent.

Most merchants hired scribes to do their reading and writing for them, but the Merchant had begun as a scribe and preferred to keep his own accounts. He doubted anyone else on the Council except the Priest could read or write, and he enjoyed the feeling of mastering a skill most of them hadn't even tried. And he found the world of lists and tallying figures far more comfortable than the unsettled and unsettling world where war might be preferable to the uncertainties.

THE WISE OLD MAN

Preparing for bed, the Wise Old Man decided in the unlikely event he was again chosen for the Council at the next Festival, he'd defy tradition by refusing the mask.

Sometimes the work had been rewarding. He'd visited the city twice since the new ordinances had taken effect and felt a surge of pride that he'd had a part in giving the city new life. On the other hand, his first term as leader of the Council had been a disaster, and he wished his second term were behind him or, at least, more than eleven months away.

His heart had almost broken when he'd first had Tatros' message read to him, and he hoped the scribe had taken his oath on the Trinity seriously and was not, even now, sharing the contents of the message with everyone in the street.

He'd been surprised and frightened by the Warrior's sudden illness, and his heart, already broken, had almost failed when he'd learned it had been an attempted assassination. Despite his initial dislike and distrust, he'd had to admit the man had proven himself the most able figure on the Council. Which was probably why he'd been marked for murder.

The Priest, usually a source of solace and support, had his own problems. While he hadn't given many details, he was obviously concerned about a schism in the Faith. They'd both noticed that while some aspects of the Faith had become a refuge for the poor and some in the army, too many priests and priestesses had considered their oaths less important than their comforts and had all but become merchants—or harlots—selling their services to the wealthier classes, who'd become almost as irreligious as the people of Shicassa.

He'd found himself sympathizing with the Youth; even he had been tempted to vote for war. It was against his nature to rush impetuously into drastic action, but he couldn't deny Tatros' schemes and insults galled him almost to illness. The Artisan's vote for war had been a surprise; the man was normally even-tempered, almost phlegmatic, but he'd been almost as outraged as the Youth.

He'd wished to talk with the Warrior who had, immediately after the noon meal, saddled his horse and ridden away. He'd left word he'd be at the next regular Council meeting in a fortnight but had left no way to contact him. Probably the wisest course, the Old Man decided, although he'd worry until he saw the man again.

He wanted to find a way to uncover the traitor on the Council but could do nothing alone; he needed allies he could trust. While he and the Crone had their differences, he was sure he could trust her. Strange to realize it, but he could trust the Fool for the same reasons he could trust the Crone. They'd almost certainly saved the Warrior's life. And, of course, he could count on the Priest. With himself and the Warrior, that was half the Council. He'd have to approach them one at a time and see if any of them could think of a way to draw the spy into the open.

THE ARTISAN

In the fortnight since the last Council Meeting, the Artisan had tried to lose himself in his craft, hammering his rage out against hot steel. He wondered why the Warrior hadn't voted for the war. The Artisan was a patient man—working with metal required it—but when he was angered, he stayed angry until action was taken. With every blow of the hammer, he imagined the blow was at Tatros' head. He'd broken tools and left himself with repairs to make on his projects.

As he quenched the steel and heard the liquid hiss, he also heard someone enter the shed. Turning, he saw the Warrior unclasping his cloak. He nodded to the man and said, "I'm glad to see you again."

"And I you."

The question that had nagged him for a fortnight shot to his lips and he doubted he could stop it, even had he wanted to. "Why did you vote against war with the man who tried to kill you and insulted the Council?"

The Warrior set his cloak aside and stretched his legs. "Because we would have warned the spy, who would have put Tatros on his guard. When we take action, I want it to be at a time and place of our choosing, not his. As long as he believes we are still arguing and haggling, he is more likely to delay, perhaps see if he can find some other way to annoy us. That is another reason I was reluctant to mention the possibility of a spy on the Council; I did not want to warn him or her."

The Artisan stood considering the answers for a time, then nodded. "I can see the sense in both sets of reasons, but I'd still like to see Tatros' head on a pole."

"It will get there, sooner or later."

"Where have you been?"

"Riding the borders, noting the most likely approaches for armies from any direction. The Youth had given me good information but I needed to see it. A river can be crossed, as can hills. I needed to find the most likely spots for crossings and the best march-route to them. And I wanted to meet the farmers at the frontiers. The watchtowers are too vulnerable. I suspect the soldiers in them are the worst of garrison troops, but the farmers will sound the alarm." The Warrior held out his hands to the forge, warming them.

The Artisan began putting his tools away for the evening, "We're not at war with anyone but Tatros."

"Not that we know of. That is one of the reasons I am not sure having a Warrior on the Council is in your best interests. As a member of the Council, it is my duty to seek good relations with the neighboring city-states, while as a warrior I have to trust no one and anticipate the worst."

The Artisan grinned. "At least being a warrior doesn't often leave you disappointed. Would you take the evening meal with me?"

"I would be pleased. After the meeting tomorrow, I will be leaving for the camp. I want the spy to think I am afraid, and I have work to do at the camp."

As they walked into the residence, the Artisan said, "There are others who want to speak with you as well."

"There will be time for all of them."

When they entered the dining hall the Youth looked up from his meal, sprang to his feet, and rushed toward them, catching the Warrior in a hug that almost left bruises. As the Warrior extricated himself, the Artisan glanced around the room, seeing smiles on all the faces, and he wondered which smile was another mask.

THE RASH YOUTH

Saddling his horse, the Youth glanced at the Warrior. The man had visited with each member of the Council but had said nothing about the conversations, and had hardly spoken at the Council meeting, only commenting he had nothing to report.

At least he hadn't argued when the Youth had insisted on riding to the camp with him. The Youth sprang into the saddle and used his knees and the reins to guide his mount beside the Warrior's and they set out for the camp. While they both wore cloaks, the Youth felt that the worst of winter had passed. Within weeks, the farmers would begin preparing the ground for planting.

"Unless you want to take the chance of being able to win back the valley without damaging the crops, you're going to have to move soon," the Youth observed.

"Or wait until the harvest begins," the Warrior replied.

"You're a more patient man than I."

The Warrior grinned. "I do not have to uphold your reputation for rashness."

The Youth chuckled. "As long as you don't mind my upholding it."

With a wry smile, the Warrior said, "It is your duty."

When they topped the rise before the camp, the Youth hardly recognized the place. He'd seen the new buildings, of course, but the men moved with a sense of purpose and half the camp, it seemed, was drilling with weapons.

They drew their horses to a halt just outside the stable built at the campside corner of the fenced pasture for horses and goats, turning over their mounts to one of the stablemen.

As they strode to the practice field, the Warrior remarked, "He and his fellows are indifferent fighters but are excellent with animals. We have only had to dismiss about fifty men, ten of them captains or petty-captains. Most of them wanted out after they had finally learned the army works. Once they realized they would no longer be paid to sit by the fire and drink, they decided to fail at something less strenuous."

After donning the bulky padded practice armor they chose shields and wooden swords. Already familiar with the use of a light sword without a shield, the Youth paid close attention to the instructions given by the Warrior or shouted by Hondros.

He learned to keep his sword poised for the strike without betraying the timing or the target of his attack. His shield had to be used with as much skill as a weapon. While the edge or the flat of the shield could be used as a weapon, the shield could also be used against him. If he hid behind it, it blocked his own view and if an opponent trapped it, he would be helpless.

He took some hard blows but he administered a few as well, and the Warrior kept him busy until he was breathing heavily and sweating. Hondros nodded approval. "You're quick and you learn quickly. You could be a great fighter."

Flushed with pleasure at the praise, he watched the other men practice. It was not only easier learning from the mistakes of others, it was also far less painful. Alternately drilling with the men and resting, the day passed quickly into twilight and the evening meal.

After the meal, he drank the Warrior's wine ration with Hondros and the Warrior sipped water. "You said 'fighter' today," remarked the Youth to Hondros, "rather than 'soldier' or 'warrior.'"

Hondros sipped at his wine before he replied. "A soldier fights because circumstances require it. A fighter fights because his nature demands it. A warrior is a fighter who can lead and command others. He also," with a glance at the Warrior, "plans the time and place for battle or how to deal with an enemy who has those advantages."

By the time he was ready to ride back with the Warrior to the next Council meeting, he could, with sword or sword and shield, win more often than not against either the Warrior or Hondros, and he'd become an adequate archer.

THE WARRIOR

Silently tapping his fingertips on the table before him, he waited for the inevitable. The Merchant had announced food stocks for the city were adequate, although the Wise Old Man added that they'd had to hang a constable for theft. Then the Farmer breached the subject of the valley and asked what measures were being taken for its recovery.

The Warrior leaned forward to look directly at the Farmer. "I should have an answer for you by the next meeting. I believe there may be a diplomatic solution."

The faces under the masks around the table were other grim masks, and the Artisan and the Rash Youth looked as though they were biting back comments, but his answer seemed to settle the matter until the next meeting.

The only remaining matter was the handing of the staff from the Artisan to the Merchant, and the Merchant called the meeting ended.

As the others filed out of the chamber, the Warrior stopped by the Merchant and murmured, "I need some of that help you had offered."

He suspected even behind the mask the Merchant's face would have been unreadable. "I'll see you in my quarters immediately."

They paced quickly to the Merchant's rooms and as soon as they'd entered the man closed the door behind them and settled in his chair behind the table. "What help can I offer you?"

The Warrior remained standing. "I know the man Tatros left in Sweetwater Valley. If I could meet him—there is a place half a league from where we signed the truce—perhaps we could reach some accommodation. I will go alone to meet him. Could you send a courier to invite him to the meeting?"

"How soon did you want to meet him?"

"In one week, at noon."

The Merchant leaned back, his fingers steepled. ""You know what a risk you're running, I hope."

"I do, but I believe I can trust Khaimon. We may not agree but I think he will deal honestly."

"Where, exactly, did you want to meet him?"

"As I said, half a league from the olive grove where we signed the truce. It is west of there, by a small stream a hundred paces or so from an uncleared forest. The stream wanders around a rocky bank so there is a tongue of land at that point."

"Will you be staying here until then?"

The Warrior rested his right hand on the pommel of his dagger. "It would probably be wiser to wait at the camp, and the ride from there is no longer."

The Merchant paused, his fingers toying with the base of his chased silver goblet. "As you wish. I'll send the courier today."

"Thank you." The Warrior turned to leave.

"The Trinity be with you,"

At least two of them, the Warrior thought. I'll be bringing the third.

He next visited the Fool, who he found in the garden with the Harlot, watching the Farmer prepare the earth for the new planting. Sitting on the bench across the path from them, the Warrior said, "I have wanted to thank you both for your support."

"We thank you," the Fool replied. "We appreciate your getting the Youth away from the residence. With him around, we always seemed to smell something burning."

"I can promise something to put out that fire by the next meeting," the Warrior said. "Consider it a reward for patience."

To the Crone, the Wise Old Man, the Priest, and the Artisan he delivered the same message but he took the Youth aside. "You might want to visit the city, sample the wine and the harlots. And, if you want to see things unfold, be at the camp in four days."

The Youth grinned broadly. "Finally! I'll ride out with you today."

"No need. I would prefer you to use your ears in the city, but be careful. I suspect there are more than two daggers for hire."

"What do you want me to learn?"

The Warrior shrugged. "If I knew that, I would not need you in the city."

"Four days, then," the Youth said, grinning.

After taking the noon meal at the residence with the Priest and the Wise Old Man, the Warrior readied his mount and rode alone to the camp. When Hondros met him at the stable he said, "I need you to choose your best petty-captain and the twenty best men for moving rapidly and silently and tell them I will need them ready to march at a half-day's notice, but I want at least a company of men to march out with them."

"Worried about spies?" Hondros asked.

"Would you not be?"

"Probably. Any other orders?"

"After tomorrow, no one is to leave the camp except for firewood or for marches, and I want the cavalry to patrol up to a day's ride around the camp. Let anyone in; let no one out."

Hondros' smile was bleak. "It sounds as though we're going to have some brisk days ahead in the blood trade."

"Rely upon it."

"I also want to send a message to Khaimon, the Shicassan commander in the valley. The messenger is to speak of his message to no one but Khaimon." He repeated the time and place for a meeting.

Two days later he called in the cavalry and the next night he conferred with the men Hondros had chosen for the strike force. The following night they were to slip out of camp with three days' rations and, traveling at night, infiltrate the forest near the tongue of land where he was to meet Khaimon. If Khaimon appeared alone or with a man or two, they were simply to remain hidden, but if Shicassan troops tried to enter the wood, they were to be captured alive if possible or killed if they refused to yield. And the survivors were to see what happened when he met Khaimon. Half the men chosen were proficient with the bow, in case they found cavalry slipping into the forest.

As the men left the room in twos and threes, Hondros said, "I presume you don't trust this Khaimon."

"You would be wrong," the Warrior replied. "I trust Khaimon very much but, if I am correct, the spy also knows about the meeting."

"How could he have learned it?"

"Because I think I told him."

"And if there's no ambush waiting for you?"

"Then I will have wasted an opportunity and the best I can hope for is a pleasant but useless conversation with Khaimon."

When the last of the men had gone, he and Hondros returned to their pallets, but the Warrior had to coax himself into sleep.

* * *

Three days later, the Youth rode into the camp in time for the noon meal. As they ate, he said, "I'm not sure my time was well-used. The city is a nest of rumors with a dozen new ones hatching every hour. Everything from the Council is in negotiations with Tatros to hand the city over to him to an invasion by the matriarchy. There are even stories you were assassinated and the Council is keeping it secret."

"One of the problems with keeping secrets is that it breeds rumors," the Warrior said. After washing down the last of his flatbread with a drink of water, he added, "We will practice today, rest tomorrow, and, if you are so minded, you can take a ride with me the day after tomorrow."

"Where are we going?"

Those words reassured the Warrior. He wanted only one man on the Council to know. "We will be riding north."

"Scouting terrain for an invasion? Excellent!"

With the Youth so enthused, the Warrior decided not to disappoint him yet.

* * *

On the day of the meeting, the Warrior rose early, washed himself, and armored himself in the rich plate mail. Breakfast was a few dried dates, flatbread, and tea. When he arrived at the stable he found the Youth already waiting.

"The horses are saddled," the Youth said. "Let's be on our way."

Shaking his head at the Youth's impatience, the Warrior swung into his saddle and they set out. After two leagues the Warrior slowed his mount to a walk. "We are not reconnoitering," he said. "That has been done long ago. I am riding to a meeting with the Shicassan in command of their soldiers in Sweetwater Valley."

"To what end?" the Youth demanded.

"First, to find an ally. Khaimon is a man in a trap and Tatros holds the key. I think I know a way to pick that lock. And I hope to find out who our traitor is."

"Do you think this Khaimon knows that?"

"I very seriously doubt it. But, apart from the Merchant and a handful of men in the army I am sure I can trust, no one in Valtierra knows I am meeting Khaimon, and no one else knows the time or place. If the soldiers I have sent ahead find no ambush, I have guessed wrong but, if there are Shicassans sent to kill me, the Merchant is our traitor."

"That greasy bastard's head will go on a pole. He's mine!"

"You are welcome to him. I must finish getting the valley back. But you will probably have to wear out a horse or two to get him. Once he learns his plan has failed, he has to be clever enough to know we have discovered his game." He urged his mount back into a canter.

Leagues later, he drew his horse to a halt ant pointed out to the Youth the tongue of land that was their objective. A glance overhead and then down at the shadows told him it was nearly noon, and a single rider appeared on the horizon, reflected sunlight blazing off his mail.

"Stay here," the Warrior said. "We are to meet alone." He paused. "Do not be surprised at anything you see, and do nothing to interfere."

Urging his charger to a walk, he looked at the trees. A movement caught his eye and he realized he was staring at a bloodstained hand holding up three fingers. He hoped that meant there were three survivors. Only three ambushers would've been an insult.

He and Khaimon stopped about the distance of three spear shafts apart and both dismounted. As soon as they were near enough, the Warrior said, in undertones, "I am trying to find a way to save you and your family. Tatros has assassins in those trees, so we have to fight."

Khaimon's eyes widened then narrowed. "I sent no one to ambush you."

"I know that, but the spy in the Council had more than enough time to arrange it. I do not want to kill you but if you simply surrender, Tatros will kill your family. If it seems you have died fighting me, he will not dare touch the family of a dead hero."

Khaimon's smile was devoid of joy or humor as he stepped back and drew his sword.

The Warrior drew his war hammer from his belt and, as Khaimon made a tentative cut, beat the weapon aside, spun, and, drawing the blow as much as he could, struck the side of Khaimon's left leg above the knee with the hammer's tang. With the curved spike of the hammer he caught Khaimon's leg behind the knee then slammed into him, bearing him to the ground.

"Scream as I strike with my dagger but stop the scream by the time my hand is just above your face," the Warrior muttered, as he drew his dagger. Raising it high, he plunged it down into the ground on the opposite side of Khaimon's head from the forest. To the ambushers, it must look as though he'd stabbed Khaimon through his open helmet.

Leaving his dagger in the ground, the Warrior wanted to applaud as Khaimon twitched most realistically, then the Warrior hauled himself to his feet. "Let those weasels slink back to Tatros," he roared at the trees. "Let them tell him what happens to those who break faith."

He watched as three men scurried from the woods, one of them nursing what was probably a broken arm.

His own men emerged from the wood and they watched as the would-be assassins disappeared over the horizon, then he bent, extending a hand to Khaimon.

Khaimon accepted the assistance and, working together, they hauled him to his feet. "That was a nice piece of work with the war hammer," he said. "Dumped me on my ass before I could draw a breath." He stared into the Warrior's eyes. "I'm glad to be alive, and glad my family's safe—for the time being. But why go through with the charade?" He bent and drew the Warrior's knife from the dirt and handed it to him.

"In the first place," the Warrior said, mounting his charger, "I did not want to see you dead. In the second place, I have a use for you."

Khaimon climbed a little stiffly into his own saddle. "I hope you don't think I'd betray Shicassa."

"No, I want you to help save it. We will talk later."

Within a few moments they'd joined the Youth who, had he not been in a saddle, would've been pacing. "Khaimon," the Warrior said, "this is the Rash Youth." The two nodded to each other. "The Youth is anxious to be about some private business."

The Youth nodded again. "If matters here are finished…"

"Be careful," the Warrior warned him, "all sorts of vermin have teeth."

As the Youth turned his horse's head and moved away at a canter, the petty-captain of the men in the forest joined Khaimon and the Warrior. "Three out of fourteen," he said, "and a princely prisoner to boot."

"He is not a prisoner," the Warrior said, "he is a guest. Were any of your men wounded?"

"None seriously."

"Excellent. I will see you back in camp. You and your men have earned prizes."

"I'd better not tell the men," the petty-captain replied. "They'd be likely to run back faster than your horse can carry you."

The Warrior kicked his horse into a canter until he and Khaimon were well out of earshot of his soldiers, then he let the charger slow to a walk. "The one who is betraying Shicassa is Tatros. The fool will not be happy with anything less than a war."

Khaimon nodded glumly and added, "He won't need a war to devastate Shicassa. He's handed the place over to the merchants. He taxes them heavily, but they don't mind sharing the plunder. I've heard some people are starving. The army's rations haven't been cut, but if you're not one of his favorites or a merchant, or in the army, you're probably living on flatbread made of whatever you can find. What are your plans?"

"Do you still have friends in Shicassa and in the army?"

"Some. Most people are afraid to trust anyone."

"Then we need to get you back into Shicassa. I do not want an invasion in force, I just want to be rid of Tatros and those closest to him in the army. Unless the Shicassans are sheep, the merchants will probably be hanged by those they have stolen from."

"That leaves the question of who would take the throne." Khaimon glanced at the Warrior. "And who would be controlling him or them."

"As for who would lead Shicassa, you seem to have most of the qualities needed of a prince. Or someone you believe you can trust. It does not matter to me. It is not in Valtierra's interests to have a ruler subject to us. It would be pleasant to have a friendly neighbor for a change."

Khaimon laughed. "When I told you you could do worse than become the Warrior, it seems I understated."

THE MERCHANT

Looking over his cup as he sipped, the Merchant studied the other members of the Council in the dining hall. The Rash Youth had ridden away four days ago, probably to join the Warrior at the camp. With a little luck, he'd ride with the Warrior to see Khaimon. He hadn't considered it necessary to inform Khaimon of the meeting. If Tatros wanted his man in Sweetwater Valley dead, he could arrange it himself.

Killing the Warrior would cut off the Council's arms and, if the Rash Youth were killed, it would cut out their heart. That left one more to finish. The deaths of the Warrior and the Youth were necessary but killing the Fool would be a pleasure. The slippery bastard had frustrated him for the last time. It was enough to know the Warrior and, perhaps, the Youth were dead, but he wanted to watch the Fool die.

The task needed planning but he wanted to watch the knife go into the Fool's chest, see him cough out his red life, and he'd personally give the bastard another grin—across his throat. How such an inane jester could've thwarted him, even embarrassed him so often was a mystery, but the final laugh would be his.

Tatros was necessary for the time being. Eventually, the merchants would own him as surely as they did the Prince of Shielba. He would either be a figurehead or a corpse. Benett was theirs already and, with Valtierra joining the others, they'd be able to dictate terms to the other city-states. With her craftsmen and her fertile land, Valtierra was in a position to be the leader of the city-states.

It wasn't simply Valtierra's leadership that was important, it was the alliance. Sooner or later, some force would sweep from the north or from the west, some force strong enough to gobble up the city-states, and the only protection for Valtierra lay in leading a greater state. With all the city-states under Valtierra, they could withstand the threat.

He bore the others on the Council no ill-will, although the Harlot and, especially, the Crone could be annoying, and the Old Man ought to be dithering over his grandchildren instead of sitting in the Council.

As he watched the others, the Crone climbed to her feet, reminding him that, of them all, she was the most dangerous, the one most likely to see through him.

Only a little longer. With the Warrior and, perhaps, the Youth dead, most of the rest of them would be ready to collapse with just one more push. He'd cut off their arms, he would cut out their heart sooner or later, and then he'd kill their laughter. As leader of the Council, he was sure he could convince the others that war would be so devastating that accepting Tatros' rule would be the lesser evil. He could even convince them the Council would continue, still able to administer its own laws in the city.

He set the cup down and, when he looked up again, the Youth was stalking into the dining hall, his sword bare in his hand.

THE RASH YOUTH

Despite the weariness of a long, hard ride that had exhausted his horse, the Youth felt as strong as if he'd just risen from a restful sleep. Every sense was heightened and his sword felt as light as a wand. A glance around the room was enough. The Merchant reached again for his cup, the face below the mask pale.

"Traitor," the Youth roared, and stalked toward the Merchant. The others in the room sat in stunned silence as he advanced on the spy. Time seemed to slow; he saw the Merchant almost convulsively grasp his cup while his left hand fumbled for his dagger. The man got to his feet quicker than the Youth would have credited and the hand with the cup swung upwards as the Merchant tried to dash wine in his face.

The Youth sidestepped and lunged, plunging his blade a hand's length into the other's chest. Twisting the blade, the Youth sprang back, avoiding the flailing left arm with the dagger.

The eyes behind the mask widened and the mouth gaped as the Merchant stared down at the blood spurting from his chest. Numb fingers dropped the dagger, which clattered on the tabletop, and the Merchant said, "You've killed me!"

"Not yet," the Youth rasped, and whipped his blade around for a slash that opened the Merchant's neck and more blood geysered.

Stumbling forward, the Merchant fell over the table to sprawl on the floor, blood still gushing from his wounds to pool on the floor.

Sensing someone approach, the Youth spun, his blade in a guard position.

The Fool gestured at the corpse. "He was always one to leave a mess for others to clean up." As the Youth lowered his blade, he added, "You'd best clean that off. Nothing rusts steel like blood."

The energy lent by rage had gone with the anger. His feelings numb and his body suddenly weary, the Youth trudged into the kitchen for water and cloth to clean his sword.

When he returned, the Youth held out a cup of wine to him, which he gulped down. "Did he cut you?" the Fool asked.

The Youth shook his head.

Turning to the Harlot, the Fool said, "See him to his room. I'll get the Artisan from his forge. This will require a meeting in the morning." To the Farmer he said, "Take this carrion out and bury it. Perhaps dead he'll be worth more as fertilizer than he was ever worth alive. And," he added, "no one is to leave the residence tonight."

Feeling lost as well as numb, he allowed the Harlot, her hand on his arm, to guide him to his room, not sure he could've found them without her help. In his room he gestured that he wanted to be alone and sat on the bed. For a long moment, he simply sat, staring at nothing, then dropped back. He felt the Harlot tug off his boots and cover him with a blanket but it all seemed very far away as he lay gazing at the ceiling but not seeing it.

THE FOOL

They weren't paying the kitchen women enough, he decided. The women were to cook and clean, but they'd probably just recovered from cleaning up vomit, and now they had to wash up blood.

The door to the forge stood open and he waited until the Artisan had put aside his work. "There'll be a meeting in the morning. You'll lead it. The spy was the Merchant and the Youth has solved that problem. But you need to return to the residence to make sure no one else leaves during the night."

As they walked back to the residence, the Fool smiled and breathed deeply. The sudden changes had been exhilarating. Any fool could plan. The real challenge lay in adapting to changes. The Youth had almost lopped the snake's head off, but that left a lot of serpent in the city, but he'd already decided how to deal with that.

As they entered, the Harlot returned to the hall. "The Youth is exhausted but he just lies in bed, his eyes staring at the ceiling."

"His blood is still up. How do you feel?"

With a wan smile she replied, "Better when I was helping someone else. Now, I have to deal with my own feelings."

He nodded. "Just remember the third member of the Trinity always collects his due. It's never too late for a good man to die, and never too early for a bad one."

He stood and walked to where the Artisan was talking with most of the other members of the Council. "You'll be leading the Council meeting tomorrow morning," the Fool said. "It was the Merchant's turn but he won't be able to attend. The next leader was to have been the Warrior, but he's not available. So, as the last leader before the Merchant found he couldn't cheat the Destroyer, the task falls to you."

"Very well." The Artisan peered at him. "Despite the sarcasm, you don't seem like the Fool I know."

"I'll try to be more irreverent and irrelevant tomorrow. I suppose seeing a merchant actually paying his accounts is shocking enough to make even a Fool speak common sense."

He turned and, seeing the Harlot get up from the table, fell into step beside her. "I'll walk with you to your room, if I may."

"I'll be glad of the company. And if you'd like to tarry for a time, I'd be pleased."

The Fool sighed dramatically. "As long as I'm not the one pleased, I don't suppose it's against the Council rules."

The Harlot's lips threatened to smile.

THE CRONE

The rap at her doorframe came just as she was reaching for her staff. "A moment," she said, and grasped the stick and opened the door. The Fool stood waiting and even the mask couldn't hide his grim expression.

"I'd like to speak with you before the Council," he said.

She waved him into the room and hobbled to her couch. "This is a bit unusual."

"These are unusual times. Any suggestion I make in Council will be discounted because of my office." He sat down on the stool. "The Rash Youth has rid us of a spy but there must be more of them in the city. It might be a good idea to call a constable, a magistrate, and an interrogator. A large one. If we send the Rash Youth for them, he can spread the misinformation that the Merchant is being questioned to find out who he was dealing with."

"Very clever," the Crone said. "Have you any other suggestions?"

"I'd be interested to know what the Warrior has in mind. Perhaps the Youth could give us a few answers. Not too many—we can't be certain the Merchant was the only spy on the Council. And we still don't know how the Youth discovered the Merchant. I had my suspicions, and I'll wager you did, too, but the Youth seemed certain."

"Certainty, even when he's wrong, is one of his traits," the Crone observed.

"I'm willing to give him the benefit of any number of doubts, but I would like to find out how the Youth discovered him."

The Crone gestured, hiding a wince of pain. "The Merchant let us see the little plots so we'd assume we knew the depths of his dishonesty. He was deeper and more clever than we believed."

The Fool got up from the uncomfortable stool. "As long as we agree, I can be my usual playful self. I suppose we should eat alone—it seems to be the custom on days of a Council meeting." He offered an arm to the Crone and helped her stand, handed her the staff, and slipped out the door.

Leaning on her stick, the Crone followed but the Fool had already turned the corner to the cross-corridor by the time she'd gotten out the door.

When she reached the dining hall she found all the others at table, nursing their scanty meals and their thoughts. A glance around showed that while the blood had been washed away, the floor was still stained, which did nothing to make the morning more pleasant. Like the others, she ate alone and in silence.

A glance at the Youth suggested he'd already taken his tray back or had eaten nothing and was only sipping at a steaming cup of tea.

To the Crone, the meal was adequate; another reminder of her age. Her taste seemed to have become as infirm as her limbs and her other senses. She still saw clearly what was immediately before her but the far end of the room was blurred. The mind's eye was sharper; she still saw the past and hints of the future with great clarity.

Finally the Artisan stood and led them to the Council chamber, and each member took his or her place at the table.

After the Artisan had tapped the staff of office three times, he said, "I'd like to hear from the Youth how he can be so certain the Merchant was the spy."

Still looking unsteady, the Youth stood and trod to the center of the arc. "The Warrior was the one who discovered it. He told the Merchant of his plans to meet Tatros' commander in Sweetwater Valley. No one else knew about it. I simply assumed we were going scouting, but an ambush was set. Or almost set. The Warrior had anticipated it and sent men ahead."

"What happened to the Shicassan commander?" the Artisan asked.

The Youth paused. "He and the Warrior fought. I rode part of the way back with the Warrior."

The Crone wondered who else had noticed the evasion.

"It seems the commander was the one who suffered for Tatros' provocations," the Fool said. "A shame a man had to die in the place of a weasel."

Smiling to herself, the Crone almost applauded the Fool's capacity for misdirection.

The Farmer leaned forward. "Does this mean we'll be taking the valley back soon?"

"The Warrior didn't tell me and I didn't ask," the Youth replied. "I believe he knows what he's doing. He flushed out the spy and seems confident he can accomplish all the Council has asked of him."

After the Youth saw no one else had a question, he returned to his seat.

"We do have another problem," the Crone observed. "We can't be certain the Merchant was the only spy in the Council, and we know he wasn't the only spy in Valtierra. I propose we have the Wise Old Man choose a trustworthy magistrate and constable and an interrogator, and send someone to bring them to the residence. We should give the impression the Merchant is alive and is being persuaded to name his confederates. The Rash Youth would be the natural choice to send but I don't believe he has the knack for prevarication. I'd suggest we send the Fool."

She could almost feel the heat of his glare, but only added, "I call for a vote on this proposal."

Only the Fool voted against the proposal and, after seeing he would be sent to the city, said, "I'll try to frighten the rest of the vermin into doing what they do best—duck into dark little holes or flee like rats."

The Wise Old Man leaned forward and looked around the table. "We also need to choose a new Merchant. I suggest we extend the term of the Artisan to the end of the month. We can't expect a new Merchant to immediately lead the Council. Let the Artisan recommend a new Merchant."

Only the Artisan voted against the proposal and the Fool showed his teeth in a sardonic smile.

"If there's nothing else…" When no one spoke, the Artisan rapped the base of the staff three times against the tiled floor.

The Fool waited until the others had gone, then leaned over the Crone. "I thought we agreed to send the Youth for the constable and the others and to spread the word the Merchant was likely to give up his fellows."

"You saw and heard him," the Crone replied. "He has no talent for dissembling. And can you see the Artisan or the Farmer trying to invent?"

The Fool rolled his eyes. "Your point is taken. At least, the Artisan has a worse task. I don't have to speak to any merchants. I'll see the Wise Old Man for names of constables we can trust."

As the Fool walked away the Crone looked down at her gnarled old hands. Sometimes they still surprised her. Sometimes she forgot she was an old woman in the ruins of a body. Her mind was still sharp and her wits still quick. The unfairness sometimes chafed her spirit. So many men and women had young, strong bodies but stunted minds or minds weak from lack of use.

She wondered what the Warrior was planning but only out of curiosity. She trusted the man to avoid a war if at all possible. She hoped he was better than she at seeing possibilities.

THE WARRIOR

Khaimon was an exceptional commander, with a sharp eye for detail and a good sense of the mood of the men under him. He'd noted many of the men in Tatros' army scented success the way a horse could smell water but most of them hoped their lives wouldn't be the price of that success. Among the more eager soldiers discipline was lax, a sign of overconfidence. Most of the rest of them simply eked out what comfort they could.

Khaimon verified that, along the watchtowers, a blaze was set at the sight of a fire in the tower to the east and the fire extinguished when the fire in the eastern tower was put out. A fire on a watchtower at any other time was a signal for danger. With little to do but watch Valtierra and set a single fire each night, the men in the watchtowers had grown careless.

"If you could get past the guardtowers," the Warrior asked, "could you get into Shicassa and find enough friends to kill the guards at the city's main gate?"

Khaimon snorted, then raised his cup to his lips, drank, and replied, "There's no 'if.' I could get past the watchtowers drunk and crippled. Once past them, I have enough friends among the peasants and the army to reach Shicassa in no more than two days, and I have enough friends in the city to stay hidden. The guards would be more difficult, but I think I could do it. But, as I said, I've no heart for betraying the city. Letting an enemy army enter …"

"Not an army," the Warrior said softly, "two or three companies. I have no desire to take the city. But if we can kill Tatros and most of his cutthroats, the army of Shicassa could bring order to the city."

"You're trusting a lot to events beyond your control."

The Warrior sipped his tea, holding the cup with both hands to let them soak up the warmth. "What else can I do? Lead an army against Shicassa in a war that will destroy Shicassa and cripple Valtierra? That is where this is heading. Either there will be one provocation too many and the army of Valtierra will attack with real hatred—that is a horse no one can ride—or wait for Tatros to attack us and lose our farms and crops? If we lose, Valtierra will be ruined and if, as I believe, I can defeat your army, Shicassa would be destroyed."

"That's very good wine," Khaimon said, raising his cup. "A pity you've never developed a taste for it." Even in banter, the worry never left his eyes. "You're right, of course, but you're gambling heavily on a single throw of the knuckle-bones."

"If you have a better plan, I would be pleased to listen."

"Unfortunately, I don't." Khaimon stared at the fire. "I appreciate your trust, but are you sure you want to take that gamble? I assume you'd be leading your small force, and that leaves you—and them—vulnerable."

"I take you to be an honest man." The Warrior poured himself another cup of tea. "I do not take you to be a stupid one. You know I will do my best to limit the killing and avoid the looting. If you were to kill us, the army would be outraged; they would leave Shicassa a dead city with nothing standing higher than a man's knee."

Khaimon slowly nodded. "You're right, of course. I just wanted to make sure you'd thought it all out. How soon do you want to start?"

"As soon as the first foggy night."

"You've chosen the right season for it. The warm winds are due any day now."

"I will ride with you to the river. Most of the farmers along the shore have small boats for fishing, and we should have no trouble getting you across."

THE RASH YOUTH

When he reached the camp he immediately noticed an air of expectation. Men were industriously refurbishing their armor and weapons, honing anything with a cutting edge.

He found the Warrior in his quarters putting a fine edge on his sword.

The Warrior clapped him on the shoulder. "What happened?"

"The Merchant died. The Council has kept it secret and hopes to either find the other spies or force them to run. Each member of the Council approached me to tell you that you have their support."

"I am grateful." He offered the Youth a bowl of hummus and some flatbread. "I noticed you said, 'the Merchant died,' not, 'I killed the Merchant.'"

"I did kill him," the Youth replied. "But it wasn't a fight and I didn't feel like having a drink of wine and a harlot afterward."

"That is reassuring." The Warrior poured a cup of wine and handed it to the Youth. "You are growing up." He grinned. "If you continue to grow, you will be the Wise Old Man in a few years."

The Youth sipped the wine and nodded at the bowl and platter. "I really haven't gotten my appetite back yet."

"You had better regain it soon, if you are coming with us. The footsoldiers leave tonight. The three best companies will be rested this afternoon and they are eating well before sleeping. After we start, there will be little sleep and less food." The Warrior dipped a piece of flatbread in the hummus and ate.

Cautiously, the Youth did the same and, while the flavor might not be as rich as he remembered, it was still welcome and needed. The Warrior was right. He'd need all his strength and stamina in the next few days. Then he realized what the man had said. "Why are we moving at night?"

"Because this will be a raid, not an invasion. I do not want most Shicassans to see us coming before we have already gone."

The Youth grinned and almost meant it. "That's more ambitious than my becoming old or wise." He ate another mouthful and drank more of the wine. It was soldiers' wine; more sour than he favored. "If you're only taking three companies…"

"Three companies and half the cavalry."

"Then what are the other men preparing for?"

"They have other work to do. I want two companies to appear to threaten the Shicassans in Sweetwater Valley without actually entering it. I have chosen a position where they have the best defence in case the Shicassans attack them.

If that happens, they should be able to simply walk into the valley. The other companies will take up blocking positions in the southeast and west. They will have half the remaining cavalry to let them communicate with each other."

The Youth realized he'd eaten the rest of the bread and hummus and finished the wine in the cup. "How long will you leave them there?"

"Until this is finished, one way or another."

The Warrior set his weapons beside his pallet and lay down. "There is another pallet in the corner. Choose the softest part of the floor." Within moments the Warrior's breathing had become steady and he'd begun to snore. The Youth had endured worse. He found the pallet and laid it out on the floor. Copying the Warrior, he placed his weapons within hand's reach and lay down, but sleep was an eel—too slippery to catch.

He stared at the ceiling beams. The Warrior was willing to let him ride with the army. It'd be his first taste of real battle. He couldn't consider the brief fight with the assassin a battle, and much less his execution of the Merchant. He tried to remember if the man had a family, couldn't. That, at least, was a consolation. Another was the man deserved far worse than a couple of blows with a sword. Still, it nagged at him. Perhaps, he supposed, because he'd known the man.

He drew his cloak over himself—the room was chilly—and tried to set his racing mind at rest. For the first time since he'd been a boy, he found himself praying to the Sustainer, asking his blessings on the Warrior, the city, and himself. With a trace of superstition, because he didn't want the Destroyer to take offence because he'd been neglected, he prayed if the Destroyer won the day, he could die well and quickly.

The Warrior had said, 'Until this is finished, one way or another,' which meant he wasn't certain of the outcome either, yet he'd gone immediately to sleep. If it finished one way, they'd take Shicassa. If it was the other, they would all be dead and the rest of the army would have to do what the best could not.

He'd scarcely closed his eyes when a callused hand shook him awake.

"Be prepared to march in half an hour," the Warrior said, and strode out the door. The Youth found a breastplate and brigantine waiting for him, along with chain trousers, and a horseman's oval shield, all carefully blackened. He dressed and armed himself quickly and stepped out the door.

"You'll need this," a man said, handing him a rucksack and a waterskin.

About three companies of infantry were falling into ranks and a company of cavalry stood by their horses' heads. The sun was just setting and dark figures stood out against the pink-orange sky.

"Ready?" asked a familiar deep voice, and he nodded.

The men moved out with hardly a jingle of harness, although the horses' hooves thudded on the hard-packed earth. Before they'd gone a league, the

Warrior said softly, "Out," and the cavalry mounted and moved away from the file, roving along the flanks.

The Youth walked until his breathing had become labored and his legs ached. He could barely see the ground ahead of him despite the rising quarter-moon, and the Warrior, clad in plate, seemed to have only started to march. He guessed it to be near midnight when the Warrior finally called a halt and the Youth sat and panted, too tired to eat, although he took two drinks of water.

After his second drink the Warrior leaned toward him and murmured, "Drink any more and you will make yourself sick."

"How do you do this?" the Youth asked.

"Mostly by practice. You are doing better than most beginners—you have built stamina on the practice field. And do not whisper. The sound carries farther than a murmur."

"Why all this?" The Youth gestured broadly with his hand and arm. "We're still leagues away from any Shicassans."

"That we know about," the Warrior replied. "Do you want to tell a man's family he died because you did not take the proper precautions?"

Valuing his breath too much to spend it on an answer, the Youth shook his head.

In what seemed only a dozen heartbeats, the Warrior extended a hand to the Youth, who was embarrassed to realize he needed the help. A glance at the men behind him showed that none of them had sat down, and he felt a new respect for them. He might be able to best any of them with a sword but they could march half a dozen leagues in armor to the fight. The ache in his legs became worse, but he set his jaw and forced himself to keep pace with the Warrior.

Through the night the torment grew worse. The waterskin and rucksack seemed filled with rocks and the leagues ahead seemed to grow longer. Twice more they halted, and the Youth ate a little flatbread and trail meat at the second halt. When the Youth was sure he was going to spend the rest of his life marching in darkness, the Warrior gestured broadly to his right toward a forest and the Youth followed him into the trees.

As soon as they'd marched as deeply into the woods as the Warrior thought sufficient he called another halt.

By the time he'd recovered his breath, the Youth's legs began to cramp. Fighting the morning chill, he wrapped himself in his cloak but still shivered.

The Warrior had moved among the men and sentries took up positions at the edge of the group but still out of sight of the edge of the forest.

When he was able to speak again, the Youth asked, "What became of the cavalry?"

"They are east and west of us. They will be patrolling routes they have patrolled several times in the last two months. They will attract no particular attention."

"What do we do now?"

The Warrior spread his blanket on the ground. "We rest. Tomorrow night, we cross the river into Shicassa."

THE PRIEST

He had enough to pray about. He could pray the ploy suggested by the Crone would work, although it placed him in a dilemma. If he hadn't lied, he'd at least supported a lie. In fact, he had voted to have someone tell the lie. Whatever the Trinity might demand in punishment, he prayed it fell on him, not to others who'd taken no vows. He did pray, earnestly, for the Warrior and the Youth, who'd ridden away from the residence still troubled. So many things he couldn't pray for because he couldn't know what they were. The soldiers had left the camp, according to the Farmer, some moving toward Sweetwater Valley, others marching around the city to the south. That wouldn't set well with the matriarchs, although the Matron hadn't seemed concerned by the news.

The Wise Old Man had obviously been shocked by the revelation of the spy but seemed to have recovered. He was no more dour than usual, but he seemed frailer, which could just be the change in the season. He prayed the Wise Old Man survived his term. Too many changes, each unfolding on the heels of the one before, had stripped away even a semblance of calm.

The Artisan and the Farmer seemed untouched by the chaos around them, and he wondered if they were lucky enough to be as impervious as they seemed or whether they simply hid their fears better. Either way, he envied them. He'd seen the Farmer as stoic about a bad crop year, so the man was likely as solid and stolid as the earth he worked.

The Mother had been unnerved enough she was seldom seen except at meals, and she sometimes had the meals taken to her room.

Of the others, one seemed to have grown. He'd noticed after the killing of the Merchant, it had been the Fool who'd taken command and had started the ploy the Crone had proposed. He was reminded again there was more to the young man than quick words, a grin, and a capacity for irreverence.

He'd watched the Fool closely after that and had again observed a cleverness and even a profundity to the man he'd only noticed recently.

The rap at the door disturbed his reverie and he barely remembered to put on his mask before he said, "Come in."

Adara, the priestess, opened the door and walked into the room, her manner subdued. She glanced around the room before responding to his gesture by sitting in the other chair. "A very plain room," she said.

"I prefer not having distractions." He kept his smile to himself. She probably, along with many others, assumed the Council lived in opulence. Almost all the outsiders who'd visited the residence had seemed disappointed.

"I know you meant well when you suggested you might help me become the Priest—or Priestess—but after having spoken with you I realized that not only would I not want the office but also that I wouldn't be a good member of the Council." She looked down at her palms as though she'd written what she wanted to say on them. "I'm not sure I'd be as quick as you to admit to error or to try to change. For the Council, that is an invaluable trait. It's more a luxury I can ill-afford in my calling."

"I appreciate your honesty. But was that the only reason you came?"

"No," she admitted. "I have two other reasons. The first is the poor have needs that can't be met with Faith; they need hope for something better, if not for themselves, then for their children."

"I've been thinking about that myself. The people of the fourth quarter are the crippled, the drunkards, the beggars, the widowed—the lost. They're part of the city but the city neglects them. Were they simply lazy wastrels, I'd have no qualms about their plight, but often their suffering is through no fault of their own." He paused a moment to stare into her eyes. "Would you speak of them before the Council?"

"Me?"

"I can think of no one better. I have no gift for oratory. I suppose it's because I'm so reflective. But you, you can speak with words of fire. I don't think the Council lacks concern, but it's simply never had the problems presented to it by someone who cares deeply and brings real passion for the people. I can't promise we can solve the problems but we can seek help from the others, and I can promise, if we don't do something the problem will only become worse." He stood, poured two cups from the flagon on his table, and offered her one.

"I don't drink wine," she said.

"It's water, flavored with lemon, something I learned from the Warrior."

She accepted the cup, sipped, and gestured. "If you believe it will do any good, I'll speak with them." She took another sip. "What do you intend to do after your term on the Council is over?"

He sat back down and considered the question. "I really hadn't given it much thought. So much has happened so quickly I hadn't taken the time to think that far ahead." Gazing at a spot above Adara's head he paused before continuing. "Perhaps I'll move to the fourth quarter. I'd rather be around people whose faith is real, not something they practice only when it's comfortable to do so. I couldn't do what you do, but I could try to bring something to the people."

The tone of Adara's voice was almost a command. "I don't think you should do that. I think you should be the Priest for as long as possible. For the same reasons I shouldn't be the Priest, you should be. The Creator gave each of us gifts, and the best way to worship Him is to use those gifts in the best possible way."

Surprised, he searched her face, half expecting to find sarcasm or, at least, irony there. Finally realizing she was serious he shook his head. "I'm not sure I'm the best person to be the Priest."

"I'm sure enough for both of us." She stood. "If you're not sure your faith is strong enough…well, all of us have our times of doubt. But you'll always do what you think is right." She turned and walked out of the room, closing the door softly behind her.

The Priest found himself wondering if the feeling welling in his throat was a laugh or a sob. Perhaps both, he decided.

THE WARRIOR

Aside from an hour's sentry watch, the Warrior allowed the men to rest, drink water, and nibble rations. He wanted to be sure they did nothing to disturb the birds and squirrels to give the watchtower across the river any warning he and his men were so near.

Just after full darkness had fallen he looked to the river. Fog was already beginning to drift in pale wavering lines across its surface.

Within half an hour he heard men moving from around the hill behind him and he sent a team of men to replace the farmers carrying the boat. He wanted men who could move quietly. Sound carried all too clearly at night. The fog was now rising as though the water was boiling, although he could still see the watchtower. While the tower itself was still above the fog, it was blind to anything lower than the woods. Within minutes the tower was almost invisible.

While they were hauling the boat toward the water he chose the four best climbers; a tall, lanky man and three short lithe ones. They'd already stripped off their armor and carried only knives or short swords.

The fog had risen almost to the forest's edge by the time they'd joined the men at the river's edge. For a moment he listened intently but heard only the water lapping at the banks. After making sure the oarlocks had been padded, he joined two rowers, the four climbers, two other soldiers, and a petty-captain.

They glided across the river almost silently, the fog so thick he could barely see the nearest man, and he felt the strange sensation he was only a spirit, lost in a land of ghosts. Some of his old seasickness returned but he fought it, swallowing hard. He hoped that on their return they'd be able to take the bridge upriver. He'd have taken the bridge but the place was too well-guarded to capture quickly, and time was essential.

A hiss from the prow of the boat caused the rowers to stop and the boat bumped against the bank. The first man out of the boat carried a coil of rope, the other end of which was held by a man on the opposite bank. The four unarmored men followed him and disappeared into the fog. Again, the Warrior was struck with the sense of seeing spirits disappear. He followed them, leaving the rowers and the petty-captain to row back across the river, playing out a second rope.

Listening intently, the Warrior heard nothing but the river itself. More men joined him, ferried across on two boats, and more boats were being shoved into the river on the opposite bank.

Within a quarter of an hour of his landing, the lanky man loped back to where the Warrior waited, a smear of blood across his tunic.

"Are you wounded?"

"It's Shicassan blood. We have the watchtower. I left the others to light the fire as soon as they see the signal."

The Warrior nodded. "They've brought your arms and armor on the second boat."

Two more boats lurched out of the fog, bumping the bank, and men sprang ashore. One of the first was the Youth. "They're bringing up more boats, and the cavalry are preparing to cross."

On the heels of his words they heard splashing and before long the first of the cavalry rode out of the river, the horse shaking itself of water. The captain of the cavalry peered about then rode toward them.

"As soon as you've assembled your men I want them ahead of us and on both flanks. We are moving into country we do not know. If you find farmers, confine them to their homes but do not molest them in any way. We have enemies enough; we do not need to make more. Be sure your men understand that." The Warrior turned his head in the direction of the watchtower. "Go that way. It is upslope and you should be out of the fog when you reach the tower. Ride a tenth of a league before you spread your forces." As the man waved acknowledgement, the Warrior began to move up the grassy slope himself, only half-aware of the stream of infantry following him.

A brightness appeared above and ahead of him and he knew his men had lit the signal fire. He'd leave two of the less able men to remain in the watchtower to light the fire again tomorrow night.

The men assembled at the base of the tower and formed their groups, each man resting his left hand on the shoulder of the man to his left. As soon as the murmur ran down the line and the nearest captain said, "Ready," the Warrior gave the order to move forward, while he and the Youth strode half a dozen paces ahead of the line.

"How long do you hope to keep this many men hidden?" the Youth asked.

"If we march until two hours past dawn and move again at twilight tomorrow, we should reach the gates of Shicassa by the second hour after midnight the day after tomorrow. Khaimon told me the Shicassan soldiers prefer to rise late." The land continued to rise, less steeply, and in less than an hour's march they were above most of the fog.

The ground was covered with the skeletal remains of last year's crops, still waiting the touch of the plow. The plain over which they marched was gently rolling terrain. Twice they found farmhouses and, at each, two men were detailed to watch the farm to make sure no one left it to spread the alarm. In each case, the men relieved a cavalryman who mounted and ranged ahead.

Five men were left at a village. They were to keep the villagers confined to their houses and to detain any travelers.

During a brief halt, the Youth got enough control over his breathing to ask, "Is it wise to leave so few men to guard so many?"

"I doubt there will be trouble as long as we do not seriously annoy them. The farmers and villagers will not want to risk their lives to defend a prince they despise. That is why the men are instructed to treat them, and especially their women, with respect and to assure them that we acknowledge their ownership of the land. Since Tatros has never done as much for them, while they may not be our allies, at least they won't be our enemies." He stood. "Time to march again. We still have another three leagues to cover."

THE FOOL

The Fool had come to the first meal early and had hardly sampled his hummus when the Priest entered. To the Fool's surprise, the Priest approached him.

"May I join you?"

Still more surprised, the Fool gestured to the place opposite him at his table.

The Priest always knelt at table, sitting on his heels because of his gray robe, which made sitting cross-legged physically impossible or impossibly embarrassing. He knelt and leaned back. "Would you support my proposal to have someone speak to the Council at the next meeting?"

"That shouldn't be a difficulty. We've had several people at the meetings." Usually, they were magistrates or constables reporting to the Council. "If I might ask, who did you have in mind?"

The Priest had fumbled out his smooth black prayer stone from his robe and was holding it tightly. "I'd like Adara, a priestess who tends the people in the fourth quarter, to speak for the people there."

Today was truly a day of surprises, the Fool thought. He wasn't sure the Priest had even known the city possessed a fourth quarter, much less known anyone from there. "I'll favor it. Whoever she is, she'll certainly be more comely than the last two people who spoke to us." Seeing the slight stiffening of the Priest's lips, he grinned. "I'm sorry. I was only annoying you out of habit."

The Priest did smile then before staring into the Fool's eyes. "Why do you do it? I'd noticed a cleverness in you, now and then, but when the Youth killed the Merchant you immediately took command of all of us. It showed strength of character and real intelligence. Why do you waste your gifts?"

The Fool's cheeks burned and he dropped his gaze. "It's not I who chose to be the Fool. I was selected, I suppose, for my quickness with words, which commonly make people laugh. But if I were to reveal a serious side, I'd betray the mask. Like it or not, I'll wear this for almost another year."

"So," the Priest said, "you do this as a duty."

The Fool shrugged. "Who's to say where the mask ends and the person begins? I've always appreciated humor and wit. And sometimes they're the best tool for prying into a question, but they do make most people unlikely to believe you have a soul or a mind."

"I'll never make that mistake about you again,'" the Priest said earnestly.

Producing another grin, the Fool replied, "I suspect it would be better for both of us if you maintained the charade."

The Priest left the table to return within minutes with his own light meal. "Since there are only the two of us here, have you any suggestions about how I can deal with the others?"

The Fool considered the question. "For something not requiring a Council action, a simple majority should be enough. Either you or I could approach the Crone. I don't see any difficulty in getting the Harlot's vote. I'll speak with her. As for the Matron and the Mother, I think both can be gently shamed. Both consider themselves nurturers, so asking their help in aiding the city's lame and young will appeal to them. The Farmer shouldn't be too difficult, either. The farmers often have large families, which are helpful in doing the work of a farm, but only one son can inherit the farm, which leaves the rest of them landless, so they flock to the city. Point out to the farmer, subtly, that he'd actually be helping his own children. The Artisan is likely to resist strongly—the guilds want to keep their numbers limited, and one way out of the fourth quarter is having a trade. Since we don't have a new Merchant, I can't propose anything. The Old Man is likely to favor the idea, after he gets over the newness of it."

"What about the Youth and the Warrior?"

"The Youth has a sense of fairness. I believe if you strike that note with him, he'll all but sing. And the Warrior is, I believe, a convert. As the Mother would put it, he's become a son of the city. He'll want what's best for Valtierra. I think you can count on his vote. So, you not only have a majority, you have enough to make a change."

The Priest stared at him. "And you do all these calculations before each vote?"

"Only the important ones. I can afford to be trivial when the issues are trivial."

The Farmer trod into the room, apparently ready for a day in the fields.

Lowering his voice, the Priest asked, "What do you think is going on in the north?"

"I'd rather not know the particulars, but I'd guess the Warrior is taking action. If I knew too much about it, I'd have to express an opinion. As it is, I can simply wish them well." As they finished speaking, the Harlot entered the hall then stopped as she saw the Priest with the Fool.

The Fool waved her over to the table and gestured to the place at the table to his right. Reluctantly, she knelt then sat, her lower legs turned to the right. The Priest appeared to be preparing to rise but the Fool said, "This is ridiculous. You're both good people, so you should learn to enjoy each other's company." The Fool noted, with amusement, the Priest was clutching his prayer stone so tightly his fingers were white.

After clearing his throat, the Priest said, "I hope you slept well."

"Yes, thank you," the Harlot replied. "I always sleep better when it's cold. I can bundle myself up and enjoy my rest. I have more trouble sleeping in summer."

"I do too," the Priest said, and an awkward silence descended on the table.

"I'd better get my breakfast," the Harlot said, beginning to rise.

"If you haven't already tried it," the Priest said, "you might add a bit of honey to the tea."

"That's how I like it best. The Fool puts both honey and lemon in his tea. He apparently can't make up his mind whether he prefers sweet or sour."

The Fool smiled. "I like them both. Why make a decision when one doesn't have to?"

As the Harlot padded to the kitchen on soft slippers, the Priest said, "I feel I should be going."

"Nonsense," the Fool replied, "Why don't you simply enjoy the Harlot's company? No one is asking you to bed her, but there are forms of intimacy you can enjoy together, if you'll set aside your misperceptions."

"There are also the perceptions of others," the Priest said. "If I were seen talking with a harlot…"

The Fool laughed. "Why should the misperceptions of others matter to you? Doesn't your Trinity perceive with clear eyes? So why concern yourself with the false impressions of greater fools than I?"

The Priest chuckled and, while he still held the prayer stone, his fingers had regained some of their color. "All right. For a little while. But I do need to see some of the others."

The Harlot returned with a light meal and a large cup of tea. After sitting again, she asked, "What were you discussing?"

"The Priest would like to invite someone to the Council to speak about conditions in the fourth quarter. I believe it's past time to discuss those problems and actually try to find a way to solve some of them."

"Really?" The Harlot turned to the Priest. "You have my vote. My profession is one of the few ways out of the quarter." Even shadowed by the mask the Fool could see the Priest's eyes widen.

"I never thought…"

"That I was once a child in the fourth quarter?" The Harlot kept her tone light, not accusatory. "We were all children once. If we're lucky, like the Fool, we remain, in some ways, child-like. Or if we're lucky enough to know someone like the Fool who reminds us." As she smiled at him with her white, even teeth, the Fool could feel the blush redden his cheeks.

"Let me get you another cup of tea," the Priest said to the Fool, and took his cup. He walked into the kitchen and returned with two cups of tea. "Choose one. I'd forgotten which cup was yours."

"I doubt we need worry about any more poisonings," the Fool said, as he took the nearer cup. "I can't believe there'd be two poisoners on one Council" He sampled the tea. "Very good. Did you decide to try honey and lemon?"

"I'm beginning to appreciate new experiences," the Priest replied. "And the other thing we were talking about before you arrived is what's happening in the north."

The Harlot swallowed a bit of bread and asked, "Have you heard something from them?

"No, the Priest replied, "we were just wondering what might be happening and wishing the Warrior and the Youth well."

"I said a prayer for them both," the Harlot said, "and for the men with them as well."

With a nod, the Priest rose, taking his tea with him. "I must be going, but I'll look forward to speaking with both of you in the future." He took a drink of his tea to keep from spilling it as he walked but, probably, also to prove that both cups of tea were safe, the Fool suspected.

As the man left the room the Harlot nodded after him. "That man is a source of surprises."

With a grin, the Fool replied, "After all, he is only a man, and a lovely woman makes fools of us all."

THE RASH YOUTH

They'd just stopped marching and had hidden in a grove when two cavalrymen escorted two men on an ox-drawn wagon toward them. The Youth walked with the Warrior to meet the party.

One of the cavalrymen rode to them and said, "The older man claims Khaimon sent them. Said they had provisions for us."

By the time the man had finished speaking, the wagon stopped with a final creak and a squeal of steel brakes against an iron-rimmed wheel. With the Warrior, the Youth strode to the wagon. The driver, a pock-marked man of middle age, very carefully kept his hands on his knees and his gaze on the oxen, but the older man, with a carefully trimmed moustache and chin beard, grinned and clambered down from the wagon's seat.

"The Warrior and the Youth, I presume," the man said and, at a nod from the Warrior, continued, "Khaimon thought you and your men could use some food and water."

"How did you find us?" the Warrior demanded.

"I didn't, really," the man replied. "Khaimon figured you'd be in the general area and sent me, with Petrakis, here, to drive the wagon. I have water in the barrels, and flatbread and sausages."

The Warrior's smile was bleak. "I hope you will not mind sampling them for us."

"Not at all," the man replied. "I've developed an appetite on the ride. You choose what you want me to eat."

"Kostas," the Warrior said, calling on the captain of the first company, "take a cup and fill it with water from one of the barrels and bring some of the food." While the man was rummaging through the back of the wagon, the Warrior studied the man before him, then the driver. "You two have a soldierly bearing, and Petrakis has an archer's body."

"I was once one of the First Captains of the Shicassan army. Khaimon is my nephew. And Petrakis and I have served together for over three decades." He accepted the cup and the food from the captain. "Would you mind giving some to Petrakis? He's as hungry and thirsty as I am." He ate and drank with gusto After he'd finished eating, he continued, "Khaimon also wanted us to lead you to the city. There are too many guards to be rid of them all, and the palace is closest to the east gate. Khaimon thought both you and the city would be least damaged by your taking the shortest route."

"What is your name?" the Warrior asked as he gestured for his men to eat and drink.

"Rohn," the man said.

After the last of his men had eaten, the Warrior indicated the wagon. "We will share what is left," he said to the Youth. "Would you find what we have to dine on while I find a comfortable place to chat with our guests?"

The Youth followed with water and some of the bread and sausages as the Warrior led the two old soldiers to a place where the ground was soft. "You can use your cloaks to keep warm," the Warrior said. After they'd curled into their cloaks side-by-side, he laid his own cloak on the ground and sat on it. Accepting the food and water from the Youth, he asked, "Where is the Shicassan army?"

"Yanush, the new commander of the army, sent five companies south to reinforce the men in the valley you took from Valtierra. That amounts to seven companies there or on their way. The cavalry, all six companies, are north and south of the city. They'll be leaving their winter lodgings within a fortnight. Three companies of footsoldiers are quartered in the city, along with the commander. Four companies are on our border with Shielba and three more on the border with Amarr. If the commander feels they're needed, he can draw five companies from there."

"Who is this commander, Yanush?"

Rohn snorted. "A guzzler. He seems to have quickly grown a thirst for wine, but he's a fearsome man. You could make a breast-and-back for him with a couple of the shields your infantry carry. He always wears or carries a two-handed sword. They say that, to show his prowess, he killed an ox with that sword with a single blow. They say he all but decapitated it."

"I will remember not to fight him with an ox in my hand," the Warrior said.

They all chuckled, but the Youth felt a pin-prick of foreboding. Such a man would fight to the end and their tiny force couldn't afford to lose even a few men to such an ogre. While the Warrior was the most formidable opponent the Youth had ever faced, the Youth hadn't seen this giant yet.

Despite his worry, he drifted into slumber, was not even aware of having slept until he woke with a start, bitter dregs of a nightmare still clear in his mind. He'd seen an armored giant cutting the Warrior in two at the waist with a single blow of a huge sword with a flaming blade. The image and the horror were so strong it took him several minutes to realize they were still hidden in a grove leagues from Shicassa. Catching his breath, he looked around. Everyone but the Warrior was still asleep, and the Warrior stared at him.

"Bad dream?"

"Very bad. When we find the giant, let me fight him."

After a pause and a sip from his waterskin, the Warrior replied, "No, he is mine. You and Khaimon can decide between yourselves who kills Tatros, but this one is mine." After another sip of water, he added, "Maybe I am fated to lose, but I would rather face that than die a straw death."

"What's a straw death?"

"In the south, we believe you have challenges you must face. If your luck is good, you win. If your luck is bad, you die. If you hide from those challenges you may live to be an old man and die on a straw pallet, but you were dead before, when you ran from the challenge, and the body is only meat. What was important died at the time the luck ran out. When your luck runs out, you are doomed. But I still feel lucky." He paused then said, "If I am wrong and I die, kill the outlander, and do it any way you can. The Council cannot afford to lose both of us."

The Youth wanted to argue but the Warrior's tone told him any discussion would be useless. Perhaps he could find the giant before the Warrior did, and either there'd be no argument because the Youth might not be the giant-killer he thought he was, or he'd kill the giant and plead that he was only defending himself.

"It is time to get up, anyway," the Warrior said. He shook Rohn and Petrakis awake and called softly for the captains to gather.

The Youth was impressed by how quickly the men made ready to march and how promptly the captains gathered. In the old days it would've taken an hour at least. That was another reason for finding the giant first, he told himself. The Warrior was indispensable.

To the cavalry captain the Warrior said, "Have your men pad the hooves of their mounts. When we reach Shicassa, silence will be essential. The footsoldiers and I will enter first. You follow. Like Valtierra, I hear Shicassa has narrow, winding streets where you will be useless as cavalry. Dismount and either secure your horses or have one man in four hold the reins for the other three. Be prepared to defend the gate because that will be our only way out. If you can make sure the gate stays open only by destroying something, smash it, but be ready to be our rearguard."

After he'd dismissed his cavalry commander to oversee his men padding their horses' hooves, he turned to the leader of the footsoldiers. "Kostas, I want you and your men to follow the Youth and me through the gates. You decide the order of the other two companies. All of you: when we enter Shicassa, we fight only if we must. Any man who kills unnecessarily or who steals or damages property, unless they are under the direct orders of a superior, will be hanged.

"To be honest, I do not know what is waiting for us inside the gates, but we must reach the palace as quickly as possible. I want to take the head off the snake before it can coil, much less strike. So, once you are inside the gates, I want to move to the palace with all possible speed."

Rohn cleared his throat. "Khaimon plans to meet us at the eastern gate. He'll lead us to the palace, and I believe he intends to have men with torches along the way we must travel.

"Very good," the Warrior said. "If all goes according to plan, we should be at the palace before anyone is ready to oppose us. If it does not go according to plan—which is the way these things usually work out—I presume you can lead us to the palace."

"At least some of it must go according to plan," Rohn said. "Over a century ago, part of the Thele River was diverted to encircle the city. If the drawbridges are up, you're going to need far more men than you have to break into the city."

The Warrior cast a glance at the Youth. "Those knucklebones we are casting just became much larger and heavier."

THE WISE OLD MAN

Staring at his bed, the Old Man tried to convince himself to lie down and try to sleep, but his mind was still racing. Something was going on in the north and whatever the consequences would be, they would change Valtierra greatly, for better or worse.

He'd prayed for the Warrior and the Youth, asking the favor of the Sustainer for them and their enterprise, but it was out of his hands. Faith was weak solace when one realized the gods had Their own ways, which were seldom revealed to men. And which god was in ascendancy? He'd thought, many times, this was the time of the Destroyer, and he could only hope the lightnings were being flung at Tatros.

The rap at his doorpost caused his head to snap up and he realized he'd dozed. Snatching up his mask, he drew it on but left the laces loose. "Come in."

The Priest opened the door and stepped into the room. "I hope I'm not disturbing you. I saw a light under the door and supposed you'd still be awake."

With a gesture toward the other chair, the Old Man said, "What's disturbing me isn't your visit. But what are you doing prowling the halls at this hour? It must be …."

"Nearly midnight," the Priest admitted. "I've been worried about the same things you are, I suppose, but I have other matters to discuss as well. I'd like you to agree to let someone speak to the Council. It's a priestess named Adara."

"I've heard some of your brother priests speak of her, often in very uncomplimentary terms."

"And I have my opinion of some of my brother priests as well. I won't bore you or scandalize you with those opinions." The Priest sat down and leaned forward. "Adara preaches among the people of the fourth quarter. She has little patience with priests who spend much of their time at the tables of the wealthy. Many are from the richer classes; second sons of guildmasters and merchants often seem 'called' to the service of the Trinity. Their services are offered to those who can pay well for them, and when they preach, their message is often, 'Show your devotion by giving money.' To me, it's blasphemy to place one's personal comforts above the needs of the Faith."

"I'll agree with you there," the Old Man said. "I've often been grateful you were chosen the Priest instead of one of those fat, insolent hypocrites. But I've also been led to believe this Adara thinks the city owes comfort to those of the fourth quarter."

"Not comfort," the Priest replied, "unless you consider hope a comfort. I think hope is as necessary as food. Some in the fourth quarter will never be able to leave it, but they must have the hope their children can."

"Of course." The Old Man was offended the people of the fourth quarter couldn't understand the freedom they enjoyed.

"But those are only words. The merchants sometimes hire them for labor but always underpay them, while charging prices beyond the means of the people they employ. And the guilds intentionally keep their numbers small. A few people are admitted as apprentices—most of them from the craft or merchant classes—but even fewer of them are permitted to become journeymen and only a bare handful can ever become masters. I believe that, working together, we can find a way to improve the lot of those who have least. It seems only fair that most of the help come from those who gain the most from the city."

"You argue very persuasively," said the Old Man. "I wonder why you think you need the priestess to speak for you."

The Priest bowed his head for a moment before he replied, "I haven't the gift she has for showing the Council the plight of the people of the fourth quarter." After staring at the floor, he continued, "You've done well with the new ordinances, but we need to extend the new-found pride to those who've lost their pride because they've lost everything else."

The Old Man was touched by the Priest's earnestness, and it reminded him that, all too often, they tried to be true to their masks and neglected to be true to the people of Valtierra. He clapped the Priest lightly on the shoulder and said, "You have my vote."

"Thank you," the Priest said, "you have my gratitude."

"No," the Old Man replied, "you have mine." He coughed and fought back a moan at the pain in his chest. "We have a city to re-make. It's just a shame I waited so long to find my life's great work."

After a frown of concern at the Old Man's discomfort, the Priest smiled. "I'm glad to see you so excited but it'll be the work of a longer lifetime than either of us will have."

The Old Man smiled in return. "You're talking like a young man. You're looking for results. Whatever we accomplish or fail to accomplish, it's the work that's important."

THE WARRIOR

To the Warrior, the small sounds he made were as loud as a battle but, as he peered up at the imposing walls, he saw no men, heard no outcry. Rohn had led them to the place where a drawbridge stood dark against the pale stone walls.

Tendrils of fog had begun to rise from the river and he couldn't help but worry that he and his men were being flanked, but with a groaning and creaking that made him and his men seem as silent as a stalking cougar, the upper part of the drawbridge separated from the wall and leaned out until it rested on the ground before him. A single armored figure stood just inside the wall.

Moving as quietly as possible, he crossed the bridge, the Youth at his elbow and armored men at his heels, although the darkness was so dense he could barely see where he placed his feet, and the sounds of the men behind him could hide a hundred threats. There was simply nothing to do but forge ahead.

Khaimon waved him forward. Looking around, the Warrior saw no bodies but perhaps a dozen men joining them after having lowered the bridge. "How did you get rid of all the guards so quietly?"

Khaimon chuckled. "I'm too old for the sneak-sneak, stab-stab nonsense. Most of them I bribed, a few I convinced to join us. We bought this wall for the price of a keg of cheap wine. When you get old enough, you learn to appreciate cunning more than heroics. Follow me." He turned and began to stride down one of the winding streets holding a torch. His men, also bearing torches, ranged ahead on both sides of the street.

Grateful for having a guide, and light to see by, the Warrior hurried down the street past shuttered shops, watching and listening intently, ready to break into a headlong run ahead at the first sounds of alarm. His breath came quicker and his armor seemed lighter as he rushed toward a battle. Somewhere ahead and to his left, a dog howled, then yelped and was silent.

Khaimon hissed and raised an arm to signal a halt as they reached a grassy field, at the center of which stood a high walled fortress. "My men inside will be wearing a white cloth tied to their helmets or around their heads. They'll be prepared to fight beside you."

As the men behind him halted, the Warrior heard a scream from inside the fortress, then more shouts and the clangor of battle. A line of light appeared, then widened as a gate was flung open, and the Warrior raced forward.

Nearing the gate, which continued to open, he could see the interior of the fortress illumined by the uncertain light of torches and as he hurled himself through the gate he could see by the garish, flickering light, men locked in combat.

Without realizing he'd done it, he'd drawn his sword with his left hand, and he used the weapon to parry a blow aimed at one of Khaimon's men and swung the heavy war hammer in a whistling blow that deeply dented the helmet of the attacker. The man was flung aside and down.

Taking a moment to gain some view of the overall battle, he waved some of his men to guard the gates then hurled himself back into the fray. He stabbed one man in the face and drove the spiked end of the war hammer through the breastplate of another.

Men rushed from two buildings he could guess were barracks, some of them still trying to put on their armor. The first into the fight had either been guards already armed and armored or men more eager to fight than to protect themselves. The men behind him were both eager and ready, and they began to form their line, all shields and stabbing swords.

Glancing around him, he saw the Youth attack one of the enemies who'd taken the time to don armor. The Youth used his quickness and his newly-honed skills to overwhelm his opponent, finishing the combat with a thrust to the throat. Khaimon, Rohn, and half a dozen other Shicassans had broken off from the battle to rush a building about the size of the residence, but much more ornate, with a row of fluted columns.

His attention was brought back to the door of the nearer barracks by a roar, and a massive man in plate armor, wielding a two-handed sword, rushed out.

The Youth moved forward but the Warrior tapped him with the flat of his blade. "Don't condemn me to a straw death," the Warrior shouted. The Youth paused, obviously torn between attacking the giant and obeying, then joined one of the Valtierran lines forcing the Shicassans back.

The Warrior strode forward, every sense on edge, a curious lightness of spirit and body suffusing him.

The big man slashed at waist level, less to strike than to intimidate, and recovered quickly, his sword raised to strike or parry.

The Warrior sprang forward and, as the giant tried a slash from high to low and right to left, he caught the heavy blade with crossed weapons, taking most of the impact on the haft of his war hammer. The force of the blow caused a shock to shoot up his arms, but he used his weapons to sweep the heavy blade aside and down, then he ducked and spun, slamming the blunt end of the hammer into the side of the man's left knee.

The man not only looked like a bear, he roared like one, but in pain, as his knee was broken but he remained upright, swinging his sword to help keep his balance and taking all his weight on his right leg. As the Warrior sidestepped the flailing blade the big man hopped backward.

Despite himself, the Warrior was forced to admire the other man's toughness as the giant set his back against the barracks wall. The wall helped him stay upright but also left him less room in which to swing his blade. Seeing his danger, the man quickly shifted the sword in his gauntleted hands to use the guards as a sort of spike hammer and the pommel as a thrusting weapon.

The Warrior dropped his sword then, using both hands, caught his hammer on one of the swordguard's arms and hauled the big man to his left. The mercenary roared again as he was forced to put weight on his broken leg and, as he struggled to regain his balance, the Warrior brought the blunt end of the hammer crashing down on the giant's helmet, driving a dent in the steel.

Spinning, the Warrior turned the hammer in his hands and drove the steel claw of the spike through the dent and into the man's brain.

Blood shot out of the wound, spraying a flair of red on the wall, and the giant toppled like a felled tree. Wrenching his weapon free, the Warrior turned to see the battle breaking up with his men, working together, splitting their enemies into ever-smaller groups. No mercy was asked and none shown.

He turned again at the sound of screaming and, gathering a handful of men, charged toward the ornate building. He'd barely covered half the distance when the palace's large bronze doors were shoved open and Khaimon emerged, holding Tatros' severed head by the hair.

"What are you doing?" the Warrior demanded, having to shout to be heard over the screaming.

"The ugliest part of this revolt," Khaimon replied. "Tatros had two sons."

For a moment the Warrior was caught between revulsion and understanding. The man who'd threatened and used and killed the families of others had lost his own family with his life. The most distasteful fact was that Khaimon was probably right. Those boys would have been a danger to whoever ruled Shicassa for as long as they lived. Even had they not wanted to avenge their father, they'd have likely been used by others seeking power. As Khaimon had said, this was the ugliest part.

The Youth stepped forward but the Warrior caught his arm. "He has to live here. And I have no wish to die here. Help Captain Kostas assemble the men." After a moment's search he found his sword and slipped it back into its scabbard. "We will need a guide back to the gate," he told Khaimon.

Rohn stepped from behind Khaimon. "I'll take you back."

The Warrior nodded to the Youth. "You and Kostas take the lead." Watching his men file out of the fortress, he said to Khaimon, "I hope this is the end of the conflict between Valtierra and Shicassa. It would help if the Shicassan soldiers and farmers were called back from Sweetwater Valley." Without waiting for an answer, he followed the last of his men out of the fortress.

The way back to the city's walls seemed longer than the walk in, and he heard nothing but the men ahead of him, saw little in the darkness. By the time he'd reached the gate the cavalry were already mounting their horses. Waving to their captain, he strode across the bridge, hardly able to see it in the fog from the river.

In less than an hour the sky had turned from star-dappled black to deep blue, then to rose and gold. Away from the river the fog had thinned and the sunrise left it scurrying for shadows before disappearing.

His men had performed better than he had dared hope. Although they'd marched through the night and fought a battle, they'd lost only one man dead and three wounded, only one seriously hurt. Admittedly, their opponents had been sleep-drugged and unready but his men had fought remarkably well. He hoped that lesson had not been lost on Khaimon.

And still they marched, carrying their dead comrade and the man who'd lost an arm. He finally called a halt when they reached the grove where they'd rested the day before. The captains and lieutenants posted sentries and let the rest of the men lie down.

The Youth found as comfortable a place as any near the Warrior. "You really should've let me kill Khaimon."

"I do not think so," the Warrior replied. "Khaimon likes to think of himself as a good man and, in most ways, he is. I do not believe he enjoyed doing what he thought was necessary. I would only worry if he thought doing an evil thing has made him an evil man. Someone who has convinced himself of that is capable of anything."

The Warrior shifted, trying to find the least uncomfortable way to lie down wearing both his armor and his mask. "There was already enough killing. You fight your wars differently here in the north. Here, you fight to conquer. In the south, they fight to take. Wars between households are to the death of the last member, and whether it is between households or a household and a raider band, the battle is only over when everyone on one side or the other is dead.

"If Khaimon had let the boys live, he and everyone he cared for would have to be forever looking over their shoulders. If he had banished them, they would either recruit or be recruited. I would wager there would be any number of men prepared to support Tatros' sons for their own purposes."

He sighed. "I dislike what was done as much as you do but it was probably necessary."

The Youth's voice was slurred as he hovered at the edge of sleep. "Do you think you can trust him?"

"I am not as sure as I once was. As I said, I dislike what he did and we will have to wait to see how it has affected him. And most gratitude seldom outlasts a night or two of sound sleep. We shall see." The Warrior hadn't mentioned that, had the Youth killed Khaimon, he wasn't sure his men could have escaped the city alive or, if they did, how many dead they would've had to leave behind or how many wounded would have to be carried away by their comrades.

THE RASH YOUTH

Despite his exhaustion, the Youth was afraid he'd be too excited to sleep but he closed his eyes for only a moment before his shoulder was shaken. His hand snatched for the hilt of his sword before he realized he was staring at the Warrior's mask. The sun was high above; perhaps an hour after noon. "What…?" His mind and his mouth seemed sluggish as he tried to understand why he'd been wakened.

"Shicassan cavalry," the Warrior said, and turned to look out at the plain.

The Youth found his shield, which seemed to have become even heavier than when he'd set it down, and hauled himself to his feet. "I told you, you should've let me kill him," he mumbled.

"I don't think they're from the city." The Warrior gestured at their backtrail. "Rohn said they had cavalry stationed north and south of the city. If they patrol at all, it wouldn't be difficult for them to find our trail."

By now the Warrior and the Youth had reached the edge of the forest. A full company of cavalry milled on the plain, several leaders conferring at the center of the line. The Youth was forced to admit, to himself at least, that they presented an impressive sight. Billed, open-faced, crested helmets were topped by horsehair plumes. It took the Youth a moment to realize that the colors of the plumes and the patterns on the shields must denote different squadrons in each company. The light played off the polished helmets, breastplates and greaves of the mounted men.

Without turning his head, the Youth asked, "What do we do now?"

"That will depend upon them," the Warrior said. "If they try a cavalry charge, we remain in the woods and cut them to pieces. If they dismount, we'll go out onto the plain to meet them. On foot, we have an enormous advantage in our formations, to say nothing of our numbers. My only worry is that they'll do nothing at all, simply try to hold us here until they can be reinforced."

The Youth tried to work some of the stiffness out of his back and joints, noticing the soldiers around him doing the same. "Our men are tired and theirs are fresh. Perhaps they'll think that will give them an advantage."

The Warrior showed his teeth in an expression that couldn't be mistaken for a smile. "That would be a fatal mistake. I have learned never to count on your opponents to make large mistakes."

"What will you do if they simply try to hold us here?" The Youth stretched first one leg, then the other.

"I will give them a quarter of an hour to decide, unless we see dust raised by reinforcements. Then I will send our cavalry out. If they pursue with their whole company we will march after them, then have them caught between our horsemen and footsoldiers. If they send one or two squadrons after our cavalry, our men can crush the first group, then the other. If they do not move at all, our cavalry will turn and prepare to attack when our infantry goes out onto the plain in formation."

Glancing back in the direction of Shicassa, the Youth observed, "We may have to move quickly."

The Warrior studied the dust cloud. "Not yet, at least. It is moving too rapidly to be marching men, and it is too small to be more than two or three riders. I would guess they sent a courier to the city when they found our trail. The riders are probably bringing orders from the city. We should know very soon whether we need wet our blades again."

The Warrior had been correct. Within a few minutes the Youth was able to discern three dots at the front of the dust cloud, dots that soon grew enough to see as horsemen. They rode to the company's captain and the Youth thought one of the riders might be Rohn. They were well over bowshot away, too far to let the Youth hear them, but from the gestures and the sound of the voices, they seemed to be arguing.

The captain of the company spurred his horse forward but the man who might be Rohn moved his own horse, blocking the captain's mount, whipped out his sword, and from the sound of his voice, gave the captain a tongue-lashing.

With a disgust that could be seen in his posture, even at that distance, the captain drew his sword and flung it down, then turned his horse's head to face Shicassa and shot spurs to his mount.

Rohn sheathed his own blade and shouted a command, waiting until the rest of the company followed its captain, then waved toward the forest and rode after the men.

"You were probably right about not killing Khaimon," the Youth said. "We'd have won but it would've cost us time and, perhaps, men." He stumbled back to the place he'd chosen to rest, laid down, and was almost instantly asleep again.

THE CRONE

Waking with a start, she realized she'd drowsed and wondered how she'd been able to relax enough to sleep. She could sense something important happening just out of her sight. The other Council members felt it, too. The Fool's humor had become less barbed, though no less pointed.

She'd been told the camp was deserted except for a bare garrison whose only functions seemed to be to maintain and clean. She'd heard even the army teamsters had left the camp carrying supplies north and south.

Despite the warming weather, the city remained quiet, as though most of the citizens were holding their breaths.

Not everything had stopped. The Artisan, with the Wise Old Man advising, had interviewed over a dozen merchants before selecting a candidate. That choice had been a delicate balance between finding a man who would represent the needs of the merchants and one who could work with the Council.

Catching up her staff, she made her way to the garden. The Priest sat at his usual bench, his prayer stone in his hand. Moving around the outer edge of the garden, she saw the Farmer at work and was comforted by this sign of stability. While the city might be in doubt, the farmers and the land remained. She noticed the Farmer was planting flowers and smiled to herself. That was a sign he, too, had been touched by the changes. Flowers couldn't be eaten—the Farmer probably regarded them as pretty weeds—but the man was busily planting something of beauty, something that fed only the eyes, the nose, and the soul.

Following the gravel path to the poolside, she found her own favorite bench and sat down. The Priest glanced up from gazing at the pond, saw her, and stood to walk carefully around the pool, his prayer stone still clutched in his hand.

"I had been wanting to speak with you," the Priest said. "I'd like a Priestess, Adara, to be able to speak at the next Council meeting. I understand the importance of what's happening in the north but, it seems to me, saving the city is the work of all the Council. The Warrior can save us from Shicassa but it is just as important that we save the city from itself."

She felt her lips twitch into a smile. "This may be the longest meeting we will ever have held. We may have to have our meals brought to us and give the Wise Old Man time for a nap."

"It may also be the most important meeting we've ever held—and if the Warrior doesn't succeed, may be our last meeting. Have you heard anything?"

"Nothing. One courier brought word the army has won a small victory at Sweetwater Valley, but it seems only a small part of our army is engaged there. Another part of the army is in the south. I'm not sure that was a wise move. If events go against us in the north, the army will have to move those men very quickly, and withdrawing them might be seen as an opportunity by the Matriarchy."

"I suppose," the Priest said, stroking his prayer stone with his thumb, "that my calling requires faith and, just as I trust the Trinity, I believe in the Warrior."

"That's a rather different opinion than the one you expressed when he first came before the Council."

The Priest's grin was less a sign of humor than of embarrassment. "I trust the Trinity but I'm only human and I can make mistakes. That was one of mine."

"I think you can forgive yourself." The Crone paused to stare at the placid surface of the pond. "I will vote to hear the Priestess."

"Thank you." Rising to his feet, the Priest nodded to the Crone and walked the path back to the edge of the garden.

A flash of color and movement drew her attention to the door of the residence. Even with her old eyes the colors and flowing motion were enough to identify the Harlot. As she and the Priest neared each other they greeted each other and shared a few words before the Priest entered the residence and the Harlot continued around the garden. This was another change, one the Crone found as unexpected as it was unlikely. Whenever the Priest and the Harlot had been together they had pointedly been apart, scrupulously ignoring each other.

The Crone watched the Harlot stroll around the garden with a touch of envy. Even in her youth the Crone had never been as graceful or as attractive as the Harlot. She had noticed changes in the younger woman. Her reserve had added to her dignity but much of that reserve had been almost resentful. She'd seemed to have expected attack or disdain and had made it plain she refused to be treated as less than a Council member. That defensiveness had vanished, replaced by a more relaxed sense of equality.

The Harlot followed the path to the bench. "May I join you?"

"Please do." The Harlot's charm wasn't limited to men, and the trace of envy the Crone had felt evaporated. "I saw you and the Priest greet each other. You seem to have resolved at least some of your differences."

Sitting on the bench, the Harlot said, "I'm beginning to understand why we serve for two years. It took most of the first year just for us to become comfortable with each other."

With a sigh, the Crone replied, "Not always, and sometimes they never do. When I was the Mother, the Council never became a group and squabbled to the end of its term. We've been lucky. With the exception of the Merchant, we've had an excellent group." She sat musing, staring at the pond but not seeing it. "What will you do when you can finally take off your mask?"

"I hadn't given it much thought before." The Harlot shifted on the bench, bent, picked up a pebble, and tossed it into the pool. "At first, the two years seemed an eternity. Now I'm beginning to think of the future, something I'd never done before. Perhaps I'll become a merchant. There's an opportunity for another business that employs former harlots." She tossed another pebble into the pond. "One thing I've decided is that I'd enjoy being able to see the rest of you after we've all hung up our masks."

The Crone didn't even try to hide her smile. "Especially the Fool?"

The Harlot smiled back. "Especially the Fool, but I've come to care about all of you. I'm not even sure whether you've changed or I've changed the way I see you."

"Some of both, I suspect." The Crone used the tip of her staff to flip another small stone into the water. "The Wise Old Man is earning his sobriquet. I suppose, in a way, we're all becoming our masks." She peered at the Harlot. "I'm surprised you're looking forward to the future with so much hope. If the Warrior and the Rash Youth fail, our future will likely be short and bleak."

"How bright will it be if we borrow trouble? And I don't think they'll fail. I think the Warrior would rather die than fail, and he's a man who wouldn't die easily. I'm more worried about the Rash Youth. He's long since earned his name."

"We agree about that." Thre Crone again stared at the pond. "He adds life and light to the Council. No one on the Council now is dispensable, but he'd be perhaps the hardest loss to bear."

THE WARRIOR

When he woke, feeling a little refreshed, the shadows were stretching from the forest into the rolling plains. Within a quarter of an hour the men were ready and began the last leg of their march back to Valtierra, back to home. As they moved south they collected the men who had guarded the farms and villages and, in each place, the Warrior ascertained the men had done no harm. He was pleasantly surprised that out of either a sense of duty or fear of punishment, his men had been firm but not aggressive.

The Warrior led the men upriver of where they'd crossed. The bridge was all but invisible in the rising fog and the men he'd sent ahead had taken the small fortress and captured the half-dozen men who'd been posted to guard the bridge. His men quickly cleaned the place of arms and armor, throwing them into the river as they crossed.

Half a league downriver they reached the woods from which they'd launched their raid. The two wagons of provisions he'd ordered prepared were waiting for them and he let the men eat and rest. The campfires they lit were the signal for the men in the Shicassan watchtower to return to Valtierra, and they arrived before midnight.

His cavalry and their horses were as exhausted as the footsoldiers and he let all the men sleep until midmorning, the soldiers who had brought the provisions taking sentry duty.

The men of the dead man's company dug the man's grave deep and buried him standing up, with his weapons, facing Shicassa. The man who'd lost his arm had died during the night and was buried the same way.

While the infantry and most of the cavalry returned to camp, he sent couriers to the men on the other borders to return as well, while he rode with half a company of cavalry to the two companies he'd left threatening Sweetwater Valley.

He'd left First Captain Hondros in command of the two companies and Hondros greeted him with a grin. "The first day we were here, some of the more excitable Shicassans tried to attack us, about two companies. We lost three men. Perhaps a dozen of them were still alive and able to take to their heels. This morning our scouts saw movement in the Shicassan camp and we waited for an attack, but they were clearing out. We're waiting until they're out of sight of our scouts before we enter the valley, but it looks deserted."

"Excellent," the Warrior said. "Take both companies in but if it is as it seems, leave one to protect the farmers coming back and take the other company back to camp."

"It's finished, then?"
"It is never finished but, for now, we can all rest."

THE HARLOT

"You've been uncharacteristically quiet," the Harlot observed.

The Fool leaned back in the nest of cushions that had become 'his.' "Sometimes one can be too happy for humor," the Fool replied. "The Warrior and the Rash Youth are back, safe and hale. War with Shicassa no longer looms like a thunderhead. The meeting tomorrow looks to be exciting. The wine in this cup is very fine, and I'm with the person I most enjoy being with. I'd put those in no particular order except the last, which is actually the first."

The Harlot chuckled. "Strangely enough, I'm also happy for the same reasons." She sipped her wine. "One of the things I can't tell from the mask is in which ear you wear your ring."

The Fool's stunned expression, mouth agape, was as visible as if the Fool had removed his mask. Finally he managed to stammer, "The left ear."

"Perhaps, in a few months, when we're rid of the masks, that'll change."

The Fool took a deep drink of wine. "Are you sure? You don't even know what I look like."

The Harlot chuckled again. "I've seen you without the mask—not that formed leather headpiece—but the one you present to the world, even when you're not wearing the leather one, and I like what I see. You can't possibly be as ugly as the Fool's mask, but even if you were, I'd still find you charming." She laughed. "You're blushing again."

After a few moments the Fool regained his composure, took her hand, and kissed it.

For that matter," the Harlot said, "you still don't know what I look like, either."

"I've seen behind your mask, too," the Fool said, "and if your face had less than a hundredth of your beauty, you'd still be lovely."

"The idea of a Fool being courtly seems somehow…quaint. But I appreciate it." She brought his hand to her lips and kissed it.

"It's going to be difficult for us," the Fool said. "Until we can take the masks off, we're still bound by duty."

The Harlot smiled. "Do you appreciate a cup of cool water more when it's a cool day or when you're working in the heat?"

"Well said," the Fool observed, "but it seems to have warmed considerably in here, and I think I'd best get back to my own room."

She stood up as he did and they embraced, then he hurried out of the room.

THE CRONE

The Priest had been right; the priestess, Adara, had spoken with fire. She had not pled, she had demanded justice for the people of the fourth quarter.

The priestess' visit to the Council had followed the acceptance of a new Merchant, whose new mask was fresh from the hands of the artisans who'd crafted it. Then the Warrior had made his report. Although it had cost six men's lives, the valley had been recovered, Tatros was gone, and war had been averted.

Then the Council had taken up the matter of the fourth quarter.

"The army can take up to two hundred men, but it will come at a cost," the Warrior said. "Half that many men have left, but as our soldiers age, I do not want to have them forced to beg or starve. They have given more to the city than all but their comrades."

"The constables can be drawn from the army and from the fourth quarter," the Wise Old Man added, "and magistrates from former captains and petty-captains."

Everyone had suggestions and the Artisan finally agreed to allow the numbers of apprentices and journeymen admitted by the guilds to increase by half, and the number of masters to grow as well.

The new Merchant was easily intimidated into agreeing to accept new taxes, and the Priest was sure priests and priestesses could collect alms for the poor and, with a little supervision, deliver them in the form of goods.

When the discussion had run its course, the Artisan asked, "Do any of you see any dangers?"

The Rash Youth was, of course, the first to speak. "We will need to watch our neighbors. This Khaimon may be a good man but we can't count on his gratitude. Valtierra and Shicassa still have their differences. We can't expect those to disappear like fog in the morning sun."

With his usual insouciant grin, the Fool said, "We also can't count on the next Council to be made up of as exemplary a group as this one is, but that's for them to worry about. And, of course, the people who choose them."

The Wise Old Man coughed for a moment, cleared his throat, and sipped at his water before he said, "Many things can go wrong, but we've made a beginning. If we do nothing more, we have, at least, done our share. Others will have to finish our work, but we've given them a start and a direction."

"A beginning, yes," the Warrior agreed, "but we should post warning signs as well. The army must never be strong enough to take power from the hands of the Council. We have made a start by having our men take pride in being the army of Valtierra. We need to remind them that they are not merely fighting for a city but for the people and the rights of Valtierra.

"The old Merchant was right in one sense, even if for the wrong reasons. We should try to form a league of the city-states. While we have an uneasy balance now, that balance could easily be tipped by any number of events. A major invasion from the north or the west could leave each city-state too weak to defend itself. A common alliance could solve that, but a famine would likely tear any alliance apart. A few hard winters like the last one could do that. So could some dangers we cannot even mark."

The Crone leaned forward. "All this advice is necessary, but it is in the future. The danger from outside Valtierra has been ended for now, and the steps we take here may be the best way for Valtierra to mend. The city may not kill itself, but it could well cripple itself, and we've bought time and crutches for that. We must always remember the work we have yet to do, but we should also never forget what we have accomplished."

The voices fell silent as everyone measured for themselves the tasks to be done, then the Crone spoke, "I propose this meeting of the Council be finished but for the last business. It's now the Month of the Warrior, and time to turn the staff over to him."